TEN TINY
BREATHS

TEN TINY BREATHS

a novel

K.A. TUCKER

ATRIA PAPERBACK

NEW YORK   LONDON   TORONTO   SYDNEY   NEW DELHI

ATRIA PAPERBACK
A Division of Simon & Schuster, Inc.
1230 Avenue of the Americas
New York, NY 10020

First Atria Paperback edition September 2013

ATRIA PAPERBACK and colophon are trademarks of Simon & Schuster, Inc.

For information about special discounts for bulk purchases, please contact Simon & Schuster Special Sales at 1-866-506-1949 or business@simonandschuster.com.

The Simon & Schuster Speakers Bureau can bring authors to your live event. For more information or to book an event, contact the Simon & Schuster Speakers Bureau at 1-866-248-3049 or visit our website at www.simonspeakers.com.

Designed by Nancy Singer

Manufactured in the United States of America

10 9 8 7 6 5 4 3 2 1

Library of Congress Cataloging-in-Publication Data

Tucker, K. A. (Kathleen A.)
 Ten tiny breaths : a novel / K.A. Tucker. — First Atria Books trade paperback edition.
    p. cm.
1. Sisters—Fiction. 2. Self-realization in women—Fiction. 3. Drunk driving—Fiction. 4. Post-traumatic stress disorder—Fiction. 5. Orphans—Fiction. I. Title.
 PR9199.4.T834T46 2013
 813'.6—dc23
               2013005585

ISBN 978-1-4767-4032-4
ISBN 978-1-4767-4033-1 (ebook)

To Lia and Sadie
May your angels always protect you

To Paul
For your continued support

To Heather Self
All the purple and green feathers in the world

PROLOGUE

"Just breathe," my mom would say. "Ten tiny breaths . . . Seize them. Feel them. Love them." Every time I screamed and stomped my feet in anger, or bawled my eyes out in frustration, or turned green with anxiety, she'd calmly recite those same words. Every single time. Exactly the same. She should have tattooed the damn mantra on her forehead. "That makes no sense!" I'd yell. I never understood. What the hell does a tiny breath do? Why not a deep breath? Why ten? Why not three or five or twenty? I'd scream and she'd simply smile her little smile. I didn't understand it then.

I do now.

stage one

■ ■ ■

COMFORTABLY NUMB

ONE

A soft hiss . . . my heart thumping in my ears. I hear nothing more. I'm sure my mouth is moving, calling out their names . . . Mom? . . . Dad? *. . . but I can't hear my voice. Worse, I can't hear theirs. I turn to my right to see Jenny's silhouette, but her limbs look awkward and unnatural and she's pressed up against me. The car door opposite her is closer than it's supposed to be.* Jenny? *I'm sure I say. She doesn't respond. I turn to my left to see only black. Too dark to see Billy, but I know he's there because I can feel his hand. It's big and strong and it envelops my fingers. But it's not moving . . . I try to squeeze it but I can't will my muscles to flex. I can't do anything except turn my head and listen to my heart pound like an anvil against my chest for what feels like an eternity.*

Dim lights . . . voices . . .

I see them. I hear them. They're all around, closing in. I open my mouth to scream, but I can't find the energy. The voices get louder, the lights brighter. A reedy gasp sets my hair on end. Like a person struggling for his dying breath.

I hear a loud snap, snap, snap, *like someone pulling stage-light levers; light suddenly pours in from all angles, illuminating the car with blinding intensity.*

The smashed windshield.

The twisted metal.

Dark smears.

Liquid pools.

Blood. Everywhere.

It all suddenly disappears and I'm falling backward, crashing into cold water, sinking farther into the darkness, picking up speed as the weight of an ocean swallows me whole. I open my mouth to search for air. A lung's worth of cold water greets me in a rush, filling me inside. The pressure in my chest is unbearable. It's ready to explode. I can't breathe . . . I can't breathe. Tiny breaths, *I hear my mom instruct, but I can't do it. I can't get even one. My body's shaking . . . shaking . . . shaking . . .*

"Wake up, dear."

My eyes fly open to find a faded headrest in front of me. It takes me a moment to find my bearings, to calm my hammering heart.

"You were gaspin' for air somethin' fierce," the voice says.

I turn to find a lady peering down at me, concern on her deeply wrinkled face, her twisted, old fingers on my shoulder. My body curls into itself before I can stop the knee-jerk response to her touch.

She removes her hand with a gentle smile. "Sorry, dear. Just thought you should be woken up."

Swallowing, I manage to croak out, "Thank you."

She nods and shifts away to take her seat on the bus. "Must have been some kind a nightmare."

"Yeah," I answer, my usual calm, vacant voice returning. "Can't wait to wake up."

■ ■ ■

"We're here." I give Livie's arm a gentle shake. She grumbles and nuzzles her head against the window. I don't know how she can sleep like that, but she's managed to, snoring softly for the past six hours. A line of flaky, dried spit snakes down her chin. *Super attractive.* "Livie," I call again with an impatient bite in my tone. I need off this tin can. Now.

I get a clumsy wave and pouty "don't bug me, I'm sleeping" lip.

"Olivia Cleary!" I snap as passengers rustle through the overhead compartments and gather their belongings. "Come on. I've got to get out of here before I lose my shit!" I don't mean to bark, but I can't help it. I don't do well in confined spaces. After twenty-two hours on this damn bus, pulling the emergency hatch and jumping through the window sounds appealing.

My words finally sink in. Livie's eyelids flutter open and half-dazed blue eyes stare out at the Miami bus terminal for a moment. "We made it?" she asks through a yawn, sitting up to stretch and scope out the scenery. "Oh, look! A palm tree!"

I'm already standing in the aisle, preparing our backpacks. "Yay, palm trees! Come on, let's go. Unless you want to spend another day going back to Michigan." That gets her body moving.

By the time we step off the bus, the driver has unloaded the luggage from the undercarriage. I quickly spot our matching hot-pink suitcases. Our lives, all of our belongings, have been reduced to one suitcase each. It's all we managed to throw together in our rush out of Uncle Raymond and Aunt Darla's house. No matter, I tell myself as I throw an arm over my sister's shoulders in a side hug. We have each other. That's all that matters.

"It's hot as hell!" Livie exclaims at the same time that I feel a trickle of sweat run down my back. It's late morning and the sun is already blazing down on us like a fireball in the sky. So different from the autumn chill we left in Grand Rapids. She pulls off her red hoodie, soliciting a string of catcalls from a group of guys on skateboards.

"Picking up guys already, Livie?" I tease.

Her cheeks turn pink as she slinks over to hide behind a concrete pillar, partially out of view.

"You do realize you're not a chameleon, right? . . . Oh! The one in the red shirt is coming over here right now." I stretch my neck expectantly toward the group.

Livie's eyes flash wide with terror for a second before she realizes I'm only joking. "Shut up, Kacey!" she hisses, smacking my shoulder. Livie can't handle being the center of attention for any guy, and the fact that she's turned into a knockout over the last year hasn't helped.

I smirk as I watch her fumble with her sweater. She has no idea how striking she is, and I'm okay with that if I'm going to be her guardian. "Stay clueless, Livie. My life will be so much easier if you're oblivious for the next, say, five years."

She rolls her eyes. "Okay, Miss *Sports Illustrated*."

"Ha!" In truth, some of the attention from those asshats probably is directed at me. Two years of intense kickboxing has given me a rock-hard body. That, topped with my deep auburn hair and watery blue eyes, garners loads of unwanted attention.

Livie is a fifteen-year-old version of me. Same light blue eyes, same slender nose, same pale Irish skin. There's only one big difference, and that's the color of our hair. If you put towels over our hair, you'd think we were twins. She gets her shiny black color from our mother. She's also two inches taller than me, even though I'm five years older.

Yup, to look at us, anyone with half a brain can tell we're sisters. But that's where our similarities end. Livie's an angel. She tears up when children cry; she apologizes when someone bumps into her; she volunteers in soup kitchens and libraries. She makes excuses for people when they do stupid things. If she were old enough to drive, she'd slam on the brakes for crickets. I'm . . . I'm not Livie. I might have been more like her before, but not now. Where I'm a looming thundercloud, she's the sunshine breaking through.

"Kacey!" I turn to find Livie holding a taxicab door wide open, her brows raised.

There's no way we can fit a cab into our tight budget. "I hear Dumpster-diving for food isn't as fun as it's cracked up to be."

She slams the cab door, her face twisting. "Another bus it is." She gives her suitcase an irritated tug over the curb.

"Really? Five minutes in Miami and you're already starting with the attitude? I've got sweet-fuck-all left in my wallet to get us past Sunday." I hold out my wallet for her to inspect.

She flushes. "Sorry, Kace. You're right. I'm just out of sorts."

I sigh and immediately feel bad for snapping. Livie doesn't have an attitude-riddled bone in her body. Sure, we bicker, but I'm always to blame and I know it. Livie's a good kid. She's always been a good kid. Straitlaced, even-tempered. Mom and Dad never had to tell her anything twice. When they died and Mom's sister took us in, Livie went out of her way to be an even better kid. I went in the opposite direction. Hard.

"Come on, this way." I link arms with her and squeeze her closer as I unfold the piece of paper with the address. We visit the bus terminal's information desk. After a long and laborious conversation with the elderly man behind the glass partition— complete with a game of charades and a pencil diagram on a city map circling three transfers—we're on a city bus, and I hope we're not heading toward Alaska.

I'm glad to be sitting again because I'm beat. Aside from my twenty-minute catnap on the long-distance bus, I haven't slept in thirty-six hours. I'd much rather ride in silence, but Livie's fidgety hands in her lap kill that idea quickly. "What is it, Livie?"

She hesitates, furrowing her brow.

"Livie . . ."

"Do you think Aunt Darla called the cops?"

I reach down to squeeze her knee. "Don't worry about it. We'll be fine. They won't find us, and if they do the cops will hear what happened."

"But he didn't *do* anything, Kace. He was probably too drunk to know which room was his."

I glare at her. "Didn't *do* anything? Did you forget about that disgusting old-man hard-on that pushed up against your thigh?"

Livie's mouth puckers like she's about to vomit.

"He didn't do anything because you bolted out of there and came to my room. Don't defend that asshole." I'd seen the looks Uncle Raymond had given Livie as she matured over the last year. Sweet, innocent Livie. I'd crush his nuts if he stepped foot inside my room and he knew that. Livie, though . . .

"Well, I just hope they don't come get us and bring us back."

I shake my head. "That's not going to happen. I'm your guardian now, and I don't care about any stupid legal paperwork. You're not leaving my side. Besides, Aunt Darla hates Miami, re-member?" "Hate" is an understatement. Aunt Darla is a fanatical born-again Christian who spends all of her free time praying and making sure everyone else is praying or knowing that they should be praying to avoid hell, syphilis, and unplanned pregnancy. She's certain that major cities are the breeding ground for all evil in the world. She wouldn't come to Miami unless Jesus himself were holding a convention.

Livie nods, then lowers her voice to a whisper. "Do you think Uncle Raymond figured out what happened? We could get in real trouble for that."

I shrug. "Do you care if he does?" Part of me wishes I'd ig-nored Livie's pleading and called the cops about Uncle Ray-mond's "visit" to her room. But Livie didn't want to deal with police reports and lawyers and Children's Aid, and we'd certainly have had to deal with the full gamut. Maybe even the local news. Neither of us wanted that. We'd had enough of it after the accident. Who knows what they'd do with Livie, since she's a minor. Probably stick her in foster care. They wouldn't give her to me. I've been classified as "unstable" by too many professional reports for them to trust me with someone's life.

So Livie and I struck a deal. I wouldn't report him if she left with me. Last night turned out to be the perfect night to run. Aunt Darla was away at an all-night religious retreat, so I crushed three sleeping pills and dumped them into Uncle Raymond's beer after dinner. I can't believe the idiot took the glass I poured for him and handed to him so sweetly. I haven't said ten words to him in the last two years, since I found out he lost our inheritance at a blackjack table. By seven o'clock, he was sprawled out and snoring on the couch, giving us enough time to grab our suitcases, clean out his wallet and Aunt Darla's secret money box under the sink, and catch the bus out that night. Maybe drugging him and stealing their money crossed the line. Then again, Uncle Raymond shouldn't have gone all creepy pedophile.

■ ■ ■

"One-twenty-four," I read the number on the building out loud. "This is it." This is real. We stand side-by-side on the sidewalk outside our new home—a three-story apartment building on Jackson Drive with white stucco walls and small windows. It's a neat-looking place with a beach-house feel to it, even though we're half an hour from the beach. But if I inhale deeply, I can almost catch a whiff of sunscreen and seaweed.

Livie runs a hand through her wild dark hair. "Where'd you find this place again?"

"Www.desperateforanapartment.com," I joke. After Livie

stormed into my room in tears that night, I knew we needed out of Grand Rapids. One internet search led to another and soon I was emailing the landlord, offering him six months' rent in cash. Two years of pouring overpriced Starbucks coffee, gone.

But it's worth every drop.

We climb the steps and walk up to a gated archway. Now that we're closer, I can see the cracks and stains marring the exterior walls. "The picture with the ad looked great," I say with a hint of wariness as I grab and pull the gate handle to find that it's locked. "Good security."

"Here." Livie pushes on a cracked, round doorbell to the right. It makes no sound and I'm sure it's broken. I stifle a yawn as we wait for someone to pass through.

Three minutes later, my hands are cupped around my mouth and I'm about to yell the landlord's name when I hear shoes dragging across concrete. A middle-aged man with rumpled clothes and a scruffy face appears. His eyes are uneven, he's mostly bald on top, and I swear one ear is bigger than the other. He reminds me of Sloth from that old eighties movie my father made us watch, *Goonies*. A classic, my dad used to say.

Sloth scratches his protruding gut and says nothing. *I'll bet he's as intelligent as his movie twin.*

"Hi, I'm Kacey Cleary," I introduce myself. "We're looking for Harry Tanner. We're the new renters." His shrewd gaze lingers on me for a while, sizing me up. I silently praise myself for wearing jeans to cover the sizeable tattoo on my thigh in case *he* dare judge *me*. His focus then shifts to Livie, where it rests too long for my liking.

"You gals sisters?"

"Our matching suitcases give it away?" I answer before I can stop myself. *Get inside the gates before you let them know what a smart-ass you can be, Kace.*

Luckily, Sloth's lips curve upward. "Call me Tanner. This way."

Livie and I exchange a shocked look. Sloth is our new landlord? With a loud clank and creak, he ushers us through the gate. Almost as an afterthought, he turns to me and extends his hand.

I freeze, staring at those meaty fingers but not moving to take them.

Livie deftly swoops in and grabs hold of his hand with a smile, and I ease back a few steps so there's no illusion that I'll be having anything to do with this guy's hand. Or anyone's hand. Livie's great at saving me.

If Tanner notices, he says nothing, leading us through a courtyard with mangy shrubs and dehydrated plants surrounding a rusted hibachi. "This here's the commons." He waves his hand dismissively. "If you wanna grill, suntan, relax, whatever, this here's the spot." I take in the foot-high thistles and desiccated flowers along the borders and wonder how many people actually find this space relaxing. It could be nice, if someone tended to it.

"There must be a full moon or something," Tanner mutters as we trail behind him toward a row of dark red doors. Each has a small window next to it and all three floors are identical.

"Oh, yeah? Why's that?"

"You're the second apartment I've rented this past week through email. Same situation—desperate for a place, don't wanna wait, will pay in cash. Strange. I guess everyone's got somethin' to run from."

Well. How about that? Maybe Tanner *is* smarter than his movie twin.

"This one here just arrived this morning." He thumbs a stubby finger at Apartment 1D before leading us to the apartment next to it with a gold "1C" sign on it. His huge set of keys jangles as he searches for one in particular. "Now, I'll tell you what I tell all my tenants. I've only got one rule but it's a deal breaker. Keep thy peace! Don't be throwin' no wild parties with drugs and orgies—"

"Sorry, can you specify—what qualifies as an orgy in the State of Florida? Are threesomes okay? What if blow-ups are involved, 'cause, you know . . ."

Tanner scowls at me and Livie sharply jabs me in the shoulder blade. After clearing his throat, he goes on as if I hadn't spoken. "No feuds, family or otherwise. I don't have patience for that crap and I'll boot you out faster than you can lie to me. Understand?"

I nod and bite my tongue, fighting the urge to hum the *Family Feud* theme song as Tanner pushes the door open.

"Cleaned and painted it myself. It's not new, but it should provide what you're looking for."

The apartment is small and meagerly furnished, with a green-and-white tiled kitchenette area lining the back. The white walls only enhance the hideous puce-and-orange floral couch. Cheap forest-green carpet and the faint scent of mothballs pull together the seventies white-trash look nicely. Most notably, it's nothing like the picture in the ad. Surprise, surprise.

Tanner scratches the back of his graying head. "Not much to it, I know. There are two bedrooms over there and a bathroom between them. Put in a new toilet last year, so . . ." His lopsided gaze shifts to me. "If that's all . . ."

He wants his money. With a tight smile, I reach into the front pocket of my backpack and slide out a thick envelope. Livie ventures farther into the apartment while I pay him. Tanner watches her go, biting his lip as if he wants to say something. "She seems a bit young to be out on her own. Do your parents know you two are here?"

"Our parents are dead." It comes out as harsh as I intended and it does the trick. *Mind your own damn business, Tanner.*

His face turns ashen. "Oh, um, sorry to hear that." We stand uncomfortably for all of three seconds. I fold my hands under my armpits, making it clear that I have no intention to shake any hands. When he spins on his heels and heads out the door, I release a small sigh. He can't wait to get away from me, either. Over his shoulder, he hollers, "Laundry room's underground. I clean it once a week and expect all tenants to help out with keeping it tidy. I'm in 3F if you need anything." He disappears, leaving the key sitting in the lock.

I find Livie investigating the medicine cabinet in a bathroom made for hobbits. I try to step in but there isn't enough room for both of us. "New toilet. Old, repulsive shower," I mutter, my foot tracing the grungy, cracked tile floor.

"I'll take this room," Livie offers, squeezing past me to head to the bedroom on the right. It's empty except for a dresser and a twin bed with a peach crocheted spread over it. Black bars line the single window that faces the exterior of the building.

"You sure? It's small." I know without looking at the other room that this one is the smaller of the two. That's how Livie is. Selfless.

"Yeah. It's okay. I like small spaces." She grins. She's trying to make the best of it, I can tell.

"Well, when we throw those all-night ragers, you won't be able to fit more than three guys in here at once. You do realize that, right?"

Livie tosses a pillow at me. "Funny."

My bedroom is the same except it's slightly bigger and has a double bed with an ugly-ass green knit blanket. I sigh, my nose scrunching with disappointment. "Sorry, Livie. This place looks nothing like the ad. Damn Tanner and his false advertising." I tilt my head. "I wonder if we can sue him."

Livie snorts. "It's not so bad, Kace."

"You say that now, but when we're fighting roaches for our bread . . ."

"You? Fighting? *Big* shocker."

I laugh. Few things make me laugh anymore. Livie trying to be sarcastic is one of them. When she tries to pull off airy and cool, she ends up sounding like one of those radio announcers doing a dramatic rendition of a cheesy murder mystery.

"This place sucks, Livie. Admit it. But we're here and it's all we can afford right now. Miami's freakin' expensive."

Her hand slides into mine and I squeeze it. It's the only one I can handle touching. It's the only one that doesn't feel dead. Sometimes I have a hard time letting it go. "It's perfect, Kace. Just a little small and mothbally and green, but we're not that far from the beach! That's really what we wanted, right?" Livie stretches her arms above her head and groans. "So, now what?"

"Well, for starters, let's get you enrolled in the high school this afternoon so that big brain of yours doesn't shrink," I say, popping open my suitcase to empty its contents. "After all, when you're making a bazillion dollars and curing cancer, you'll need to send money my way." I rifle through my clothes. "I need to enroll at a gym. Then I'll go see how much Spam and creamed corn I can buy for an hour with my sweaty, hot body on the corner." Livie shakes her head. Sometimes she doesn't appreciate my sense of humor. Sometimes I think she wonders if I'm serious. I stoop to yank the covers from my bed. "And I definitely need to bleach the shit out of this entire place."

■ ■ ■

The building's laundry room beneath our apartment is nothing to write home about. Panels of fluorescent lights cast a harsh light over faded robin's-egg-blue concrete floors. A floral scent barely masks the musky odor in the air. The machines are at least fifteen years old, and they'll probably do more damage than good to our clothes. But there's not a cobweb or a piece of lint anywhere.

I shove all our sheets and blankets into two machines, cursing the world for making us sleep in secondhand bedding. *I'm buying new bedding with my first paycheck*, I commit to myself. Dumping in a mixture of bleach and detergent, I set the water to its hottest setting, wishing it were labeled "boil the hell out of any living organism." That would make me feel marginally better.

The machines need six quarters per load. I hate pay laundry machines. Earlier, Livie and I accosted strangers at the mall with our dimes and nickels, asking for a trade. I have just enough in my stash, I realize, as I begin sliding the coins into their designated slots.

"Any free machines?" a deep male voice calls out from directly behind me, surprising me enough that I yelp and throw the last three quarters in the air. Luckily, I have catlike reflexes and I catch two of the coins midair. My eyeballs glue onto the last one as it hits the ground and rolls toward the washer. Dropping to my hands and knees, I dive for it.

But I'm too slow.

"Dammit!" The side of my face hits the cold pavement as I peer under the machine, searching for a glint of silver. My fingers can just fit underneath . . .

"I wouldn't do that if I were you."

"Oh, yeah?" Now I'm pissed. Who sneaks up on a female in an underground laundry room, other than a psycho or a rapist? Which maybe he *is*. Maybe I'm supposed to be quivering in my sandals right now. But I'm not. I don't scare easily and, frankly, I'm too damn annoyed right now to be anything else. Let him try to attack me. He'll be in for the shock of a lifetime. "Why is that?" I force out between clenched teeth, trying to remain calm. *Keep thy peace*, Tanner warned us. No doubt he sensed something about me.

"Because we're in a cool, damp underground laundry room in

Miami. Creepy eight-legged insects and things that slither and crawl hide out in places like this."

I recoil as I fight the shiver running through my body, envisioning my hand reemerging from underneath with a quarter and a bonus snake. Few things freak me out. Beady eyeballs and a writhing body is one of them. "Funny, I've heard creepy *two*-legged things lurk in these places too. They're called creeps. A plague, one might say." As I'm leaning far over in my skimpy black shorts, he's got to be getting a nice view of my ass right about now. *Go ahead, perv. Enjoy it, 'cause that's all you're getting. And if I sense so much as a brush against my skin, I'll take you out at the kneecaps.*

He answers with a throaty laugh. "Well played. How about you get up off your knees?" The hairs on my neck prickle at his words. There's something decidedly sexual in his tone. I hear the sound of metal against metal as he adds, "This creep has an extra quarter."

"Well, then, you're my favorite kind of—" I start to say, reaching for the top of the machine as I stand to meet this asshole face-to-face. Of course the open bottle of detergent is right there. Of course my hand knocks it clean off. Of course it splatters all over the machine and the floor.

"Dammit!" I curse, dropping to my knees again as I watch the sticky green soap ooze everywhere. "Tanner's gonna evict me."

Creep's voice drops low. "What's it worth to you for me to keep quiet?" Footsteps approach.

On instinct, I adjust my position so I can dislocate his joint with a kick and make him crumple in agony, just like I'd learned in my sparring sessions. My spine tingles as a white sheet sails down to cover the floor in front of me. Sucking in a breath, I wait patiently as Creep passes my left side and crouches.

The air leaves my lungs in a swoosh, and I'm left staring at a set of deep dimples and the bluest eyes I've ever seen—cobalt rings with light blue on the inside. I squint. *Do they have turquoise flecks inside them? Yes! My God!* The blue floors, the rusty old machines, the walls, everything around me vanishes under the weight of his gaze as it strips me of my protective bitch coat, yanking it clean off my body, leaving me bare and vulnerable in seconds.

"We can soak it up with this. I needed detergent anyway," he says with an amused boyish grin as he drags his sheet around to clean up the spilled liquid.

"Wait, you don't have to . . ." My voice fades, the weakness in it nauseating me. Suddenly I'm feeling all kinds of wrong for labeling him creepy. He can't be a creep. He's too beautiful and too nice. I'm the idiot throwing quarters all over the place and now he's sopping up my detergent off this dirty floor with his sheets to help me!

I can't seem to form words. Not while I'm gawking at Not Creep's ripped forearms, feeling heat ripple into my lower belly. He's wearing a button-down shirt with the sleeves rolled up and the top buttons undone, exposing the beginnings of a killer upper body.

"See something that interests you?" he asks, his taunt snapping my eyes back to his smirking face, blood rushing to my cheeks. Damn this guy! He seems to flip-flop from Good Samaritan to Evil Tempter with each new sentence out of his mouth. Worse, he caught me ogling his body. Me! Ogling! I'm around first-class bodies every day at the gym and they don't faze me. Somehow, though, I'm not immune to his.

"I just moved in. 1D. My name's Trent." He looks up at me from under impossibly long lashes, his shaggy, golden-brown hair framing his face beautifully.

"Kacey," I force out. *So, this guy is the new tenant; our neighbor. He lives on the other side of my living room wall! Gah!*

"Kacey," he repeats. I love the shape of his lips when he says my name. My attention lingers there, staring at that mouth, at his set of perfectly straight, white teeth, until I feel my face explode with a third wave of heat. *Dammit! Kacey Cleary blushes for no one!*

"I'd shake your hand, Kacey, but—" Trent says with a teasing smile, holding up detergent-covered palms.

There. That does it. The idea of touching those hands slaps me across the cheek, breaking this temporary daze, pushing me back to reality.

I can think straight again. With a deep inhale, I struggle to reactivate my shields, to form a barrier against this godlike creature, to end all reaction to him. It's so much easier that way. *And that's all this is, Kacey. A reaction. A strange, uncharacteristic reaction to a guy. An incredibly hot guy but, in the end, nothing you want to get mixed up with.*

"Thanks for the quarter," I say coolly, standing and sliding the coin into the slot. I start the washer.

"It's the least I could do for scaring the crap out of you." He's up and shoving his sheets into the machine beside mine. "If Tanner says anything, I'll tell him I did it. It's partially my fault anyway."

"Partially?"

He chuckles as he shakes his head. We're standing close now, so close that our shoulders almost touch. Too close.

I take a few steps back to give myself space but I end up staring at his back, admiring how his blue checkered shirt stretches across his broad shoulders, how his dark blue jeans fit his ass perfectly.

He stops what he's doing to glance over his shoulder, blazing eyes leveling me with a look that makes me want to do things to him, for him, with him. His attention drags down the length of my body, unashamed. This guy is a contradiction. One second sweet, the next second brazen. A mind-blowing hot contradiction.

A warning siren goes off in my head. I promised Livie that the random one-night hook-ups would stop. And they have. For two years, I haven't given anyone the time of day. Now, here I am, day one in our new life, and I'm ready to straddle this guy on the washer.

Suddenly I'm writhing in my own skin, uncomfortable. *Breathe, Kacey*, I hear my mom's voice in my head. *Count to ten, Kace. Ten tiny breaths.* As usual, her advice doesn't help me because it makes no sense. All that makes sense is getting away from this two-legged trap. Immediately.

I move backward toward the door.

I don't want these thoughts. I don't need them.

"So, where are you . . . ?"

I run up the stairs to safety before I hear Trent finish his sentence. Not until I'm aboveground do I search for a breath. I lean against the wall and close my eyes, welcoming that protective coat back as it slides over my skin and reclaims control of my body.

TWO

A hissing sound . . .
 Bright lights . . .
 Blood . . .
 Water, rushing over my head. I'm drowning.

"Kacey, wake up!" Livie's voice pulls me out of suffocating darkness and back into my bedroom. It's three a.m. and I'm drenched with sweat.

"Thanks, Livie."

"Anytime," she answers softly, lying down beside me. Livie is used to my nightmares. I rarely go a night without one. Sometimes I wake up on my own. Sometimes my screams send Livie running to my room. Sometimes I start hyperventilating and she has to dump a glass of cold water over my head to bring me back. She didn't have to do that tonight.

Tonight is a good night.

I stay quiet and still until I hear her slow, rhythmic breathing again, and I thank God for not taking her from me too. He took everyone else, but he left Livie. I like to think he gave her the flu that night to keep her from coming to my rugby game. Congested lungs and a runny nose saved her.

Saved my one ray of light.

■ ■ ■

I get up early to say goodbye to Livie on the first day at her new high school. "You have all the paperwork?" I ask her. I signed everything as Livie's legal guardian and made her swear that I was if anyone asks.

"For what it's worth . . ."

"Livie, just stick to the story and everything will go smoothly." To be honest, I'm a little worried. Depending on Livie to lie is like expecting a house of cards to stand up to a windstorm. Impossible. Livie can't lie if her life depends on it. And it kind of does in this case.

I watch her finish her cereal and grab her school bag, pushing her hair back behind her ear about a dozen times. That's one of her many tells. A tell that she's panicking.

"Just think, Livie. You can be anyone you want to be," I offer, rubbing her biceps as she's about to head out the door. I recall finding one shred of solace when we moved to Aunt Darla and Uncle Raymond's—a new school and new people who knew nothing about me. I was dumb enough to believe the break from pitying eyes would last. But news travels fast around small towns, and soon I found myself eating lunches in the bathroom or skipping school altogether to avoid the whispers. Now, though, we're worlds away from Michigan. We really do have a chance to start over fresh.

Livie stops and turns to stare at me blankly. "I'm Olivia Cleary. I'm not trying to be anyone else."

"I know. I just mean, no one knows anything about our past here." That was one of my negotiating points for coming here: no sharing our past with anyone.

"Our past isn't who we are. I'm me and you're you, and that's who we need to be," Livie reminds me. She leaves, and I know exactly what she's thinking. I'm not Kacey Cleary anymore. I'm an empty shell who cracks inappropriate jokes and feels nothing. I'm a Kacey imposter.

■ ■ ■

When I searched for our apartment, not only was I looking for a decent school for Livie; I needed a gym. Not one where pencil-thin girls prance around in new outfits and stand near the weights, talking on their phones. A fighter's gym.

That's how I found The Breaking Point.

The Breaking Point is the same size as the O'Malley's in Michigan, and I instantly feel at home when I step inside. It's complete with dim lighting, a fighting ring, and a dozen bags of various sizes and weights, hung from the rafters. The air is infused with that familiar stench of sweat and aggression—a by-product of the fifty-to-one male-to-female ratio.

As I step into the main room, I inhale deeply, welcoming the sense of security the room brings with it. Three years ago, after the hospital released me from long-term care—after extensive physiotherapy to strengthen the right side of my body, shattered in the accident—I joined a gym. I spent hours there each day, lifting weights, doing cardio, all the things that strengthened my broken body but did nothing to help my devastated soul.

Then one day, a ripped guy named Jeff with more piercings and tattoos than a jaded rock star introduced himself. "You're pretty intense in your workouts," he said. I nodded, uninterested in any direction the conversation could go. Until he handed me his card. "Have you tried O'Malley's down the road? I teach kick-boxing down there a few nights a week."

I'm a natural, apparently. I quickly excelled as his star pupil, probably because I trained seven days a week without fail. It has turned out to be the perfect coping mechanism for me. With each kick and each hit, I'm able to channel my anger, my frustration, and my hurt into one solid blow. All the emotions I work hard to bury in my life, I can release here in a nondestructive way.

Thankfully, The Breaking Point is cheap, and they let you pay month-to-month with no enrollment fees. I have enough cash set aside for one month. I know it should be going toward food, but not working out isn't an option for me. Society is better off with me in a gym.

After I enroll and get the grand tour, I drop my gear by an available sandbag. And I feel the men's eyes on me, the questioning stares. *Who's the redhead? Doesn't she realize what kind of gym this is?* They're wondering if I can throw a punch worth shit. They're probably taking bets already on who gets me in the shower first.

Let them try.

I ignore the attention, the flagrant comments and snickers, as I stretch my muscles, afraid I'll strain something after missing three days. And I smirk. *Cocky assholes.*

Taking several breaths to soothe my nerves, I focus on the bag, this gracious thing that will absorb all my pain, my suffering, my hatred, without protest.

And then I release it all.

■ ■ ■

The sun isn't even up yet when the worst kind of old-man heavy metal blasts through my room. My alarm clock reads six a.m. *Yup. Right on schedule.* It's the third day in a row that my neighbor wakes me up to this racket. "Keep thy peace," I mutter as I jerk my covers over my head, replaying Tanner's words. I guess keeping thy peace means not kicking down thy neighbor's door and smashing thy electronics against the wall.

That doesn't mean thou can't exact thy revenge.

I grab my iPod—one of the few non-clothes possessions I grabbed in our dash—and scroll through the playlists. There it is:

Hannah Montana. My best friend, Jenny, loaded all this tween shit as a joke years ago. *Looks like it's finally going to come in handy.* I push away the ache that goes along with the memories tied to it as I hit "Play" and crank the volume to max. The contorted sound bounces off the walls of my room. The speakers might blow, but this is worth it.

And then I dance.

Like a maniac, I bop around my room, waving my arms, hoping this person hates Hannah Montana as much as I do.

"What are you doing?" Livie yells, barreling into my room in rumpled pj's, her hair untamed. She leaps onto my iPod to slam the power button off.

"Just teaching our neighbor a lesson about waking me up. He's some kind of dickhole."

She frowns. "Have you met him? How do you know it's a guy?"

"Because no chick blasts that shit at six in the morning, Livie." I know it can't be Trent because his apartment is on the other side.

"Oh. I guess I can't hear it in my room." Her brow puckers as she studies the adjoining wall. "That's dreadful."

"Ya think? Especially when I worked until eleven last night!" I'd started my first shift at a Starbucks in a nearby neighborhood. They were desperate, and I have a stellar reference letter thanks to my old manager, a twenty-four-year-old mama's boy named Jake with a crush on the badass redhead. I was smart enough to play nice with him. It paid off.

With a pause and then a shrug, Livie shouts, "Dance party!" and cranks the volume back up.

The two of us jump around my room in a giggling fit until we hear the pounding on our front door.

Livie's face drains of all color. She's like that—all bark, no bite. Me? I'm not worried. I throw on my ratty purple housecoat and proudly strut over. *Let's see what he has to say about that.*

My hand is on the lock, about to throw the door open, when Livie whispers harshly, "Wait!"

I pause and turn back to find Livie waggling her index finger, like my mother used to do when she was scolding. "Remember, you promised! That was the deal. We're starting fresh here, right? New life? New Kacey?"

"Yeah. And?"

"And, can you please try not to be an ice queen? Try to be more like the Before Kacey? You know, the one who doesn't stonewall everyone who comes close? Who knows, maybe we can make some friends here. Just *try*."

"You want to make friends with old men, Livie? If that's the case, we could have stayed home," I say coolly. But her words sting like a long needle shot straight into my heart. Coming from anyone else, they would have slid off my tough Teflon exterior. The problem is, I don't know who Before Kacey is. I don't remember her. I hear that her eyes shined when she laughed, that her rendition of "Stairway to Heaven" on the piano made her dad tear up. She had hordes of friends, and she snuck in hugs and kisses and hand-holding with her boyfriend whenever she could.

Before Kacey died four years ago, and all that's left is a mess. A mess who spent a year in physical rehabilitation to repair her shattered body, only to be released with a shattered soul. A mess whose grades took a nosedive to the bottom of the class. Who sank into a world of drugs and alcohol for a year to cope. After Kacey doesn't cry, not a single tear. I'm not sure she knows how. She doesn't open up about anything; she can't stand the feel of hands because they remind her of death. She doesn't let people in, because pain trails attachments closely. The sight of a piano sends her into a dizzying haze. Her only solace is to beat the crap out of giant sandbags until her knuckles are red and her feet are raw and her body—held together with countless metal rods and pins—feels like it's going to crumble. I know After Kacey well. For better or for worse, I'm sure I'm stuck with her.

But Livie remembers Before Kacey and for Livie, I'll try anything. I force a smile. It feels awkward and foreign and, judging by the wince on Livie's face, probably looks a little bit menacing. "Okay." I go to turn the handle.

"Wait!"

"God, Livie! What now?" I sigh with exasperation.

"Here." She hands me her pink and black polka-dot umbrella. "He could be a serial killer."

Now I tip my head back and laugh. Such a rare sound but it's genuine. "And what should I do with this? Poke him?"

She shrugs. "Better than beating the snot out of him like you'll want to do."

"Okay, okay, let's see what we're dealing with here." I lean over to the window beside the door and push back the gossamer curtain, looking for a graying man with a faded too-small T-shirt and black socks. A tiny part of me hopes that it's that Trent guy from the laundry room. Those smoldering eyes invaded my thoughts several times without invitation over the past few days, and I've had a hard time kicking him out. I've even caught myself staring at the adjoining wall between our apartments like a creeper, wondering what he's doing.

A corn-silk blond ponytail wags back and forth outside our door instead. "Seriously?" I snort, fumbling with the lock.

Barbie's standing outside. No joke. A real-life five-foot-nine, highly toned blond bombshell with plump lips and giant periwinkle-blue eyes. I find myself speechless, taking in her tiny cotton shorts and the way the Playboy logo distorts as it stretches across the front of her tank top. *Those are so not real. They're the size of hot-air balloons.*

A soft drawl breaks my trance. "Hi, I'm Nora Matthews, from next door. Everyone calls me Storm."

Storm? Storm from next door with giant balloons sewn onto her chest?

A throat clears and I realize I'm still staring at them. I quickly avert my gaze back to her face.

"It's okay. The doctor gave me a free upsize while I was asleep," she jokes with a nervous giggle, earning a choking cough of shock from Livie.

Our new neighbor, Nora, aka "Storm," with giant, fake boobs. I wonder if Tanner gave *her* a "no orgies, keep thy peace" speech when he handed her the keys.

She extends a toned arm and I immediately tense up, fighting the urge to visibly recoil. This is why I hate meeting new people. In this diseased day and age, can't we all just wave at each other and move along?

A raven head of hair pops into my view as Livie dives to grab Storm's outstretched hand. "Hi, I'm Livie." I silently thank my sister for saving me yet again. "This is my sister, Kacey. We're new to Miami."

Storm offers Livie a perfect smile and turns back to me. "Look, I'm so sorry about the music." *So she can tell I'm the instigator.* "I had no idea someone moved in next door. I work nights and my five-year-old has me up early in the morning. It's all I can do to stay awake."

It's then that I notice the whites of her eyes are bloodshot. Guilt stabs me now that I know there's a kid involved. *Dammit.* I hate feeling guilt, especially for strangers.

Livie clears her throat and shoots a "remember not to be a bitch" gaze at me.

"No big deal. Just maybe, not quite so loud? Or so eighties?" I suggest.

"My dad got me hooked on AC/DC. I know, not cool." She grins. "I'm taking requests. Anything but Hannah Montana, please!" She holds her hands in front of her in surrender, causing Livie to giggle.

"Mommy!" A tiny version of Storm in striped pajamas appears, tucking herself behind her mother's shapely long legs as she peers up to examine us with her thumb in her mouth. She's about the most gorgeous little girl I've ever seen.

"These are our new neighbors, Kacey and Livie. This is Mia," Storm introduces us, her hand stroking the little girl's dark blond waves.

"Hi!" Livie hollers with that tone reserved for little kids. "Pleased to meet you."

No matter what kind of mess I've turned into, little kids have the power to temporarily melt the layer of protective ice coating my heart. Them and potbellied puppies. "Hello, Mia," I say softly.

Mia ducks back with hesitation, glancing up at Storm.

"She's shy around strangers," Storm apologizes, then looks down to address Mia. "It's okay. Maybe these girls will be your new friends."

The words "new friends" is all it takes. Mia steps out from behind her mother's legs and wanders into our apartment, dragging a faded yellow fleece blanket behind her. At first she simply takes in our place, likely investigating it for hints about her new "friends." When her eyes finally rest on Livie, they don't shift again.

Livie drops to her knees to meet Mia face-to-face, a giant grin stretched across her face. "I'm Livie."

Mia holds up her blanket, her face serious. "This is Mr. Magoo. He's my friend." Now that she's talking, I can see a giant gap where she's lost her two front teeth. She's instantly that much cuter.

"Nice to meet you, Mr. Magoo." Livie squeezes the fabric between her thumb and index finger, mock-shaking his hand.

Livie must have passed the Mr. Magoo test, because Mia grabs her arm and tugs her out the door. "Come meet my other friends." They disappear into Storm's apartment, leaving Storm and me alone.

"You guys aren't from around these parts." It's a statement, not a question. I hope she leaves it at that. "Have you been here long?" Storm's evaluating eyes float over our sparse living room, much like her daughter's had, pausing at a framed picture of us with our parents on the wall. Livie pulled it off Aunt Darla's family room wall as we ran out the door.

I silently admonish Livie for hanging it up there for all to see, to ask questions about, even though I have no right. There are a few times when Livie digs her heels in. That was one of them. If it were up to me, the picture would be in Livie's room where I could work up to visiting it occasionally.

It's too hard for me to look at their faces.

"Just a few days. Isn't it homey?"

Storm smirks at my attempt at humor. Livie and I ransacked the local dollar store for some basic necessities. Aside from that and the family picture, the only thing we've added is the scent of bleach in place of mothballs.

Storm nods, folding her arms over her chest as if to ward off a chill. There is no chill. Miami is hot, even at six a.m. "It's what works for now, right? That's all we can ask for," she says softly. Somehow I get the feeling she's talking about more than the apartment.

There's a squeal of delight next door and Storm laughs. "Your sister's good with kids."

"Yeah, Livie has some sort of magnetic power over them. No kid can resist her. Back home she volunteered at our local day care a lot. I'm sure she'll have at least twelve of her own." I lean in for a mock whisper behind my hand. "Wait till she learns what she needs to do with boys for that to happen."

Storm chuckles softly. "I'm sure she'll learn soon enough. She's striking. How old is she?"

"Fifteen."

She nods slowly. "And you? Are you in college?"

"Me?" I heave a sigh, fighting the urge to clam up. She's asking a lot of personal questions about us. I hear Livie's voice inside my head. *Try . . .* "No, I'm working right now. School will come later. Maybe in another year or two." *Or ten.* I'll make sure Livie's set up before me, that's for sure. She's the one with a bright future ahead of her.

There's a long pause as we're both lost in our own thoughts. "It's what works for now, right?" I echo her words and I see understanding in her blue eyes, thinly veiling her own dark closet of skeletons.

stage two

...

DENIAL

THREE

I wander half-asleep into the kitchen to find Livie and Mia at the little dining table, playing Go Fish.

"Good morning!" Livie sings.

"Good morning!" Mia mimics.

"It's like *eight* a.m.," I mutter as I grab the generic jug of OJ I splurged on the other day from the fridge.

"How was work?" Livie asked.

I take a giant gulp right from the container. "Shit."

There's a sharp gasp and I find Mia's short finger stabbing the air in my direction. "Kacey just said a naughty word!" she whispers.

I cringe as I catch Livie's unimpressed glare. "I get one, okay?" I say, looking for a way to excuse myself. I'll have to watch my language if Mia's going to be hanging around.

Mia's head cocks to one side, likely considering my logic. Then, given any good five-year-old's limited attention span, my heinous infraction is quickly forgotten. She smiles and announces, "You guys are coming over for brunch. Not breakfast and not lunch."

Now it's my turn to glare at Livie. "Are we now?"

Lowering her brow, Livie gets up and comes to my side. "You

said you'd try," she reminds me in a low whisper so Mia doesn't overhear.

"I said I'd be nice. I didn't say I'd swap muffin recipes with the neighbors," I respond, trying hard not to growl.

I get an eye roll. "Stop being dramatic. Storm's cool. I think you'd like her if you'd stop avoiding her. And all other living creatures."

"I'll have you know I've graciously served over a thousand cups of coffee this week to living creatures. Some questionable ones, too."

Crossing her arms, Livie's glare dissipates, but she doesn't say anything.

"I'm not avoiding people." *Yes, I am.* Everyone, including Barbie. And Dimples next door. Definitely him. I'm sure I've spotted his lean frame watching out the window as I came home at night a few times, but I ducked my head and sped past, my insides constricting at the thought of seeing him face-to-face again.

"Really? 'Cause Storm sure thinks you are. She came out to talk to you the other day, and you rushed into the apartment like lightning before she could say 'hi.'"

I hide behind another sip of juice. Busted. I *totally* did that. I heard her door unlock and the beginnings of a "Hello, Kacey," and I hurried to shut our apartment door.

"I *am* like lightning. Lightning Girl has a nice ring to it," I say.

Livie watches as I scan the meager contents of our fridge and my stomach protests with a perfectly timed growl. We agreed to spend as little as possible until I earned a paycheck or two so we've been living off store-brand cereal and bologna sandwiches for more than a week. Given that I need more calories than the average twenty-year-old to function, this diet left me sluggish. I guess offering to feed us earns Storm at least five points in the potential friend bank.

My tongue slides over my top teeth. "Fine."

Livie's face brightens. "That's a yes?"

I shrug, acting nonchalant. Inside, panic is rising. *Livie's get-ting too attached to these people.* Attachments are bad. Attachments lead to hurt. I make a face. "As long as she's not making bologna."

She giggles, and I know it's more than my lame joke. She knows I'm trying, and that makes her happy.

I change the subject. "How's your new school, by the way?" I'd worked the afternoon shift all week so we haven't communicated at all, besides exchanging a few kitchen-counter notes.

"Oh . . . right." Livie's face pales as though she's seen a ghost. She reaches for her backpack, with a glance back to see Mia busy playing her own card game at the table. "I checked my email account at school," she explains as she hands me a piece of paper.

My back stiffens. I knew this was coming.

Dearest Olivia,

I assume that sister of yours has convinced you to run off. I can't possibly understand why but I hope you are safe. Please send me a message to let me know where you are. I will come get you and bring you home, where your parents want you to be. That will make them happy.

I am not upset with you. You are a sheep led astray by a wolf.

Please let me bring you home. Your uncle and I miss you terribly.

Love,
Aunt Darla

Heat erupts like a volcano inside me as my blood boils. Not from the wolf comment. I don't care about that; she's called me worse. But she's using our parents as a guilt trip, knowing full well it would hurt Livie. "You didn't respond, did you?"

Livie shakes her head solemnly.

"Good," I say through clenched teeth, crumpling the note into a tight ball. "Delete your account. Get a new one. Don't ever respond to her. Not once, Livie."

"Okay, Kacey."

"I mean it!" I hear Mia's tiny gasp and I quickly temper my tone. "We don't need them in our lives."

There's a long pause. "She's not a bad person. She means well." Livie's voice turns soft. "You didn't exactly make things easy for her."

I push down the lump of guilt forming at the back of my throat, fighting to take over my anger. "I know that, Livie. I do, really. But Aunt Darla's way of 'meaning well' doesn't work for us." My hands rub my forehead. I'm no idiot. For the first year after the accident, I put all my effort, focus, and thought into fixing my body so I could move again. Once released, my focus shifted to shoving the memories of my former life into a bottomless well. There were impossible days, though—holidays, birthdays, and the like—and I quickly learned that alcohol and drugs, while capable of destroying lives, also had a magical power: the power to dull pain. More and more, I relied on those weapons against the constant and overwhelming rush of water swelling over my head, threatening to drown me.

That and sex. Meaningless, mindless "take what I want" sex with strangers whom I didn't care about, and who didn't care about me. No expectations, at least not on my part. Guys from parties, guys from school. If it was awkward for them afterward, I didn't care. I never let them get close enough to me to find out. It was the perfect coping mechanism.

Aunt Darla knew what was going on, but she just didn't know how to handle it. At first she tried connecting me with her priest so he could confront and rid me of the demons within. This all had to be the work of demons, after all, but when the demons proved resilient to her church's powers, I think she decided ignorance was best. "It's just a phase," I'd hear her whisper to Livie with a comforting pat. A disgusting, self-deprecating phase that she wanted no part of. From that point on, she put all of her focus on her non-broken niece.

I was fine with that until I woke up to Livie smacking my back to keep me from choking on my own vomit, tears streaming down her cheeks, sobbing hysterically, saying over and over again, "Promise you won't leave me!"—her words a knife stabbing my heart.

I stopped everything that night. The drinking. The drugs. The random sex. The sex, period. I haven't so much as looked at a guy since. I'm not sure why. I guess it's all linked together in my mind. Luckily, I found a new release with kickboxing soon after. Livie has never completely approved of or supported my newest addiction, but she happily takes it over the other stuff.

I slam the fridge door, not wanting to think about Aunt Darla or the depths of my self-destructive past anymore. "What time's breakfast?"

"Brunch!" Mia corrects me with a loud sigh.

. . .

The delicious smells of bacon and coffee spark hunger pangs as we follow Mia into her place. I mentally pat myself on the back for making the right choice. If nothing else, the western omelets Storm is serving will give me loads of energy for the gym today.

My eyes drift over Storm's apartment and I feel a degree of awe. It's a mirror image of ours, except it's *nice*. She's filled the living room with a dove-gray sectional, sparkly throw cushions, and little glass tables with pretty crystal lamps. A flat-screen television sits on a stylish teak armoire. The hideous green carpet peeks out beneath a cream shag rug. Her walls are a light gray and splashed with candid black-and-white photos of Mia. While our apartment looks like a cheap rental, Storm's looks like a trendy girlish boutique.

I have to admit, as I sit at the table and quietly listen to Storm, Livie, and Mia banter back and forth, I'm starting to like Storm whether I want to or not. Though one would never know by looking at her, Storm is street-smart and she acts a lot older than her twenty-three years. It takes no time to see that. She's laid-back and she cracks a witty joke here and there in that soft but husky voice of hers. She fumbles with her hair a lot and laughs easily, and I see nothing but sincerity and interest in her eyes. For someone so beautiful, she doesn't come across as vain or self-absorbed. Mostly she listens, though. And watches. Those shrewd orbs take everything in. I catch her studying the tattoo on my thigh, her eyes narrowing slightly as I'm sure she's zeroing in on the hideous scar beneath it. It's the one major scar that's not caused by surgery but from a jagged chunk of flying glass.

She doesn't ask about it, though, and that makes me like her even more.

"Oh, man!" Storm exclaims as she sits back down after she's finished clearing the table. She yawns and I notice that her eyes are red and underlined with dark purple bags. Leaning on her elbows, she rubs her face fiercely. "I can't wait until Mia learns how to sleep in. At least during the week I can sneak in a mid-morning nap while she's at school."

"Oh, I was going to ask you. Do you mind if I take Mia to the park down the street?" Livie asks as if she'd been thinking about it and genuinely forgot. I instantly see what she's doing. That's so Livie. "I won't let her out of my sight. Not for a sec, I promise." Livie starts ticking off the items on her impressive résumé. "I've got my CPR certification, my junior lifeguard designation, a thousand hours at a private day care. I even have a printed copy of my résumé in our apartment if you want it. And references!" *Of course you do, Livie.* "We'll be back in, say, four hours, if that's okay with you?"

"Yeah, Mommy! Say yes!" Mia bounces up and down on the couch, waving her arms frantically. "Say yes! Yes! Yes! Mommy, say yes!"

"Okay, okay. Calm down." Storm laughs, patting the air. "Of course you can, Livie. You spend so much time with her as it is, I'm not worried about your credentials. I should be paying you, though!"

"No. Absolutely not." Livie brushes her words away, earning a sharp glare from me. *Is she nuts? Does she enjoy eating bologna? Must we move on to Spam?*

Livie helps Mia with her shoes. "Bye, Mommy!" Mia shouts on her way out. Livie avoids making eye contact with me. It's as if she has a line to my brain and can read my scathing thoughts.

As soon as the door closes, Storm's forehead drops to the table. "I thought I was going to die today. Oh, Kacey. I swear, your sister's like an angel fluttering around with little satin wings and a magical wand. I've never met someone like her. Mia's already so in love with her."

The layer of ice over my heart melts. I decide maybe I can "try" to be friends with Storm Matthews, giant fake breasts and all.

■ ■ ■

"See you later, Livie," I grumble, grabbing my things for Starbucks, a scowl twisting my face.

"Kace . . ." There's a long pause. Livie's gulp fills the silence between us and I know something's bothering her.

"Ugh, Livie!" I roll my head back. "Spit it out. I don't want to be late for my stellar job."

"I think I should have stayed in Grand Rapids."

That freezes my feet. Anger sparks inside me at the thought of my little sister left back there, not with me. "Stop saying stupid shit like that, Livie." I tap her nose, making her flinch. "Right now. Of course you shouldn't have stayed in Grand Rapids."

"How are we going to survive, though?"

"With ten hours of prostitution for each of us. Maximum."

"Kacey!"

I sigh, turning serious. "We'll figure it out."

"I can get a job."

"You need to concentrate on school, Livie. But . . ." I waggle my finger at her. "If Storm offers you money again, take it."

She's already shaking her head. "No. I'm not taking money to hang out with Mia. She's fun."

"You're supposed to be having fun with people your own age, Livie. Like boys."

Her jaw tenses. "When they're not idiots, I'll do that. Until then, five-year-olds make more sense."

I stifle a laugh. That's part of Livie's problem. She's too smart. Genius smart. She's never related to kids her own age. I think she was born with the maturity of a twenty-five-year-old. Losing my parents only exacerbated that problem. She's grown up too fast.

"What about you? It's never too late for the Princeton dream," she says quietly.

An unattractive snort escapes me. "That dream died years ago for me, Livie, and you know that. You'll go to Princeton. I'll apply somewhere local as soon as I have the money." *And somehow forge my transcript to erase two years of appalling grades.*

Her brow creases in that worried Livie way. "Local, Kacey? Dad would hate that." She's right, he would. Our dad went to Princeton. *His* dad when to Princeton. In his view, I may as well enroll in a school with golden arches for a crest and take "Flipping Burgers 101" if I'm not going to Princeton. But Mom and Dad are gone, and Uncle Raymond blew our entire inheritance at a blackjack table.

I remember the night I found out about that as if it were yesterday. It was my nineteenth birthday, and I asked Aunt Darla and Uncle Raymond for our money so we could move out. I wanted to become Livie's legal guardian. I knew something was up when Aunt Darla's gaze wouldn't meet my eyes. Uncle Raymond stumbled over his words before blurting out that there was nothing left.

After smashing almost every dish on the kitchen counter and jamming my foot into Uncle Raymond's jugular so hard his face turned purple, I dialed the cops, ready to charge my aunt and uncle with theft. Livie grabbed the phone from me and hung up before the call went through. We wouldn't win. I'd likely be the one arrested. As smart as Mom and Dad were, they didn't plan on dying. All the money left after the debts were paid went to Uncle Raymond and Aunt Darla to "care" for us. Secretly, I'm kind of glad Uncle Raymond did all that he did. It gave me another legitimate excuse to take my sister and leave that part of our lives behind for good.

I pat Livie's back, trying to appease her guilt. "Dad would be happy that we're safe. End of story."

■ ■ ■

The next afternoon I'm in the laundry room, when Storm skips down the steps, smiling but sallow-eyed. Livie took Mia to the park after school again and I'm giving serious consideration to smacking her upside the head for refusing to take money.

"Tanner must have his panties in a bunch over this." Storm slides her foot across the sticky green stain left by my detergent. I duck my head, silently reminding myself to come back and scrub the floor. The thought of Tanner in any kind of underwear makes bile rise in my throat.

I quietly continue my sorting until I notice Storm is standing there idly, watching me. It's obvious she wants to talk to me, but she probably doesn't know where to start.

"How long have you lived here?" I finally ask.

I think my voice startles her because she jumps and begins tossing in Mia's little T-shirts and tiny pairs of undies. "Oh, three years, I think? It's a pretty safe building, but I still wouldn't come down here at night."

Her words return my mind to thoughts of Trent and the unwanted feelings he elicited from me so effortlessly. We've been here several weeks and I haven't run into him since that first day. If I dig deep inside, if I care to pay attention to what I'm trying to bury, I catch a glimpse of disappointment over that fact. But I quickly crush it with a hammer and throw it into the well with all the other unwanted feelings.

"What are the other people like in the building?"

She shrugs. "A lot of people move in and out. Rent's cheap, so we get a lot of college kids. They've all been nice, especially to Mia. Mrs. Potterage on the third floor helps babysit after school and when I work. Oh,"—she points a finger at me—"avoid 2B like the plague. That's Pervie Pete."

My head tilts back with a groan. "Fantastic. No building is complete without a resident perv."

"Oh, and a new guy moved in next to you. 1D."

I can't control the heat from crawling up my neck. "Yeah, Trent," I say casually as I set the machine. Even hearing his name out loud sounds hot. Trent. Trent. Trent. *Stop it, Kace.*

"Well, I haven't talked to this Trent, but I saw him and . . . wowza." Her eyebrows waggle suggestively.

Great. My gorgeous Barbie neighbor thinks Trent is hot. All she has to do is adjust her shirt and she'll have him on his knees. I realize my teeth are clenched painfully and I focus on relaxing my muscles. *She can have him and all the trouble he comes with. Why do you care, Kace?*

Slamming the door to her machine shut and hitting the On switch, Storm exhales deeply, blowing her long bangs off her face. "Are you going to be here for a while?" She glances at the newspaper and marker I've brought down with me. "Would you mind just turning my stuff over when it goes off? I mean, if you're around and it's not too much trouble."

I look at her again, at her drawn skin and the purplish lines marring her pretty blue eyes, and see just how worn she is. Young, single mom with a five-year-old and she works six days a week, up until three a.m. every night.

"Yeah, no problem." That sounds like something a nice, normal person would do, I tell myself. Livie will be proud.

"Are you sure? I don't want to impose."

I notice that she's biting her lip and her shoulders are pinched together, and it dawns on me that she's nervous. Asking for my help likely took a ton of courage, and she must be desperate enough to do it. Realizing that makes me want to slam my head into a wall. Clearly, I haven't tried very hard to be approachable, like I promised Livie I would be. And Storm's nice. Really, genuinely nice.

"Why, ma'am, I reckon it'd be my honor to wash your drawers," I drawl in a fake southern accent, picking up the paper to fan myself with it.

Her face lights up with surprise as she giggles. She opens her mouth to answer, but nothing comes out. Me having a sense of humor has floored her. *Dammit, Livie's right. I am an ice queen.*

I quickly add, "Besides, I owe you for last week. It's the least I can do after pulling out Hannah—the dirtiest of all weapons."

I smile and it's not forced. "I'll just be going through the jobs section, so I may as well do that in this paradise."

She frowns. "Starbucks not working out?" Livie must have told her, because I sure didn't.

"It's fine, but the pay's shit. If I want to live on Spam and scrape blue spots off of bread for the rest of my life, I can make it work."

She nods, thinking. "You guys should come over for dinner tonight." I open my mouth to decline the charity, but before I can she adds, "As my thanks to Livie for taking care of Mia today." There's something in that tone, a mixture of forced bravery and authority, that makes me slam my mouth shut. "I'm going to start cooking now. It'll be ready by the time these loads finish."

"And . . ." She shifts her feet a bit hesitantly, as if she's not sure if she should say what's on her mind. ". . . do you know how to mix drinks?"

"Uh . . ." I blink rapidly at the sudden change in topic. "Isn't it a little early in the day for that?"

She smiles, her perfect teeth gleaming. "Like martinis and Long Islands?"

"I pour a mean tequila shot," I offer halfheartedly.

"Well, I can talk to my boss and see if he'll hire you, if you're interested. I bartend at a club. The money's good." Her eyes widen with those last words. "Like, really good."

"Bartender, huh?"

She grins. "So, what do ya think?"

Could I handle it? I don't say anything, trying to picture myself behind a bar. The visual ends with me smashing a bottle and kicking a grabby customer in the head.

"I should probably warn you, though." She hesitates. "It's an adult club."

I feel the frown line zip across my forehead. "Adult like . . ."

"Strippers."

"Oh . . ." *Of course.* I look down at myself. "Yeah, I'm a keep-clothes-on-in-crowds kind of girl."

Storm's hands wave my words away. "No, don't worry. You wouldn't have to strip. I promise."

Me? Work in a strip club? "You think I'd fit in, Storm?"

"Can you handle being surrounded by sex, booze, and loads of cash?"

I shrug. "Sounds like my teenage years, minus the cash."

"Can you learn how to smile a bit more?" she asks with a nervous giggle.

I flash her my best fake grin.

She nods with approval. "Good. I think you'll do well behind the bar. You have a look they'll like."

I snort. "What look? The I-just-got-off a bus from-Michigan-and-I'll-do-anything-for-money-so-I-don't-have-to-eat-Spam look?"

The corners of her eyes crinkle as she giggles. "Think about it and let me talk to my boss. It's *really* good money. You wouldn't have to eat Spam again. Ever." With that, she skips up the stairs.

I think about it. I think about it for the next half an hour as I watch Storm and Mia's clothes spin around in circles. I think about it as the timer goes off and I flip the clothes over into the dryer and start two new loads. I think about it as I sort and fold their freshly clean clothes into neat piles and reload the hamper, paying a little too much attention to the skimpy outfits in Storm's pile. Like a tiny black top that looks like a cross between a sequined sports bra and something a wild animal mangled. I hold it up. Does she serve drinks or her body in this? That would explain her ridiculous boobs. Wow! I might be making friends with a stripper. That sounds weird. And then I realize that I'm going through her underwear. That's way weirder.

"Tell me where you wear that so I can be there to witness it."
His deep voice startles me again.

I gasp as my head whips around to see Trent strolling toward
me with a laundry bag slung over his shoulder. My breath hitches
at the sight of him, especially those deep dimples he flashes
shamelessly. It's been more than two weeks since I bumped into
him here, yet seeing him instantly ignites a fire within me.

Again with the laundry room? What are the chances? Inhaling
deeply, I force myself to relax. I'm better prepared this time. *I
won't act like a space cadet. I won't let his beautiful face disarm me. I
won't . . .* "Well, well. The Laundromat Lurker strikes again."

Trent smirks as his eyes graze over my body, stopping to sur-
vey the tattoo on my thigh for a moment before flittering back
up to my face. By the time they get there, my pulse is racing and
I think I may need to change my underwear. *Dammit! Here we go
again.* "Round two," I mutter before I can stop myself.

His eyebrow quirks with surprise as he moves toward the
open washer.

I try not to ogle his body through his fitted white T-shirt,
watching him dump a set of white sheets into the wash. "You
wash your sheets a lot," I observe coolly, thinking that's a fairly
innocuous comment.

Trent's hands pause for a second and then he continues,
chuckling and shaking his head but saying nothing. He doesn't
need to. I've clued into what my observation could imply and I
groan to myself, fighting the urge to smack myself in the forehead, my face growing even warmer. Any upper hand I thought I
had when he walked in just dissolved into a hot mess at my feet.

I'm sure his sheets see a lot of action. He's got to have a girlfriend. Someone like him *must* have a girlfriend. Or a string of
fuck buddies. Either way, now I want to crawl into a hole and
hide until he leaves.

"What can I say? It's hot in Miami without A/C," he offers after a moment as if to ease the awkwardness. That's what I fool myself into thinking, anyway, until he throws in, "Even without clothes, I wake up boiling."

Trent sleeps naked. My mouth dries as my focus uncontrollably latches onto his frame again. On the other side of my living room wall is this god, in a bed, lying naked. Though I thought it impossible, my pulse quickens even more.

I open my mouth to change topics, but I can't utter anything coherent. Words swim inside my head, stringing into gibberish. I can't come up with one damn remotely intelligent response. I, who can crack orgy jokes and crush arrogant ball sacs with the best of them, am floored. He has smoothly splintered my defensive shield with nothing but bedsheets and a visual of him naked.

And those damn dimples.

I watch the muscles in his shoulders shift as he pours detergent into the machine. Who knew doing laundry could be sexy? When he turns to me and winks, I jump.

"You okay?" he asks.

I nod and try to make an affirmative sound, but it comes out sounding like a strangled cat and I'm sure my entire head has caught on fire.

He slams the lid on the washer and pushes the coins in to start the machine, then turns to me, leaning in. "To be honest, I saw you walking past my apartment with your laundry and I grabbed the first thing I could think to wash."

Wait . . . what's he saying? I shake my head to kick the haze out of my mind. *I think he's telling me something important.*

He grins as he pushes a hand back through his unkempt hair. *I want to do that*, I think, involuntarily flexing my fingers. *Please let me do that.* In fact, I want to do all kinds of things to him. Right here in this dingy basement. On the washer. On the floor.

Anywhere. I battle the urge to lunge at him like a rabid animal. Hell, I'm panting like one right now.

"So, what do people do for fun around here?" he asks, leaning back a bit to give me space, as if he can read that I'm about to pass out from his proximity.

"Uh . . ." It takes me a moment to find my voice. And my wits. "Hang out in laundry rooms?" My words come out shaky. *Dammit—what is wrong with me?*

He laughs, his gaze settling on my lips. The feel of his eyes there makes me spew out words that my brain hasn't approved yet. "I don't know. I just moved here. I haven't had any fun yet." *Ohmigod, Kacey. Shut up! Just shut up! Now you sound like an airhead and a loser!*

With a lopsided grin, he leans against the washer and crosses his buff arms over his chest. And then he stares at me. That stare lasts an eternity, until sweat starts to trickle down my back. "Well, we need to change that, don't we?"

"Huh?" I croak, heat igniting in my lower belly. He has effectively stripped me bare of my titanium cover again. He's tossed it to another planet, where I have no hope of ever finding it. I am naked and vulnerable and his eyes are boring into my core.

His body slides across his washer until he's leaning on mine, his hip nudged up against me, his arm stretched out to the opposite corner of the machine in front of me, effectively invading all my personal space. "Change the fact that you're not having any fun," he murmurs. My breath catches. I feel as if he's reached into my body and seized my pounding heart. Does he have any idea what he's doing to me? Am I that obvious?

His index finger reaches up and runs down my temple, down my cheek, to join the rest of his hand to cup my jaw. He rubs my hanging bottom lip with the pad of his thumb as I gawk up at him. I can't move. Not a muscle. His touch has the power to paralyze me. "You are so very beautiful."

My nerves are a ball of contradictions. His fingertip feels so damn good against my lip and yet that voice is screaming, *No! Stop! Danger!*

"So are you," I hear myself whisper, and I instantly curse the traitor within.

Do. Not. Let. This. Happen.

He leans in closer and closer until his breath caresses my mouth. I'm paralyzed. I swear he's going to kiss me.

I swear I'm going to let him.

But then he stands up straight, as if remembering something. Clearing his throat, he says with a wink, "See you around, Kacey." He turns and vanishes up the stairs, his long legs taking two steps at a time.

"Ye-yeah. Fo-for sure," I stutter, leaning against the machine for support as my legs turn to jelly. I'm sure I'm two seconds away from melting into a puddle on the concrete floor. I fight the urge to chase after him. *One . . . two . . . three . . .* I struggle to shake off the uncomfortable edge that has slinked into my body. Hunching over, I lay my cheek against the machine, my flushed skin reveling in the relief of the cool metal.

He's one hell of a player. I'm usually so good at shutting them down. Being a female in a male-dominated gym, I dealt with those juiced-up egomaniacs at O'Malleys every day. *Hold my bag for me . . . Dominate me . . .* The comments were never-ending and uncreative. Then, when they decided that I must be a lesbian because I hadn't dropped my shorts for any of them, the stupid comments increased tenfold.

I've never had issues resisting the hottest of them. None of them have broken through this masterful wall of self-preservation I've constructed around myself. I enjoyed sparring with them. I loved knocking them to their knees. But never had they stirred any interest from me, physical or otherwise.

But Trent . . . there's something different about him, and I don't have to think hard to see it. Something about the way he takes over a room, the way he looks at me, as though he has already identified and can disarm every one of my defense mechanisms with no effort, as though he sees through them to the disaster lying beneath.

And he wants it.

"Fucking player," I mutter as I run to the sink. A splash of water temporarily douses the flames in my chest. He's smooth. Oh so smooth. Way more sophisticated than the asshats I normally deal with. "You're so very beautiful," I repeat, followed by a harsh mock reenactment of myself saying "So are you." I'm sure he tells everyone that. Watch, he'll meet Storm and say the exact same thing. *Oh God.* My gut spasms, my fists clench so tight that my knuckles go white. What will happen when he meets Storm? He'll fall in love with her, that's what. He's a guy. What guy wouldn't fall in love with Sweet Stripper Barbie? And then I'll become nothing more than that head case in 1C and I'll have to watch them cuddle on the couch, and listen to them have wild stripper sex on the other side of my bedroom wall, and I'll want to rip Storm's arms off. *Dammit.* I crank up the cold water and splash my face again. In no time, this guy has created permanent fissures in my carefully constructed suit of sanity, and I don't know how to fight against it, to protect myself, to keep him out.

To keep all of them out.

Ninety-nine percent of me knows I need to keep him at arm's length. There's no point in thinking about letting him get close. He'll get one look at my shit and he'll run, leaving a bigger mess behind. And yet, as I eye the washer where he just stood, where his bedsheets swirl, I give serious consideration to stealing them and leaving a "come and get it" note in their place. *No.* I shove angry hands through my thick mane, gripping the back of my head as if to keep it from exploding. I need to stay away from him. He's going to ruin everything I've worked so hard to put in place.

Suddenly, I can't get out of that laundry room fast enough.

■ ■ ■

Mia and Livie sit cross-legged on the living room floor with a Chutes and Ladders board game between them. A freshly show-ered Storm dumps a pot of spaghetti noodles into a pot of boiling water. "I hope you don't mind veal in your sauce," she says as I step in without knocking. I figure we're past the knocking stage. I just touched her thongs, after all.

"That'd be great. Your clothes are all here."

She looks over her shoulder at the hamper in shock. "Did you fold my underwear for me?"

"Uh . . . no?"

Turning a bit more to see my face, my hair still damp from the tap water, she frowns. "What happened to you?"

How do I explain that I had to have a cold mini-shower in the laundry room because that damn smooth-talking neighbor of ours cornered me? I don't.

"It was Stephen King's *Maximum Overdrive* all over again. The washing machine came to life and attacked me. Laundry and I are officially on no-speaking terms."

"I've never read that book," Storm says at the same time that I hear a tiny frightened gasp.

"I'm not surprised," I mumble as I head toward the kitchen, catching a scathing glare from Livie for scaring Mia. Our dad made us watch all the movies from his era as a way of keeping the classics alive. Most of the time, no one in my generation has a clue what I'm talking about.

Storm turns to face me wearing an apron that reads, *How's*

the sauce? Has anyone seen my Band-Aid? and a big grin. "Hey, so I spoke to my boss. Job's yours if you want it."

"Storm!" My eyes bug out.

Her long blond locks sway as she tips her head back to laugh, my shock apparently amusing. I can tell she's happy to give me the news. I get the impression that she genuinely *wants* to help us, and for no reason other than because she's just that nice.

"I haven't decided yet." *Liar, yes, you have.* Good money is good money, and as long as I don't have to strip I can handle standing in the middle of a vagina circus.

"What job is this?" Livie pipes up, her curiosity peaked.

"A job with me, where I work," Storm explains.

"My mommy gets paid to give people drinks, in a restaurant. Like this!" Mia scrambles to her feet and runs over to grab an empty cup from the counter. "Would you like a glass of lemonade, Madam?" She carries it to Livie with the utmost care and bows.

"Why, thank you, kind waitress," Livie gushes theatrically, and proceeds to gulp back the imaginary drink as if she's just crossed the Sahara Desert, finishing with a wink for Mia. But, when she turns to me, her brow is furrowed with unease. "Serving more than lemonade, I take it?"

I nod, dropping my gaze to focus on rearranging the cutlery on the table before I can meet her worried expression again. Her bottom lip is sucked into her mouth. She's trying hard to stop it from quivering, and I know what she's thinking. She's afraid I'll spiral back into that dark place where the tequila is flowing and the one-night stands are frequent. Even though I've promised her a hundred times that that phase is over, she's still terrified of losing me to it again. I can't blame her.

That's why I'm surprised by her next words. "You should take it, Kacey."

My head cocks to the side as I consider what she said.

She shrugs. "If you're serving them, you can cut them off, right?"

"Right." I nod slowly, processing that logic. Livie always finds the good in things. I steal a glance at Storm to see her intently focused on stirring her tomato sauce. I know she must have heard that. She's got to be wondering what dark skeletons these two neighbors of hers have in their closet. As usual, she has the decency not to pry.

"And there's good money in tips, from what I hear," Livie adds. "Maybe I can get a fake ID and get a job there too!"

"No!" Storm and I shout in unison, and share a silent look. A look that says this is good enough for us, but not for Livie. She's better than that.

"Mommy? Are you working tonight?" Mia's tiny voice chirps up, holding off more questions from Livie.

Storm smiles sadly at her daughter. "Yes, honey bear." It has to be hard, leaving her six nights in a row.

"Can I stay with Livie? Please, Mommy?" Mia holds her hands together in front of her as if she's praying.

"Oh, I don't know, Mia. I think you've monopolized enough of Livie's time today, don't you?"

"But, noooo . . . Mommy!" Mia whines, and stomps around the room in a circle, reminding everyone that she *is* only five years old. She stops in a huff, throwing her arms around herself, and scowls. "I don't like Mrs. Potterage!"

"She's a nice lady, Mia," Storm says with a sigh, as though she's said it a hundred times before. She leans in and whispers to me, "I don't blame the poor kid. Potterage smokes like a burning oil field. But I can usually rely on her for at least four nights a week."

"I don't mind at all," Livie jumps in with a pat on Mia's back.

"See, Mommy? Livie says yes!"

Storm cringes. "Are you sure?"

"Of course. In fact, I'm more than happy to watch her every night if you want," Livie says with complete seriousness.

"Oh, Livie. I work six days a week. That's a lot to ask of a fifteen-year-old. You deserve to go out and party, or whatever fifteen-year-olds are doing these days."

Livie is already shaking her head. "No, it's not, and I don't mind." She pinches Mia's cheek, as taken by the child as Mia is of her. "I'd love it."

There's a long pause and Storm swallows, considering it. "You'd have to let me pay you for your time. No more arguing."

Livie's hand waves dismissively. "Yeah, fine. Whatever. She'll be asleep most of the time anyway and Kacey will be at work with you, right? So at least I won't be alone."

All three turn to look at me hopefully.

I heave a loud sigh. "Just drinks, right? I'm not serving any-one . . . anything else."

Storm's eyes twinkle. "Not unless you want to."

"And I don't have to wear anything revealing?"

"Well . . ."

My head drops back and rolls from one side to the other. "Here we go."

"I was just going to say that you'll make more money show-ing a bit of cleavage than you will dressed as a Mormon. A lot more money. I'd show a teensy tiny bit of skin, if I were you."

I sigh again. "And I can quit if I don't like it? No hard feelings?"

"Absolutely, Kacey. No hard feelings," Storm asserts, holding a wooden spoon in front of her face as if she's pledging.

I pause just long enough to make Storm squirm. "Okay."

"Great!" Storm throws her toned arms around me, oblivious that the contact is making my insides churn and the voice in my head scream. She breaks away just as quickly and moves back to her pot of sauce, allowing me a chance to exhale. "You start tonight, by the way."

"Tonight! Fun." I can't keep the sarcasm from my voice as butterflies start their mad dash around my belly, killing my appetite. I hug my arms tight to my body, acknowledging that a club's worth of new people means handshakes and questions about personal shit that are none of anyone's business. I'm not ready for this. I haven't prepared . . . *One . . . two . . . three . . . four . . .* By the time I reach ten, I'm freaking out.

stage three

■ ■ ■

RESISTANCE

FOUR

The sun has set by the time we pull up to Penny's Palace in Storm's Jeep. Storm doesn't even have the thing in Park before I jump out. When she walks around to meet me on my side, she looks at me with a mixture of surprise and concern. She doesn't comment, though.

But she does make a remark about me tugging at the short black skirt I borrowed from her. "Stop fidgeting." She swats my hand away. "I never would have taken you for the nervous type."

"Easy for you to say. Your ass isn't hanging out. I can't believe I agreed to wear this Band-Aid. I'm going to bend over and show everyone my girl bits."

Storm laughs. "Of course you should wear that Band-Aid. It shows those awesome legs of yours off."

"It's showing more than my legs," I mutter, giving it another tug to cover the bottom of my tattoo. I'm not ashamed of that; I just don't want to draw more attention to myself than necessary.

"Good Lord! For such a tough act, you really are a big sissy girl, aren't you?"

She's right. I guess I'm just out of my element here and it's causing me to second-guess everything. If this were the gym, I'd have no problem in tiny shorts that hug my ass. But this isn't the gym and I'm not allowed to kick the crap out of anything here.

I cock my head to the side as I take in Storm. "Did you just call me a sissy girl?"

She doesn't miss a beat. "Did you just say 'girl bits'? This is an adult club, not a day care."

"I'll try to remember that." I chuckle as we approach the solid black metal door with a tiny peephole in it.

"You look great, Kacey. Seriously." I try not to flinch as she pats my shoulder.

Secretly, I have to admit that I do. Along with the miniskirt, I'm wearing a charcoal striped halter top and several silver jewelry pieces, courtesy of Storm's collection. She also helped me with my hair and makeup. I look more than decent. Not a knockout standing next to Storm with her turquoise dress and tanned skin and Barbie-doll curves, but decent. Decent enough that I caught myself swaggering extra slow past 1D on my way out, hoping to catch Trent's face in the window. Then I realized what I was doing, and I ran the rest of the way to Storm's Jeep, the voice inside my head scolding the snot out of me the entire way.

Storm raps against the heavy door four times. It flies open and my insides flip. Not many people intimidate me anymore. The giant man with dark skin and bulging muscles who fills the doorway, as wide as he is tall, though . . . I'm not ashamed about cowering. By the look of him, I wouldn't be surprised if he's never smiled a day in his life. He's certainly never been a cute baby. I'm sure he simply materialized out of nothingness into the beast standing before me.

"This is Nate. He's the head bouncer and Cain's right-hand man. Hey, Nate! This is my friend, Kacey." Storm doesn't wait for him to respond. She simply pushes past him, her hand giving his solid abdomen a soft punch on the way in.

"Hi," he says. The tiny word rumbles deep inside me, his voice like thunder, and I nod, temporarily mute.

He steps back to give me more space. "Come in, please."

Forcing bravado that I don't feel, I jack my chin up and step inside. Storm leads me down a narrow hallway lined with liquor cases and silver kegs, smelling faintly of beer yeast. Dark memories rise with the scent. Memories of clubs and tequila shots off guys' stomachs and white powder lines on tables in dark corners. I quickly cram them back where they belong. In the past.

"Here are the dressing rooms for the dancers . . ." Storm's index finger points to two closed doors. "I wouldn't go in there unless you want to see all kinds of 'girl bits.'" With a teasing laugh, she continues down the hall.

We pass by a broad-shouldered, towering blond guy in a tight black T-shirt and black pants. Judging by his outfit, he's definitely another bouncer but not as ominous-looking as Nate. He's cute in that "I'm from Wisconsin and I play football" kind of way. He reminds me of Billy . . .

"Kacey, this is Ben," Storm introduces us.

"Hey, Kacey." He grins, and then his head cocks to the side as if he suddenly recognizes me. "Hey, weren't you at The Breaking Point the other day?"

I look him over. I don't remember him, but then again, I don't pay any heed to the guys there. "Maybe. I just joined."

He nods slowly. "Yeah, that was definitely you." His eyes shamelessly take in my body. "You're incredible. Do you compete?"

I brush off the compliment. "Nah, it's just for fun." The truth is that I'd love to compete, but it's too dangerous for me, given my injuries. One hit to the wrong place will cause serious damage to all the work those surgeons did years ago to put me back together. I'm not about to tell Ben any of that, though.

"First night at Penny's?" he asks, leaning one forearm against a door frame.

"Yeah."

A lusty gaze wanders over me again.

"Bartending *only*," I add, crossing my arms over my chest, emphasizing the "only."

His attention skates back up to my face and he smirks. "Yeah, I've heard that before."

"And you'll hear it again from me every time you ask," I throw back coolly. What a pompous ass! He needs a good kick to the head to wipe that smirk off his mouth. Maybe I'll ask him to spar next time I'm at the gym.

Storm ushers me forward past him, hollering over her shoulder, "See ya later, Ben." She knocks on a door with a sign that reads *Bossman*. There's a caricature of a naked woman sitting spread-eagle and a pair of black lace thong underwear tacked on beside it. *How fitting!*

"And here's Cain's office. Don't worry. You'll fit in here," she whispers as she pushes through the door. I give the back of her head an arched brow. She thinks she *knows* me. She thinks I'll fit in with silicone and booze and vajayjays or whatever I'm supposed to call them. I'm second-guessing how smart Storm really is.

"Come in!" a harsh voice calls out, and my back tenses.

Inside is a small office with floor-to-ceiling shelves on all four walls, lined with more cases of booze. Tons and tons of booze. On the back wall is something that looks like a weird chemistry experiment—a bunch of upside-down liquor bottles with a mess of hoses flowing from their spouts, down into the floor. My nose catches a faint scent of cigar smoke, cedar, and whiskey lingering in the air.

"That's the bar well," Storm explains in a whisper. "All the basic liquor. It controls how much goes out. You hit a button behind the bar and it gives you one ounce. You hit it twice, two ounces—not rocket science."

"So I can't reenact my favorite scenes from *Cocktail*?" I mumble, picturing myself twirling bottles like a baton.

Storm chuckles. "You can, but it will be with the pricey bottles on the shelf, and they cost a lot when you break them."

A man with slick black hair and a navy dress shirt sits behind a giant mahogany desk with his back to us. Cain, I presume. He's on the phone with what sounds like the beer distributor. By the way he barks out "yes" and "no," I'd say he's not happy. He slams the phone down and spins around, and I prepare myself for a painful conversation.

But then his coffee-colored eyes settle on Storm and they instantly warm. He's a younger man—early thirties maybe—with attractive features and a nice sense of style. Definitely good-looking by anyone's standards. Still, he's a strip club owner, and that equals dirtbag in my book.

"Hello, Angel," he drawls, giving Storm a slow once-over. The hairs on the back of my neck prickle. I'm not going to like this guy. Not. One. Bit.

Storm ignores the leer. Or maybe she enjoys it. Frankly, I have no idea. I don't know her well enough either. "Hey, Cain." She cocks her head toward me. "This is my friend, Kacey. For the bartender position?"

My gut tenses as those dark eyes turn to appraise me, but his assessment only lasts for half a second. He bolts out of his chair and strides around the desk, extending his hand with a professional air. "Hi, Kacey. I'm Cain, the owner of Penny's. Pleased to meet you."

And here's where my little phobia makes life so damn awkward. I can't get around shaking the boss's hand when he offers it to me. Not unless I tear out of here right now, but then I'm out of a job. One I'm not sure I want, but a job nonetheless. My only real choice is to grit my teeth and hope I don't pass out from an anxiety attack when his fingers curl around my own, shoving me back into that dark place I keep trying to crawl out from.

I look at him, I look at his hand, I look at Storm. But most of all, I hear Livie's voice saying *try*.

I reach out . . .

Black spots fill my vision as his bones and muscles and gristle wrap around my hand and squeeze. My other hand blindly paws the air for support and I make contact with Storm's elbow. I grab onto it. I'm going to pass out. I'm going to keel over right here on this floor and do the funky chicken like an idiot. Nate the gargantuan will drag me out while Cain hollers, "Thanks, but no thanks, nut job," and then I'll be back to Starbucks and Livie will have to eat cat food and . . .

"Storm's told me a lot about you."

With a start, I realize Cain has let go of my hand. My lungs deflate. "Has she now?" I say in a shaky voice, stealing a glance at Storm.

He smiles warmly. "Yes. She said you've helped her out a lot. That you're smart and you're in need of a job. And that you're stunningly beautiful. I can see that now, firsthand."

I choke, my tongue disappearing into the back of my throat.

"Have you ever worked in an adult establishment?"

"Uh . . . no, sir," I answer, and silently pray to God that Storm hasn't told him otherwise. I don't know why, but I find suddenly that I *want* to impress Cain. He has an authoritative air about him, like he's much older and wiser than his appearance suggests, like he's a caring human rather than an unscrupulous strip club owner.

My answer doesn't seem to bother him. "One of my bartenders is pregnant. She and I both agree that a gentlemen's club isn't the best place for her, so . . . how many nights can you commit to?"

I look at Storm and shrug. "All of them?"

Cain's head tips back as he laughs wholeheartedly, revealing a tattoo beneath his left ear. It reads "Penny." She must be someone special if he named his club after her and tattooed her name on himself. "Don't sign your life away, sweetheart. Five or six nights will do." His eyes skim my arms now, skittering over the white scar snaking down the outside of my shoulder, and I silently chastise myself for not covering them. They probably frown upon disfigured women working in adult clubs. "You have a fighter's body," he says instead.

"No fighting. Just staying fit," I answer quickly.

He nods slowly. That seems to impress him. "Good. I like a woman who can take care of herself." He settles behind his desk again, saying, "You'll train Kacey, right, Storm?"

Storm is grinning ear to ear. "Yes, Cain."

He looks up at her again, and I see the look for what it truly is. Adoration, not lusty animalism. As though he worships her. I wonder if they've slept together. I wonder if he sleeps with all his staff. I'm sure he could if he wanted to. Will he try to sleep with me? I don't have time to think about it anymore because Storm is leading me out the door in a daze.

"Come on. We're opening soon. I need to get you comfortable."

■ ■ ■

The night goes by in a blur. Storm and I work the main bar together—Storm on the more complicated drinks, me on beer and straight shots while she teaches me the basics. The place is nothing like I expected. It's huge and three stories high in the center with a low ceiling around the perimeter, allowing sleek alcoves for the bars, shiny black high-top tables, and a hallway to the V.I.P. rooms. Apparently, Cain is strict about what happens back there. Nothing illegal, he tells all the girls. "I don't go back there," Storm says with a serious look that says "don't go back there either, Kacey."

On a raised stage in the center, the girls dance. There are three dancing at all times, each with her own little stage jutting off the main one to accommodate the group of leering men in the front row. A blue light shines down over the entire space, creating a mystical ambience. The rest of the place is dark, the air heady with booze and testosterone and lust. Music throbs through my body, its beat guiding the dancers' every move onstage.

Storm and I joke and chatter casually back and forth as we serve, and I can't help but start to relax around her. The place is busy, but people aren't climbing over each other at the bar to get a drink like at the nightclubs I've frequented. She introduces me to three girls she promises me I'll like: Ginger, Layla, and Penelope. They're all drop-dead gorgeous, giggly, and friendly. Everyone here seems to be gorgeous, giggly, and friendly, and I can't help but wonder for the hundredth time why Storm would think I'll fit in. But I say nothing, nodding to them all, making sure I've got two full hands so I can avoid all physical contact. No one seems to notice.

I get a bunch of "new girl" comments from customers who are obviously regulars, but I ignore them. I keep my head down and I work hard so Cain doesn't have any reason to expand my job description to lap dances and V.I.P. room customer support. I take orders, I serve drinks, I collect money without touching anyone's hand. In that order. Still, I feel eyes on me—drifting over my curves, sizing me up, even with plenty of flesh to look at in this place. Asshats.

The bar is my fortress. I am safe behind this half wall.

. . .

"So, how are you making out so far?" Storm asks during a two-minute lull late in the night. "Think you can handle bartending in a strip club six nights a week?"

I shrug. "Yeah, no big deal. Just a lot of boobs and ass cheeks, and I avoid the stage so I don't see . . ." My attention drifts to the stage where an Asian girl wearing nothing but a piece of silver floss wraps her legs around her neck. "That!" I jerk my head away. "How can she do it?"

"That's Cherry. She's into hot yoga."

I roll my eyes. "No, I don't mean how. I mean . . . *how!*"

"Everyone's got their price" is Storm's only response as she dispenses another round of Jim Beam.

"I guess so," I mutter, silently wondering if Storm has set a price.

"Okay, so now that you're familiar with the bar, Kacey," Storm says, "you can start smiling any time. You do know that if you smile at the customers, you're likely to get bigger tips, right?"

I smirk. "Why would me smiling make them give me more money when they can save it for the person humping their leg? Are they idiots?"

"Just . . . trust me." She sighs patiently, moving back to serve a customer, hollering over her shoulder, "You're the shiny new red-haired toy and you're forcing them to use their imagination."

Great. That's what I want to be. Some guy's wet dream.

To prove her wrong, I give the next three customers the widest grin my face can handle without splitting it in half. I even wink at one. Lo and behold, the tips double. *Hmmm. Maybe she's onto something.* If only smiling wasn't such a drain.

A middle-aged cowboy with an oversized hat and Wrangler jeans leans over the bar, his mouth twisted as if he's chewing on a piece of straw, but there's nothing there. "Ain't you a pretty sight, all toned and natural," he says as his gaze lingers too long on my cleavage. Why, I don't know. I look like a ten-year-old boy next to every other female in this place. When he sneers, I see that his teeth are stained yellowish brown from years of chewing on tobacco.

I swallow my revulsion and force a smile. "What can I get you tonight, sir?"

"How 'bout a Tom Collins and a private show?"

"One Tom Collins coming up. I'm fresh out of private shows." I keep my smile, but my level of annoyance climbs. I'm anxious to get rid of this guy. When I slide the drink across the bar to him and reach for the twenty-dollar bill, his paw closes over my forearm, his fingers coarse and impolite. He leans in and I catch a whiff of stale tobacco and booze on his breath. "How 'bout you take your break now and show me that tight ass of yours?"

"I just bartend here, sir," I force through gritted teeth, my body shifting into defensive mode. "There are plenty of girls here who can give you what you want." Everywhere I look, I see ass cheeks and nipples and worse. I played a lot of sports in high school, so I've seen my share of naked bodies in showers. Heck, I labeled Jenny the "Grand Rapids Exhibitionist" because she had no qualms about stripping down to buck in front of me. This place is different, though. They're wandering around, peddling their wares. *Selling* their bodies.

"I got money! Name your price."

"You don't have enough, trust me," I growl back, but I can tell he's not listening, his other hand disappearing below the bar, likely to adjust his growing arousal. I want to gag. I imagine he'll be rough when he finally corners a poor, desperate, and obviously blind woman. "I'd let go if I were you . . . sir."

From my peripherals, I see Nate and Ben's looming frames moving in to save me. The idea of them rescuing me bothers me. I don't need them to protect me.

I don't need anyone.

And I want to hurt this guy.

I half-lean, half-jump forward to hook my free hand around the cowboy's sweaty neck. I yank down hard and fast. He grunts as his face slams against the bar. I hold it there, my fingers digging into the base of his neck. My heart is hammering against my ribs as blood rushes to my ears. This feels good. I feel alive. "How do ya like this tight ass now?" I hiss.

Nate's hands slam over his shoulders and I hear his low rumble over the music as he drags the cowboy away, bleeding from a cut to his bottom lip. "You'll have to leave now, sir." The guy's also got a bright red mark on his forehead that will definitely bruise tomorrow. He doesn't resist, though. I doubt even the Incredible Hulk would resist Nate.

Ben hangs back. "You okay?"

"I'm fine," I assure him as Storm sidles up to me with a worried look. My attention trails after Nate and I cross glances with Cain sitting at a table off to the side. A sinking feeling settles over me. He must have watched the entire scene unfold. It dawns on me that maybe he doesn't want his customers' heads slammed against the bar. Maybe I just got my ass fired.

Cain gives me a thumbs-up sign, and I release a huge sigh of relief.

"I told you to smile, not get yourself into a bar fight," Storm jokes, nudging me in the ribs.

"He wanted a private show," I explain, my adrenaline still pumping through my body. "I gave him a public one instead."

Ben leans forward, elbows resting on the bar, an impressed smirk on his face. "You sure know how to handle yourself."

"I was raised by wolves. Had to fight for my food."

His head tilts back and a throaty laugh escapes. "Sorry if I was a douche bag earlier. I'm just used to seeing pretty, fresh girls come in here and leave worn and jaded. I hate it."

"Well, then, it's your lucky day. I'm already jaded." I give him the once-over. "And maybe you shouldn't work in a strip club."

"Yeah, that's what they tell me. But the money's too good and I'm putting myself through law school." He notices my raised brow and his grin widens. "Didn't expect that, did you?"

"You don't give off lawyerly vibes."

Ben turns his body and rests his elbows on the bar so he faces out into the crowd while he talks to me. "So I hear you just moved here?"

"Yep." I busy myself with wiping the counter down and stacking freshly washed glasses.

"You're a big talker, aren't you?"

"Us fully dressed girls have to work extra hard for our money."

His head falls back to look at me. "Fair enough. Listen—next time you're at the gym and I'm there, come get me. We can go a few rounds." He saunters away, not waiting for my response.

Oh, I'll go a few rounds with you, but probably not the kind your crotch brain is offering. I follow his movements, about to holler, "You got it, Lawyer Boy!" but the words die on my lips because I see Trent sitting at a single-top bar-height table.

And he's not watching the naked pretzel on the stage. He's watching me.

Check that. Staring at me.

Trent is here and he's staring at me.

"What the hell . . ." I grumble to no one in particular, ducking my head. I can't deal with him and what he does to me now. Here. Tonight. *Fuck!*

I sense someone step up to the bar and I cautiously look up. It's Nate, thank God. He's back from the cowboy eviction already. "Is that guy bothering you, Kacey?"

I swallow. "Nah." *Yes, but not for the reasons you think.*

"You sure?" He pivots his massive body to check the table.

Trent is still there, leaning his long body back into his chair, sipping on his straw, his focus now on Cherry. "He's been there for half an hour. He's been watching you."

"He has?" I squeak and then quickly add in a normal tone, "He's my neighbor. It's okay."

Nate's dark eyes wander around the rest of the room, looking for grabby guys whom he can toss out the door, no doubt. "You make sure you tell me if he bothers you, okay, Kacey?"

When I don't answer, he looks down at me again, that thunderous voice of his a little softer. "Okay?"

I nod. "Yup, you got it, Nate."

With a curt bob of his head, he wanders back to stand at his post like a sentry. One who could rip a guy's legs right out of their sockets if he sneezes too hard.

"What was *that* about?" Storm sneaks up behind me.

"Oh, nothing." My voice is still shaky and I can't get my tongue to work properly. I hazard another glance over at Trent. He's leaning into the table, toying with his straw, while Mediterranean Barbie—Bella, I think she goes by—presses her scantily clad body against his thigh. I watch as she gestures toward the V.I.P. room, her hand slipping over the back of his neck affectionately.

"You okay? You look like you're trying to choke someone." She's right, I realize, as I notice my fists wringing the dishcloth in my hand like it's a neck. It *is* someone's neck. Bella's . . .

"Yeah, I'm fine." I toss the cloth down and hazard one more peek at Trent, the same second his gorgeous blue eyes dart back to connect with mine. I jump. He gives me that teasing smile that peels away my defenses, leaving me as naked as the dancers onstage. Why does he affect me so? It's unnerving!

"Uh, that's not 'nothing,' Kacey. Are you looking at that guy? Who is that?" She leans over my shoulder to catch my line of sight. "Isn't that—"

My hand goes up to gently shove her face back. "Turn around! Now he knows we're talking about him."

Storm doubles over, laughing. "Kacey's got a crush," she sings. "Our neighbor's eye-humping you. Go and talk to him."

"No!" I growl back, throwing my best set of icy eye daggers at her.

She ducks her head and busies herself by clearing glasses off the bar. I can tell she's stung by the venom in my tone. Guilt instantly swells inside me. *Dammit, Kacey!*

I struggle to ignore Trent's table, but it's like passing a train wreck. It's impossible not to look. By the end of the night, I'm exhausted and annoyed by the seismic waves of jealousy crashing into me as the parade of strippers visit his table, touching him, giggling, one of them sliding up onto his lap to talk. My only relief comes from the fact that Trent politely declines them all.

■ ■ ■

Reaching into her purse, which sits between us in the console, Storm tosses a thick envelope on my lap.

Without much thought, I tear it open and flip through the bills. "Holy shit! There's got to be, like . . ."

"I told you so!" she sings, adding with a wink, "Now imagine what you'd make if you got up onstage."

There has to be five hundred dollars in here! Easy! "You've been working at Penny's for . . . four years, you said? Why are you still on Jackson Drive? You could have bought a house!"

She sighs. "I was married for a year to Mia's father. I had to claim bankruptcy after I left him because he racked up so much debt. No bank's going to give me a mortgage now."

"He sounds like a real . . . jackhole." I shift in my seat, feeling uncomfortable. Storm is getting into her private life and my defenses naturally go up. When people share, they expect you to reciprocate.

"You don't know the half of it," she murmurs, her voice drifting off. "It wasn't so bad in the beginning. I was sixteen when I met Damon. I got pregnant and he got into drugs. We needed money bad, so I started working for Cain after Mia was born. Damon said I had to get these if I wanted to make any real money." She gestures at her breasts. "Of course I was stupid enough to agree." A rare bitterness laces her words. "It hurt like hell. That's the only reason I haven't gone back to get them reduced. I swear, the things girls will do when they're blinded by love."

"So when did you finally decide to leave him?" I ask before I can stop myself.

"The second time he kicked the crap out of me."

She says it so matter-of-factly that I'm sure I misheard her. "Oh . . . I'm so sorry, Storm." And I am. The idea of someone hitting Storm instantly raises my defenses.

"The first time, I lied to everyone. Told them I ran into a wall." She snorts. "They didn't buy it, but they let me live deluded. But the second time . . ." She exhales heavily. "I came in to work with a fat lip and a bloody nose. Cain and Nate drove me right back home and stood over me while I packed Mia's and my things. Damon came in as we were walking out the door. Nate roughed him up a bit. Warned him if he ever comes near me or Mia again, he'll be peeing through a straw. And you've seen Nate." Storm gives me a wide-eyed look. "He can do it." She pulls into her parking spot outside our building and shuts the Jeep off.

"Cain set me up with the apartment and I've been here ever since, hoarding all my money until I have enough to buy a house with cash. If all goes well, I'll be out of the club scene for good in another two or three years." She adds softly, "And then my parents won't have to be ashamed of me anymore."

I snort. "Tell me about it. My parents would be rolling in their graves if they knew where I'm working . . ." My voice drifts off into an awkward silence, mentally chastising myself for bringing them up.

"Hey, Kacey?" There's that cautious, nervous Storm voice again and my shoulders tense. I know exactly where this is going. "Look, I've pieced together a few things—your parents are dead, I think it has something to do with alcohol . . . you have a lot of scars. You don't like people touching your hands . . ."

I don't let her finish. I open the door and rush out.

I decide that Storm is brilliant. A regular fucking rocket scientist.

FIVE

"Air conditioning!" I moan, peeling my sheets from my sweaty body. *We need real friggin' curtains*, I think to myself as I glare at the thin scraps of fabric hanging in front of the window. They do nothing to stop the sun from beating in. We haven't had air-conditioning since before my parents died. Aunt Darla didn't believe in paying for cool air when there are starving kids in the world. Or husbands with gambling problems. Now that we live in Miami, I don't know how depriving a tenant of air-conditioning is not illegal.

Livie and Mia are in the kitchen, humming "Pop Goes the Weasel" as they empty a brown bag of groceries. "Good afternoon!" Livie sings when she sees me.

"Good afternoon!" Mia echoes.

I check the clock. Almost one. They're right. It *is* afternoon. I haven't slept in that late in forever.

"I picked up food. There's money on the counter there." Livie's chin directs me to a small pile of bills. "I had to argue Storm down to half of what she wanted to pay me."

I smile. Storm swears she's found her angels. I'm sure that we've found ours. I need to cut my bullshit with her, I decide, then and there. I don't know how, but I need to. Strolling over to grab the money from my purse, I slap the thick envelope onto the table. "Bam! Take that!"

"Holy sh . . ." Livie's wide eyes pass from the stack of money to Mia's curious face ". . . shnikies! You just served drinks . . . right?"

So Livie figured it out on her own. I cock my head and narrow my eyes, pausing for effect as if I'm in deep thought. "Define serving drinks." I chuckle as I pull out the OJ from the fridge and chug straight from the bottle, feeling her glower at my back. "I'm kidding! Yes, just drinks. And an ass sandwich for one lucky grabber." Mia's brows spike and I wince, mouthing "sorry" to a scowling Livie. My offense is quickly forgotten, though, as she flips through the wad of money with her thumb. "Holy cow."

"I know, right?" I know I have a stupid grin on my face and I don't care. This might work. We might survive. We might not have to eat cat food.

Livie looks up with a secretive smile.

"What?"

She pauses, then, "Nothing, I just . . . you're giddy." She bites into a baby carrot. "It's nice."

Mia mimics her, scrunching her nose like a rabbit as she chews. "It's nice," she parrots.

I steal one from the bag, smash a giant kiss on Livie's cheek, and then swagger toward the bathroom.

"I'll be in the shower while you count all our money. And remind me to phone Starbucks and quit, okay?" There's no way I'm going back to minimum wage. No way in hell.

■ ■ ■

I don't care that there's no pressure. I don't care that the water has a funky chlorinated scent to it. I simply close my eyes and massage a thick layer of shampoo into my scalp, inhaling its rosy fragrance. For the first time since stealing off into the night with Livie, I think I can do this. I can take care of us. I'm old enough, strong enough, smart enough. My issues won't hold us back. Everything will be all right. We'll come out of it clean and strong and . . .

An odd soft rattling sound pulls me from my revelry. Cracking an eyelid, I spot red, black, and white stripes coiled around the pipe above the showerhead. Two beady little eyes stare intently back at me.

It takes a whole second for me to scream. Once I do, I can't stop. Scrambling backward, I slam against the opposite wall. I don't know how I manage to stay upright, but I do. The snake doesn't move. It sits in the exact same spot, shaking its tail and staring at me, as if it's deciding how it will fit its jaws around my head to swallow me whole. I continue shrieking as I hear Livie's panicked voice behind the door, but it doesn't register. Her pounding doesn't register.

Nothing registers.

Suddenly there's a loud crack and the sound of wood splintering. "Kacey!" Livie shrieks as a set of strong arms swoop in to pull me out. A towel quickly lands on me and I'm being whisked out of the bathroom and into my bedroom.

"I hate snakes. I hate snakes. Fuck! I hate snakes!" I repeat over and over again to no one and everyone. A hand smooths my hair. Not until my heart rate slows to a semi-normal pace and I stop shaking am I able to focus on my surroundings.

On Trent's furrowed brow and the flecks of turquoise in his irises.

I'm in his arms.

Naked and sitting on Trent's lap, in his arms.

My heart rate ramps back up to a dangerous level as I absorb the situation. His shirt is soaked and covered in my shampoo. I can feel the warm skin of his forearms against my bare back and under my knees as he holds me tight to him. All vital body parts are completely covered from view with a towel, but I still feel naked.

Livie storms in, eyes blazing. "Who do you think you are, barging in here?" she screams, her face as red as my hair, looking ready to claw Trent's face off.

"Trent. This is Trent," I answer. "It's okay, Livie. There's . . . there's a rattlesnake in the shower." I shudder involuntarily. "Get Mia out of here before it eats her. And get Tanner here. Now, Livie!"

Livie's attention passes from me to Trent and back to me, drifting down to my bed. She doesn't want to leave me, but finally she decides something and nods, closing the door behind her.

Trent pulls me tight against him until I feel his chest's hard ridges pressed against my arm. "You okay?" he whispers, his mouth so close that his bottom lip grazes my ear. I shudder again.

"I'm fantastic," I whisper, adding, "aside from almost dying."

"I heard you screaming from next door. I thought someone was killing you."

"Not someone. Some*thing*! Did you see it?" One arm flies out, gesturing toward the bathroom, while the other fusses to keep my towel up to cover my breasts. "I was two seconds away from being eaten alive!"

Trent starts to chuckle—a soft, beautiful sound that vibrates through my body and warms my core. "I think that's Lenny. 2B's pet snake. I saw a little bald man checking the bushes in the commons this morning, calling its name."

"*Pet?*" I spit out the word as I sit up straight. "That man-eater is someone's *pet*? Isn't there a law against owning rattlers?"

Trent's blue eyes roam over my face as he smirks, settling on my lips. "It's a milk snake. From what I know, the only thing it's going to eat is a mouse." He's so close to me now that his breath caresses my cheek. With my body pressed to him, I feel his heartbeat hammering fast against my shoulder, rivaling my own. He can feel this too. It's not just me. He lifts a hand to cup my chin. "No one's going to hurt you, Kacey."

I don't know if it's the stress of the situation, or this sizzling burn inside my belly that flares whenever Trent's around, or an uncontainable internal beast repressed for too long, but this whole situation has gone from terrifying to freaking hot in a split second.

I can't help myself.

I crash into Trent's mouth, my hand fisting the front of his shirt, snapping several buttons with no effort as I force myself onto him. There's a second of resistance—just a second where his mouth and body doesn't respond—but it quickly dissolves. His arm slides out from my knees to grip my side, scorching my bare skin. It's him that deepens the kiss, slipping his tongue into my mouth, one hand working its way through my shampoo-coated hair, gripping a handful at the nape of my neck tightly. He forces my head back as his tongue connects with mine, his mouth sweet and fresh. He's strong, that much I can sense. If I wanted to, I don't think I could fight him off. But I don't want to. Not one bit.

Without breaking his connection to my mouth, Trent somehow shifts me onto my back and now he's hovering over me on my bed, our torsos flattened against each other, my inner thighs hugging his hips while his forearms keep his full weight off my body. I don't know what's happening, what I'm doing, what has taken over all rational thought, but I know I don't want it to stop. Every fiber of my body is craving it.

Craving Trent.

I feel like I've come up for my first gasp of air after being underwater for years.

Unfortunately, it does stop. Abruptly. He breaks free and pulls away, panting as he gazes down at me with an incredulous look. His eyes never leave mine, not to wander for even a second. If they did, he'd see that my towel has slid off and I'm lying underneath him, stark naked. Body and soul.

"This isn't why I pulled you out of the shower," he whispers.

I swallow, searching for my voice. The one I find is hoarse. "No, but it's worked out rather well for you, hasn't it?"

He gives me that lopsided smile that makes my body heat up like someone has taken a blowtorch to it. But then his eyes cool, searching my face. "Isn't it exhausting?" The pad of his thumb strokes my neck softly.

"What?"

"Keeping people out."

"I'm not," I deny quickly, my voice faltering in betrayal as his words punch me in the gut. How can he see what I don't want him to see, what I work so hard to conceal? He's found a way in. Like a trespasser, he's invaded my space, breaching security and sliding in to take what I haven't offered to him.

The fire he's able to elicit in my body continues to burn, only now I find the need to battle the consuming flames. "I don't want this. I don't want you." The words taste acrid in my mouth because I know I don't mean them. *I do want this. I do want you, Trent.*

Trent crashes into my mouth, and my treacherous body leans forward, exposing me for the liar that I am. But he keeps his hands on either side of my head now, clenching my pillow tightly as if he's trying to maintain control. I, on the other hand, have lost all control, I realize, as my fingers slide under his shirt to claw at his back, as my legs wrap around him.

"You don't want this, Kacey?" he growls in my ear, pressing his erection against me.

"No . . ." I whisper, my lips trailing his neck. Then I begin to laugh at myself, at my stubbornness. At how ridiculous I must look right now, my body writhing against his. That little bit of laugher is like a lifeline. I seize it and let it drag me back from the brink. Tearing my mouth from his neck, I growl, "Get out."

He lays three more light kisses on my jawline and then softly grazes my cheek with his knuckles. "Okay, Kacey." He climbs off me and stands. I inhale sharply as his eyes draw in the length of my body with a hungry, dark look. It lasts only a second, but it unleashes a need deep in my lower belly. He turns around and heads to the door. "I'll take the heat for the doors from Tanner."

"Doors?" *Plural?*

He still hasn't turned around. "Yeah. Your front door and the bathroom door. If he's going to boot someone out, I'll make sure it's me."

And then he's gone.

Dammit! That guy is the dictionary definition of contradiction. He skates between nice guy and bad boy so fluidly, I never seem to notice the transition. It would be easier if he were a pigheaded player, but here he is, breaking down doors to save me from snakes. Then again, I go from bitch to sexual attacker and back to bitch in three heartbeats. I guess I'm not much better in terms of contradiction.

When I finally emerge from my room fifteen minutes later, our apartment has been invaded. Livie is in the kitchen, standing next to a sexy disheveled Storm with a crying five-year-old in her arms. Clearly my screams yanked Storm out of a dead sleep, because she's wearing nothing but a tank and a thong.

A police officer is interviewing a short balding man with the perpetrator coiled around his wrist. I shiver. Lenny, I presume. Trent is right. Now that I see the thing, it's not nearly as big as I first thought. Still, I fold my arms across my chest protectively, feeling its beady little eyes sizing me up.

Tanner hovers beside the busted front door, scratching the back of his head as if confused by the splinters. I have to admit, I'm more than a little impressed. Trent's a big guy, but I wouldn't have bet money that he could break through not one but two doors to save me.

Trent stands quietly beside him, his hands in his back pockets as he looks down at the mess. His shirt is half undone where I tore the buttons, drenched and clinging to a sculpted chest. Even with present company, that sight makes my mouth dry up.

Storm is the first to run to me after handing Mia off to Livie. She throws her arms around my neck. I still flinch, but not as bad as I did the first time she did it. "Are you okay?" If my rushing out of the car last night bothers her, I can't tell.

Over her shoulder, I watch the officer and the little bald man's eyes bug out, riveted by Storm's ass. The officer, at least, has the decency to flush and avert his attention to a worn spot on the linoleum. But the bald man's grin only widens. "I'll be better after I go punch that guy in the nose," I say loudly enough for him to hear me. He looks away, caught red-handed.

"That's Pervie Pete," she whispers, cringing as she stretches the back of her shirt down to cover her bare backside. It's futile. The shirt's too short and her thong is too revealing. "I'll be right back." She scurries out.

Tanner looks up from the splintered mess. "Oh, hey, Kerry."

Kerry? My brow arches. "Hey . . . Larry! How's it going?"

Livie tries to muffle her snort with her hand. At first Tanner looks confused, but then a toothy grin stretches across his face. "Kacey," he corrects himself. "Sorry . . . Kacey."

The police officer patiently scratches down notes on a pad as we replay the incident, while I catch him stealing frequent glances at a now returned and fully dressed Storm. When we're done, he gives Mia a sheriff badge sticker, which makes her grin from ear to ear. Pervie Pete apologizes profusely and takes Lenny back to his cage, swearing to a stern Tanner that he'll double-check to make sure the cage is secured well. The officer asks me if I want to press charges against Trent, and I glare at him as if he's grown an arm out of his ass.

When the officer leaves—not before giving Storm a long,

appreciative smile—Tanner and Trent are still staring at the two broken doors. "I understand that this was an emergency, but . . . er . . . I need to get this fixed, and Perv—" Tanner clears his voice, "Peter will take a while to come up with the money. I doubt these gals have insurance . . ." Tanner reaches into his back pocket to pull out his wallet. "I've got, um, a hundred bucks I can throw in."

My jaw drops. *What?* I'm expecting a tirade and an eviction notice and here Tanner is, offering to pay for our door? Livie, Storm, and I share a look of shock. Before I can get a word in, though, Trent is handing Tanner a fistful of money from his wallet. "Here. This should cover it." Tanner takes it with a nod, and then exits without another word, leaving us all speechless.

Trent walks over to Livie and thrusts out a hand. "Hi, I'm Trent. We haven't met formally."

Whatever rage Livie had running through her veins has dissipated, leaving her blushing and as awkward as a tittering twelve-year-old. She shakes his hand quickly before recoiling as if she might get pregnant from his touch, her eyes avoiding anything to do with his half-open shirt and that gorgeous toned body. I grin to myself. My chaste Livie.

Trent introduces himself to Storm next. She blushes sweetly and an unwarranted stab of jealousy pricks me. When he moves on to Mia hiding behind Storm's legs, I catch Storm's exaggerated wink of approval. I roll my eyes.

"And you must be Princess Mia? I've heard about you."

Her lips pucker and she leans out just a bit farther from Storm's cover. "You have?"

He nods. "Well, I heard about a Princess Mia who likes ice cream. That must be you, right?"

She nods slowly and whispers, "Did you hear that, Mommy? People know I'm a princess!"

Everyone laughs. Everyone but me. I'm too busy fighting this internal battle that tells me I must resist this charm. It's all an act. He's no good for me.

Actually, that's not it at all, I hate to admit.

The problem is that I know he's *too* good for me.

Trent stands up to face me. "You going to be okay?"

Always so concerned about me. I nod, my arms folding over my chest as I look down at my robe, fidgeting awkwardly under his scrutinizing gaze, remembering the feel of his body pressed against mine. And that he pulled me from the shower, buck naked and cowering.

All kinds of humiliation roils through me now.

I'm not sure if my discomfort registers with Trent, but he takes a few steps back, his fingers raking back his hair. "Well, I'll see you guys around." He winks at me. "Need to wash off all this soap. I hope *my* shower isn't as eventful."

"Yeah . . ." I mumble, feeling stupid, watching his body move away, quickly plotting how I can plant something in his bathroom so I have an excuse to bust down his door and jump in to save him. *Not a snake. He doesn't seem to be afraid of snakes. Maybe a gator. Yeah, there are lots of those in Florida. Just a quick trip to the Everglades. I'll find one, trap it, bring it back—*

"Kacey?"

I snap back to the present at the sound of Storm's voice. Her brow is arched as she looks at me, smirking. I've obviously missed a question. "What?"

Trent is standing just inside the gaping doorway, waiting.

"I'm sure Trent would love to have dinner with us as a thank-you." I see the gleam in her eye. She's playing matchmaker.

I don't like it.

Trent doesn't want this mess.

"Do whatever you want. I'll be at the gym," I answer, and my tone is an arctic breeze, freezing any mirth in the room. I spin on my heels and stalk back into my room before anyone can get a word in edgewise.

And I hate myself.

■ ■ ■

The Breaking Point is quieter than usual for the late afternoon, but I'm okay with that. I'm still reeling from today's snake excitement. And Trent. I need my nice, quiet routine. I quickly stretch and get ready to start my rounds on the bag.

"Hey, Red!" Ben's voice booms from behind.

Dammit! I turn to catch him looking up from my ass. "Ben."

He strides toward me and grabs my bag for me. "You need a spotter?"

"I guess I'm getting one either way, aren't I?" I grumble. But then his sly smirk makes me laugh for some reason, releasing the tension in my body. "Do you know what you're doing?"

He shrugs. "I'm sure you can teach me." Then he flashes that grin again as he adds, "I prefer being in control, but for you I can . . ."

Ben is jabbering away with a series of innuendos and I stop listening. Just to teach him a lesson, I surprise him with a round-house kick. He grunts as the bag slams into his hip. "Consider that your first lesson. Shut up. Don't talk to me while I'm working out."

For the next fifteen minutes, I pound away at the bag with jabs and kicks, and Ben does a half-decent job of shifting with the impact. If he's talking, I don't hear him. I'm zoned in on the sequence that propels me forward, hammering again and again, releasing all that anger with each hit.

Three idiots getting drunk one night.

Three murderers taking my life from me.

One. Two. Three.

Finally spent, I lean forward and support myself against my knees with my hands to catch my breath.

"Jeez, Kace." I look up to see astonishment on Ben's face. "I've never seen someone so completely dialed during rounds. You were like Ivan Drago. He's this Russian who—"

I cut him off, reciting the line from *Rocky IV* with a mock Russian accent. "If he dies, he dies." Another of my dad's faves.

Ben's head is bobbing, his brows arched with surprise. "You know that one."

"Who doesn't?" I can't help but chuckle again. Soon we're both laughing and I'm thinking Ben isn't such a pompous ass after all.

That's when a tall figure walks past us and drops a sledgehammer down on my shields.

Trent.

My laughter dies, all traces of ease vanish. Grabbing my water bottle, I try to hide my reaction from Ben by drawing a long swig, all the while watching Trent as he drops his stuff to the ground beside a speed bag and tugs his sweatshirt over his head by the back collar.

What the fuck is he doing here? In my *gym? This is my . . . Holy . . .* A dribble of water runs down my chin and I wipe it away with my forearm, trying hard not to gape at his defined body, covered only by a white tank. He keeps his back to me without a glance in my direction and begins punching the speed bag with a precision that surprises me. As if he's well trained. I watch for a moment, mesmerized and a little disappointed that he hasn't acknowledged me, even though I don't deserve his attention.

Maybe he doesn't know I'm here.

I doubt that.

Black curls peek out from the edges of his tank. Whatever the tattoo is, it spans the width of his upper back from shoulder blade to shoulder blade. I'd love to peel that shirt off and study his ink while he's stretched out on my bed.

"I think I've seen that guy at Penny's," Ben notes. So he's caught me staring at Trent. Great.

"You got something for him?" I tease coolly.

"No, but I hear *someone* does." I can't miss the suggestive tone in his voice.

Bloody Storm! "He's my neighbor. That's it."

"You sure?"

"Yup. I don't have a thing for *anyone*. Including you." I take a swing at my bag.

He smirks. "Aren't you gonna go over and say 'hi' to your neighbor, then?"

I answer with a roundhouse kick. Ben finally takes the hint, diving in to secure the bag. He doesn't mention Trent again.

I do my best to complete a second round, but my head's not in it anymore and it's all because of that sexy guy on the other side of the room, pounding away on the punching bag. As much as I try not to look, I find myself glancing over frequently.

This last time, I catch Trent wiping the sweat from his brow with the bottom of his shirt, pulled up to reveal a perfect eight-pack. I suck in a breath, temporarily paralyzed, my heart rate shooting through the roof, staring . . .

Something sharp snaps across my ass. "Ow!" I scream, and spin around to find Ben with his towel and a devilish grin.

"Did you just snap my ass with your towel?" I growl.

My anger doesn't seem to faze him. But my punch to his ribs does. He doubles over in pain, moaning. "Hope it was worth it, asshole." I stoop to grab my things. When I stand, I meet Trent's gaze head on. His face is blank but his eyes . . . Even from this distance, I see a world of determination, hurt, and anger in them.

He knew I was here. He knew all along.

After a long stare, Trent turns his back to me and starts pounding on the bag again, and suddenly I feel like I'm the bag, that someone is pummeling me with guilt. And pain. I'm actually hurting over Trent.

I've had enough.

I storm out to the women's locker room without another word to Ben. For half an hour I sit on the wooden bench in that room—a tiny, dark dungeon with two shower stalls and little room to maneuver—and I fight to bury all these unwanted emotions clawing their way up the well. Why does he have to be out there? Why this gym? Is he stalking me? In reality, I know that this is the only specialized gym on this side of Miami, so if he's a trained fighter, it makes sense that he'd end up here. Still . . .

I'm used to having things under control. I fight to stay numb. That's how I get through each day and it's worked well for me. Until now. Now Trent has edged into my life and I can't focus. My body is going haywire. I'm battling this internal urge to both push him away and hold him close; I'm thinking about him far too often. And even the thought of him kindles desire inside me that I haven't felt since my last random encounter more than two years ago. Only now it's a million times more acute, more needy. I rock forward and back, my forehead in my hands. *I don't want this. I don't want this. I don't want this . . .*

I hear a soft knock on the door. Hope gushes like water through a busted dam and I realize it's because I want it to be Trent. I can't help myself. I want it. I want him. *Please be . . .*

A contrite-looking Ben stands on the other side of the door, bowling me over with disappointment. "Are you okay? I'm sorry. I probably hit you harder than I should have, but you were off in la-la land."

I don't answer, adrenaline pumping through my limbs, my heart racing, frustration surging. I look up into his face and see a sweet, genuine guy. One that's become appealing. Right or wrong, destructive or not, I grab hold of Ben's shirt with two fists and haul him into the change room. He doesn't resist, though judging by his sluggish movements he's not entirely sure what's happening. I shove him into the shower stall and snap the lock on the door behind me.

"Take your clothes off. Don't touch my hands."

"Um . . ." I can tell this isn't what Ben expected. Hell, this isn't what *I* expected. But I need to dislodge this Trent problem, and mindless sex with someone else ought to do it.

When Ben doesn't move, I seize his shirt and yank him down to my mouth. He finally gets a clue. His hands tug at the back of my tank as he pulls me against him, his tongue sliding into my mouth. His kiss is sweet, but it's not like . . . *no, stop it, Kacey. You're doing this to forget about Trent.*

Just his name sets fireworks off inside my body.

"Kacey," Ben moans, his hands traveling up to my shoulders and down, over my breasts, squeezing them as they pass. He breaks long enough to yank my tank top over my head before he covers my mouth with his again. It's a confined space but he makes the most of it, lifting me onto the little bench against the wall so I'm towering over him. "I didn't think you were into me."

"Stop talking," I command as I shimmy my shorts and panties down. His hand is instantly on my inner thigh and sliding up. Up. Until it's exactly where I want it to be.

I lean back and close my eyes.

And imagine Trent doing that.

Ben doesn't waste any time, dropping to his knees to follow his hand with his mouth. "God, you're sweet," he moans. I briefly imagine fitting him with a muzzle to stop him from talking. But then he'd be no use to me. And he really *is* of use to me right now. Right or wrong, it's been so long since I allowed this or even wanted it. I lean back and relax, taking from Ben what I need.

It's all working out well.

But then Ben has to go and ruin it. He does exactly what I told him not to. He slides his hand into mine.

I feel instant shock, as though I've been plunged into a bath of ice water after sitting in a hot tub for an hour. All pleasure disintegrates and I recoil from his mouth and his touch, shoving his face away from me.

"Dammit, Ben. Just go. Now."

"What?" Confusion fills his face as he looks up at me, as if I'd just admitted to a triple homicide while whisking a bowl of cake batter.

"You touched my hands. I told you not to. Leave."

He still doesn't move, an incredulous smirk on his face. "Are you for real?"

I lean forward, unlatch the lock, and shove Ben out of the stall with the most prominent hard-on I've seen in a while. With him out, I latch the door again and crumble to the ground, hugging my knees to my body.

That didn't help after all.

In fact, that made things a thousand times worse.

Nausea churns inside me. How could I be so selfish? Ben's going to hate me now. What's more, now that the intense sex haze has worn off, I actually feel embarrassed for doing that to him. I've *never* felt guilty about my exploits. And . . . I gasp out loud. *What if Trent hears about this? Ohmigod!* My forehead drops against my knees.

I care. I care what Trent thinks. I care if it bothers him. I just . . . care. And no matter what I do, I'm not going to be able to shake that. Not with random sex, or by being a bitch, or any of the other dozen cruel methods I use to try and push him away. Somehow he's managed to slide a finger in under my titanium coat and touch me in a way that no one else ever has.

SIX

Bar-well shots are two for one at Penny's tonight, so the place is hopping, keeping Storm and me on our toes all night to the point where my body is covered by a thin coat of sweat. Cain has managed to find Nate's twin—another dark, gargantuan brute— to toss grabby patrons to the curb in the blink of an eye. In fact, the place has almost as many bouncers as it does dancers tonight. Including Ben. He hasn't said two words to me in three days, since that afternoon at the gym, and that suits me fine. I'd prefer to hang my head in shame without the constant reminder.

Cain leans over the bar as I line up ten shots of vodka. "How do you like Penny's so far, Kacey?" he asks over the music.

I respond with a nod and a smile. "It's great, Cain. The money's really good."

"Great. Saving that for college, I hope?"

"Yup." *Just likely not for me.*

"And what are you interested in?"

I pause, deciding how to answer that one. I choose honesty over a smart-ass remark. This is my boss, after all. "Not sure. I don't have a lot of direction right now." For some reason, Cain's question doesn't bother me. It doesn't feel intrusive. "I'm more concerned about getting my little sister into pre-med."

"Ah, yes. This famous raven-haired angel that Storm has praised." Cain's shrewd eyes narrow. "You're a hard worker and you're welcome here as long as you need the job, but make sure you find that direction soon. You can do better than slinging drinks. Keep up the good work." He pats the bar and continues on, leaving me staring at his back.

"What's his story?" I ask Storm.

"What do you mean?"

"Well, I think he may be one of the most interesting people I've ever met. A paradox to the strip-club-owner persona. I haven't seen him so much as squeeze an ass. He takes the time to say hi. Now he's encouraging me not to work here because I'm too good for the place."

She smiles. "Yeah, he's definitely special. He had a hard upbringing." She grabs the bottle of JD from in front of me. "Speaking of Trent . . ."

What? The sudden change of topic sends me reeling. With a smug grin, Storm jerks her chin over to a table not far from us. Sure enough, there's Trent. He's shown up for the last three nights at eleven by himself. He doesn't approach me; he just orders his drinks and sits at a safe distance. I know he's watching me, though. My skin prickles under his gaze. It's beginning to get on my nerves.

"Kace." Storm leans in. "Can I ask you something?"

"No." I grab a knife and a lime and begin slicing it into eighths.

She pauses. "Why do you keep ignoring him? He stops by every night to see you."

"Yeah, in a strip club. Every night. By himself. That's what we call a freak."

"He hardly looks at the dancers, Kace. And I've seen you looking at him all night, too."

"I have not!" I claim too quickly, my voice shrill. I've tried not to, I tell myself. Apparently I've failed miserably.

She ignores me. "I think Trent *really* likes you and he seems like a nice guy. There's nothing wrong with going to talk to him, at least. I know you're not a mean person, deep down."

I fight back the guilt swelling inside me. *Yes I am, Storm. I am mean. I do it intentionally. It's safer that way. For everyone.* "I'm not interested." I set my jaw as I keep cutting.

She lets out a huge exhale. "I was hoping you'd say that. I'm going to ask him out then, 'cause he is *fine*."

My jaw drops as my eyes fly to Storm's face, and I'm sure there's outright murder shining in them. How can she betray me like that? And she calls herself a friend?

"Ha! Gotcha!" Storm holds up a finger. "I knew it. Admit it. Admit you want to go over and talk to that sex on a stick." She slides away with a teasing grin, singing, "Trent and Kacey, sittin' in a tree . . ."

"Shut up." Right now my face feels like a burning-hot forest fire. I try to ignore Storm, Trent, and the ever-looming Nate as a customer comes up to order a drink. "Two whiskey sours, coming right up!" I announce, slamming two tumbler glasses onto the counter. I have no clue what goes in a whiskey sour, and I doubt this guy wants me experimenting. I raise an expectant brow at Storm.

She responds by crossing her arms over her chest. "Not unless you go talk to him."

I purse my lips. "Fine," I hiss. "After. Now would you help me with the drinks before I poison this fine gentleman?"

With a victorious smirk, Storm tosses two drinks together and slides them over the bar.

"That sweet southern belle thing is all an act, isn't it?"

Her smirk morphs into an innocent pout. "I reckon I don't know what you could possibly mean," she drawls, fanning herself with a dishcloth.

Somehow, whether it's her teasing or her obvious ecstatic mood over wearing me down, my mouth turns up into a grin.

"Hallelujah! Look at that! Miss Kacey is smilin' again!" She presses the back of her hand against her forehead. "Ain't it a blessed sight?"

She flinches as the piece of lime I pelt at her hits her thigh. But then I follow up with a deep bow. "Teach me, you must. Become great, I will."

Storm gives me a playful shove and then goes back to serve the next guy, while a sudden flurry of nervous activity erupts inside me. *Oh God, what have I agreed to?* My hands go to my abdomen. *One . . . two . . . three . . .* I concentrate on inhaling and exhaling. I'm not used to this feeling. It's awful and stressful and if I accept it, exhilarating. I lean down to put the knife back in its safety drawer and stand to move toward the bar exit.

A deep set of dimples meets me.

"I can't seem to get a drink at the table without being accosted," Trent murmurs with a crooked smirk, leaning across the bar. "I have no idea why."

I pull in a slow and wobbly breath. *Don't lose your cool around him, Kacey. For once!* "Some people must find you very . . . accostable," I respond as my insides liquefy. *Christ! Even my nipples are hardening.* Worse, through this thin black satin sheath, Trent will see them if he looks down.

"Is that even a word?" His eyes twinkle, and I have to pace my breathing as my heart starts hammering against my ribs. Now that I've come to terms with the fact that the bastard is going to affect me whether I like it or not, he's even hotter than before. *Breathe, Kace.*

"So, no more snake incidents?" he asks. If my cruelty the other day bothered him, either he's gotten over it or he never cared to begin with. It's a relief in any case.

"No, Superman Tanner is on it." In reality, Tanner has transformed into my mini-hero. While I showered at Storm's and headed off to the gym that day, he secured our apartment like a dutiful potbellied guard dog, not leaving until the doors were in place and new locks were installed. And then Storm heard through the apartment's grapevine that Tanner went to Pervie Pete's apartment and tore a strip out of him, threatening to make a bowtie out of his balls if there's ever another incident like that. Tanner is turning out to be a mud-covered gem.

Trent places his drink on the counter. "So, would you mind accosting . . . er . . . pouring me a drink?"

My focus drops to the limes in front of me as I work to regain my composure. He's flirting with me. I don't remember how to do that. I don't know if it's all the flesh or music around us or the fact that Storm's right, he *is* sex on a stick, but suddenly I feel the urge to try. "That depends. Do you have ID?"

His elbows support him as he leans onto the bar, frowning playfully. "For a club soda?"

That catches me off guard. He sat in a strip club all night and he's not *drinking*? I quickly regain my composure and shrug. "Suit yourself." I pull the knife out of the drawer again and I begin slicing limes, my movements focused and slow so I don't chop my shaking fingers off.

"Stubborn," I hear him mutter as he slides his ID across the bar. With a curious grin, I pick it up. It's a little hard to read it under the dim light, but I exaggerate with one closed lid as if I'm straining to read. "Trent Emerson. Six foot three." My gaze moves up and down the length of his gorgeous, hard torso, stopping at his belt. "Yeah, that's about right. Blue eyes." I don't even have to look at them to know, but I do anyway, staring intently until I feel a blush creep over my face. "Yup. Born December thirty-first?" Two weeks after my birthday.

He smiles. "Almost a New Year's baby."

"1987. That makes you almost twenty-five?" Five years older than I am. *Not too old*. Though if his ID said 1887 and he looked like that, I don't think I'd care.

"Old enough for a club soda, I think," he smirks, holding his hand out. I don't give the ID back right away. Not before noting his address in Rochester. "You're a long way from New York State," I say as I slide it back across the bar and leave it for him to pick up.

"I needed a change."

"Don't we all?" I pour his drink. From my peripherals, I notice his eyes linger on my shoulder, and I self-consciously re-angle my body. I'm sure all the scars would gross him out. Then again, he did see some of them already. Scratch that. *All* of them. This guy has seen me naked. Plenty of guys have seen me naked and I didn't care. Trent seeing me naked, though? My hand starts to shake.

"Feeling better tonight, Kace?"

I jolt at the voice, the blood draining from my face as Ben leans up against the bar next to me with a knowing smirk. He sticks his hand out. "Hey, I'm Ben. I saw you at the gym the other day when I was working out with Kacey." The way he said "working out" makes my tongue slide back into my throat.

"Trent." Trent is cordial enough, but I notice he stands up to his full height and the corners of his mouth flatten slightly. He's big. Bigger than Ben, even, though not as bulky.

"So who are you here for tonight, Trent? And last night? And the night before? Can't be the dancers, since you're busy staring at Kacey the entire time."

"Ben!" I bark, willing poison daggers from my pupils to stab him in the tongue.

He ignores me. "Yeah, Kacey talks about you all the time. She won't shut up. It's getting annoying."

I slam the drink down onto the counter with a shaky hand,

all the while mentally tearing Ben's tongue out of his mouth and shoving it up his ass so he can get a firsthand taste of what an asshole he is.

"I highly doubt that." With a soft chuckle, Trent takes his glass and steps away, a strange smirk on his face. "Better let you get back to work. Thanks for the drink."

As soon as he turns, my hand rushes to Ben's bicep to grab his muscle and twist.

He howls and jumps back, but he's grinning a split second later as he rubs the sore spot.

"What the hell was that?" I hiss.

He leans in close. "Life's too short to play whatever stupid game you're playing, Kace. You guys are both into each other, so stop screwing around."

"Mind your own damn business, Ben."

He leans in even closer, until his face is inches from mine. "I would if you hadn't dragged me into the middle of this. *Literally*. And then kicked me out. *Literally*." A pause. "Has he hurt you?"

I shake my head, knowing exactly what he's getting at.

"Then get help for whatever issues you have and move on." He grins mischievously. "Plus, I owed you. You gave me the worst case of blue balls I've ever had. That should be your stage name." Lewd eyes drift over my chest and back up. "Though I have to say it was worth it. Gave me plenty of mental images for when I'm alone."

I throw a towel at him as he walks away, howling with laughter.

If only it were that simple, Ben.

■ ■ ■

At midnight, Trent is still there, sipping his club soda, and Storm is hounding me like a hyena around a carcass. "Go talk to him again."

"No."

"Why are you being so difficult, Kacey?"

"Because I'm a difficult person." I wipe the counter as I mutter quietly, "It can't happen, anyway."

"Why not?"

I shake my head, my brow furrowing. "It just can't. He doesn't deserve to get shoved out of a shower stall."

"*What?*" I hear Storm exclaim, but I'm not listening. I don't need Ben and Storm prodding me forward. My own internal urges are doing just fine battling with my willpower. I really want to go talk to Trent. Stand next to him. Kiss him . . . Whatever switch I've relied on these past few years to block all appeal and make my life easy has failed me miserably, opening the doors to a flood of desire and emotions that I don't know how to deal with.

"He's too . . . good. And nice."

"And you're nice too. Once you stop trying to be a bitch." The way she adds that last part, it's as if she wasn't planning on saying it out loud. I catch her eyes widen in a flash.

"Nicely done, Storm," I genuinely commend her.

She sticks her tongue out at me. "He's been sitting in a strip club all night, waiting for you."

"Oh, the horror," I mutter as I point to the stage where Skyla and Candy grind against each other.

"Who are you guys talking about?" a Greek goddess with breasts to rival Storm's calls out as she places an order of drinks on her tray.

"Table thirty-two," Storm says.

With a roll of her eyes, she ascertains, "That dude's gay."

"Then what's he doing in Penny's, Pepper?" Storm asks in a sweet tone.

Pepper. Pshhh! Stupid name.

Pepper gives a lazy shrug. "China's been workin' him hard for a private dance, half off, and he won't give. He's keepin' a close eye on Ben, though."

I bite my tongue before I explain that he won't *give* because he doesn't like dirty-ass sluts. I don't know who this China is, but I want to rip her guts out. I'm not too fond of Pepper, either. *I should stalk over there and pee around his table to stake my claim. Wait . . . what? Jeez, Kacey.*

"He's just waiting for his private show with Kacey later," Storm says, and spins on her heels. I catch Pepper's eyes narrow as she studies what she must see as cash competition. I can't tell what's going on in that mind of hers. I doubt it can be much. I glare back at her all the same and she walks away as Storm returns.

"Here." Storm shoves a filled glass into my hand. "Go and talk to him again. You need a break anyway."

"Fine," I hiss. "But when we come back, we need to discuss my stage name. Maybe something like 'Salt,' or 'Lollipop' or 'Pomegranate.'"

"I hear 'Blue Balls' might fit better," Storm throws in with a sly wink.

I gasp, my finger jabbing the air pointedly at her and then searching the crowd for Ben, ready to cleave his tongue out.

"Don't worry, he just wanted to make sure you were okay," she whispers, all hints of joking gone. "I don't judge. Your secret's safe with me, you vixen." I head toward the bar exit when Storm shouts, "Hey! How about 'Vixen' as your stage name?"

I ignore her, sucking in a lung's worth of air as I lift the counter panel and walk through. I try not to fuss too much with my dress, but I do it all the same. *Hell, just admit it, Kacey. Trent intimidates you.* Just looking at him perched on his chair, leaning against the table, butterflies slam around inside my stomach. When it's obvious that I'm heading straight for Trent, I notice him sit up straighter, like he might be a bit anxious too. That makes me feel a bit of relief.

I place his club soda down on the table with a slight smile. "What are the chances that you're still here?"

"What are the chances, indeed." He offers me a wry smile in return.

"A guy moves into a new town and spends every night at the local strip club. Alone."

Trent doesn't miss a beat. "And finds two of his neighbors working behind the bar."

I pick up his empty glass. "Storm has convinced me it will be a life-altering experience."

His gaze skims the stage floor suggestively and I catch a flicker of disapproval in it. "I guess that depends on what you're doing here."

"Not that," I quickly fire back. "Clothes on at all times. It's mandatory." I bite my lip. *A little too eager to announce that, Kacey.*

Trent considers my face for a moment and then he nods. "Good."

I can't help but notice Trent's lips when he says that, noting how they remain parted after, how soft they look. "Um . . ." I shake my head, trying to uncloud my thoughts. "So you're not holding back on the strong stuff tonight, I see?"

He gives his drink a long, hard look. Another small smile. "Yeah, you better watch out. I get crazy when I drink this shit straight." He takes a sip and then asks, "So what brings you to Miami?"

"Change of scenery?" I suggest his earlier excuse, silently praying that he won't press me with any personal questions. Right now, I think I'd sing like a canary. Anything to keep him talking to me. Mercifully, Trent doesn't press.

"Have you changed your mind, sweetheart?" a lusty voice asks behind me, interrupting us. I turn to find a fake redhead moving in. She's just tall enough to prop her voluptuous breasts onto the table in front of Trent. I watch as a red claw runs down the length of his muscular forearm. This must be China.

A part of me wants to spin around and slam the bottom of my heel into her head. In kickboxing, we'd call that a Spinning Back Kick. Here, it's called "how to get my crazy jealous ass fired." There's no way I'd get a thumbs-up from Cain on that one.

The other part of me is curious about how Trent's going to handle this "accosting." After the constant parade that first night, things had been fairly tame. I have to think it's because, like Pepper, the other women presume he's waiting for Ben to start batting for the other team.

To my pleasant surprise, Trent pulls his arm off the table and adjusts himself in his chair so his body is angled toward me. "I'm fine, thanks."

With a slight pout, she purrs, "You sure? You'll regret it. I'm quite entertaining."

His eyes lock on my face and he doesn't attempt to conceal the smolder in them. "Not as much as I'll regret leaving my present company. I think she could entertain me for a lifetime."

My heart skips three beats and my breath hitches. If there was ever any doubt about Trent's interest, he's crushed it with that look, with those words. I don't notice China's scowl, which I'm sure is stripping the skin from my bones right now. I don't notice her walk away. I don't notice anything around me. Trent and I are suddenly the only two people in the bar, and that same uncontrollable urge I felt the day he saved me from the snake returns.

I close my fists into tiny balls and keep them glued to my side. I have to control myself here. I have no choice. I can't lunge at him like a hormonal freak, which is exactly what I am right now. I clear my voice, trying to play it cool.

"Are you sure? Because the most you're getting out of me are club sodas."

"I'm okay with that," I hear him whisper. "For now." His bottom lip slides in between his teeth, and the temperature in the room instantly rises twenty degrees. Penny's has turned into a bloody sauna and my mind has scattered into oblivion as I struggle to stand.

But I do manage to stand and stare at Trent as the grating announcer's voice comes over the microphone. "Gentlemen . . ." The next dancer is on her way out. I've learned how to drown that voice out, and I have no trouble doing it now as I lose myself in Trent's presence.

Until I hear:

". . . A special feature performance of the night . . . Storm!"

"You've got to be fucking shitting me!" I spin around, checking the bar to find Ginger and Penelope behind it. Everyone's attention is transfixed on the stage in anticipation as a mystical green glow hangs over it, as if the audience is waiting for a life-altering performance. Not just another naked girl in a strip club. *My* naked *friend*. "Ohmigod. This is going to be so awkward. She didn't even warn me!" I don't realize I'm moving back until I bump into Trent's inner thigh.

"You don't have to watch, you know," he whispers into my ear.

The slow throb of a dance beat starts pounding through the club, and a spotlight rises above the stage to illuminate a scantily clad female body, sitting in a suspended silver hoop. I can't look away, even if I want to.

Storm is wearing a sequined bikini that leaves nothing to the imagination. When the music picks up, she flips backward, every muscle in her arm straining as she dangles by one hand. With no visible effort, she folds her legs back over and fluidly slides her body through the hoop to hold another impressive pose. The music picks up tempo and she kicks her legs out, gaining momentum until the hoop swings back and forth like a pendulum. Then suddenly she's hanging by her arms, spinning fast, her hair flying through the air, her body contorting and diving into various graceful poses. She's like one of those people in Cirque du Soleil—beautiful, poised, doing things I never believed humanly possible.

"Wow," I hear myself murmur, mesmerized.

Storm is an acrobat.

The scrap of material covering her breasts somehow flies off.

Storm is a stripper acrobat.

Something brushes against my fingers and I flinch. My head jerks down to see Trent's hand resting on his knee, his fingertips an inch away from mine. So close. Too close, and yet I don't pull away. Something deep inside me spurs me forward. I wonder if there's any chance . . . *What if* . . . Inhaling, I look up into his face and see a world of calm and possibilities. For the first time in four years, the thought of a hand covering mine doesn't send me into a dizzying spiral downward.

And I realize that I want Trent to touch me.

Trent doesn't move, though. He stares at me, but he doesn't push. It's as if he knows this is a bridge I've all but torched and turned from. How does he know? Storm must have told him. Keeping my focus locked on those gorgeous blue eyes, I force my hand to close the distance. My fingers are trembling, and that voice screams at me to stop. She screams that this is a mistake; that the waves are waiting to crash down over my head, to drown me.

I shove the voice aside.

So slow, so light, my fingertip skims his index finger.

He still doesn't move his hand. He remains completely frozen, as if waiting for me to make my move.

Swallowing hard, I let my entire hand skate over his. I hear a sharp inhale as he gasps, his jaw clenching. His eyes are locked on mine and they're unreadable. Finally, his hand shifts and covers mine, his fingers gently slipping in between. Not forceful, not rushed.

A load roar of approval erupts from the audience, but I barely hear it over the rush of blood in my ears. *One . . . two . . . three . . .* I began taking those ten little breaths.

I can't contain the euphoria swelling inside me.

Trent's touch is full of life.

I'm sure I hear glass shattering somewhere nearby, but I'm too stunned for anything to register. "Is this okay?" he whispers, his brow pulled together. Before I can process his question, his hand is wrenched out of mine as a pair of giant mitts land on his shoulders, tearing the warmth with it.

"You'll need to leave, sir," Nate's voice thunders. "No touching the ladies."

My peripherals catch something moving beneath me. Looking down, I find a busboy sweeping up the shards of Trent's empty glass. I guess it slipped out of my free hand.

"Is it okay?" Trent asks again earnestly, like he knows it might not be okay to touch my hand. Like that's a perfectly acceptable fear to have. Like I'm not a head case.

Try as I might, I can't open my mouth or move my tongue. I'm suddenly a statue. Petrified.

"Kacey!"

Nate yanks Trent back and out the door and I do nothing but watch him go, that intense pleading gaze riveted to my face until it's out of sight.

As I wander back to the bar in a daze, everything seems wobbly. The walls, the people, the dancers, my legs. I mumble an apology to Ginger for taking more than fifteen minutes. She waves me away with a smile as she pours someone a drink. I stiffly turn back to see that a shapely Native American woman has taken center stage, doing some sort of rain-dance reenactment in a scant feather costume. Storm is nowhere to be seen.

The world moves forward, oblivious to this significant shift in my tiny universe.

stage four

■ ■ ■

ACCEPTANCE

SEVEN

"So, what'd ya think?" Storm interrupts the silence in the car on the ride home.

I frown, not understanding her question. My mind is still stuck on Trent, on the feel of his hand; on me, standing there like an idiot, not saying a thing. I'm so wound up over Trent and that pivotal moment that for once I'm not fazed by the confines of Storm's Jeep. He held my hand. Trent held my hand and I didn't drown.

I notice that Storm's small fists are curled tightly around her steering wheel and she's looking everywhere but at me. She's nervous. "What do I think about what?" I ask slowly.

"About . . . my show?"

Oh! Right. "I don't know how those boobs of yours don't throw your balance off."

Her head tips back and she laughs. "It took some getting used to, believe me."

"Seriously, that was the most amazing thing I've ever seen. What the hell are you doing in a strip club? You could be in Cirque du Soleil or some shit like that."

I catch a hint of sadness in her giggle. "Not a lifestyle I can handle anymore. That means training all day and shows all night. I can't do that with Mia to care for."

"Why is this the first show I've seen?"

"I can't do that every night. It's hard enough to stay upright and get a bit of a workout in every day."

Huh. Storm works out. I had no idea. "Why didn't you tell me?"

She shrugs. "We all have our secrets."

My eyes drift out the window. "Well, that's one hell of a way to reveal a secret."

She chuckles, nodding in agreement. There's a pause. "How was your little chat with Trent?"

"Oh, life-altering." His touch still lingers on my fingers and I can't shake the pleading sound of his voice. Raw shame has settled on my shoulders. I should have answered him. Instead, I let Nate toss him out like a drunken ass.

I hate being in my skin right now.

We drive a few more minutes without talking. Then Storm breaks the silence with a full-on assault. "Kace, what happened to you?" My jaw instantly clenches, unprepared, but she rushes on. "I still don't know you at all. Given I've pretty much bared all— literally—I was hoping you'd trust me enough to do the same."

"You want me to spin around on a hoop and take my top off?" I joke, my voice flat. I know that's not what she means.

"I asked Livie and she wouldn't tell me. She said *you* needed to," Storm says in a low voice, like she knows she wasn't supposed to ask Livie in the first place.

My gut sinks to the floor. "Livie knows better than to tell anyone my secrets."

"You need to start talking to someone, Kacey. That's the only way to get better."

"There's no getting better, Storm. This is it." *There's no coming back from the dead.* I try to keep the coldness from my voice, but I can't help it. It's there.

"I'm your friend, Kacey. Whether you like it or not. I may

have known you for only a few weeks, but I've trusted you. I've trusted your sister with my five-year-old, invited you into my home, and got you a job. Not to mention that you've folded my underwear and seen me naked."

"All that without giving you my number. Oh, the guys at my gym would be so proud of me."

We pull into the parking lot outside our building as my hand works fretfully over the door handle. Now that Storm's Jeep has morphed into a confessional tin can, it's overwhelming to be inside it.

"What I'm trying to say is that I'm not an idiot. I don't do that with everyone. But there's something about you. I could see it from day one. It's like you're fighting against being yourself. Every time a little bit of the real you escapes, you shut it down. Cover it up." Her voice is so soft, and yet it makes me break out in a cold sweat.

The real me. Who is that? All I know is that since moving to Miami, my carefully crafted defenses have been attacked from all angles. Even Mia and her gap-toothed grins have managed to worm their way into the cracks of my armor. No matter how many times I tell myself I don't care, I'm starting to find my heart beating a little bit faster and my shoulders lifting a little bit higher when I make my new neighbors laugh.

"You don't have to tell me everything, Kace. Not all at once. Why not just one little thing every day?"

I rub my brow as I try to find a way out of this. After the last time I blew her off, I thought she'd give up. But she's just been biding her time. What if I bolt out of this car right now? Maybe this is a turning point in our friendship. Maybe she'll write me off if I do something like that again. A sinking feeling in the pit of my stomach tells me that will bother me. And Livie. That will outright crush her and I can't do that. I hear Livie's voice in my head. *Try.* I know I have to. For Livie.

"Four years ago, my parents, my boyfriend, and my best friend died in a drunk-driving accident."

There's a long pause. I don't even have to look to know that tears are running down Storm's cheeks. People crying over it doesn't faze me anymore. I've permanently shut off that tear-jerking switch.

"I'm so sorry, Kacey."

I nod. Everyone apologizes and I don't know why. They weren't the douche bags in the other car.

"Do you remember any of it?"

"No," I lie. Storm doesn't need to hear how I remember every single moment trapped in the mangled Audi. She doesn't need to hear how I listened to the hissing sound of my mother's last breath, the noise that haunts me every night. Or how on one side my friend Jenny's broken body molded itself against the car and how on the other, my hand lay trapped in my boyfriend's, sensing every degree drop as the heat left his corpse. How I had to sit in that car, surrounded by the bodies of those I loved for hours while the emergency crew struggled to cut me out. I shouldn't have survived.

I don't know who let me live.

Storm's soft voice pulls me from my thoughts. "Were you driving?"

I turn to glare at her. "Do you think I'd be sitting here now if I had been?"

She flinches. "Sorry. What happened to the drunk driver?"

I shrug noncommittally, staring straight ahead again. "He died. He had two friends in his car. One died. One walked away." I answer, my words oozing with bitterness.

"God, Kacey." She sniffles. "Have you had therapy?"

"What is this, the Spanish Inquisition?" I snap.

"I'm . . . I'm sorry." The car is filled with Storm's muffled sobs.

Though she's trying to contain them, to be strong, I can tell she's still crying by the way she keeps sucking in her breaths.

My anger morphs into guilt and I bite my lip. Hard. The coppery taste of blood coats my tongue. Storm's been nothing but kind to me and I'm nothing but a bitch to her. "I'm sorry, Storm," I force out the words. Even though I mean them, they're still hard to get out.

She reaches for my hand but, remembering, places her palm on my forearm.

That little gesture is enough to melt my icy defenses and I start rambling. "I was in the hospital and rehab for almost a year. Doctors visited me there. Not much after that, though. Apparently they thought zombie drugs and daily rounds of 'Kumbaya' would solve all my problems. When I got out, my aunt insisted I talk to the counselors at her church. They suggested she put me in a serious rehabilitation program because I'm a broken young woman full of rage and hatred who could become harmful to herself and others if let loose." That last part is almost word for word what they said. My aunt's answer to that was to leave a Bible on my nightstand. In her view, reading the Bible fixes everything.

"Where's this aunt now?"

"Back in Michigan with her disgusting husband who tried to molest Livie." Silence. "Is that what you wanted to hear, Storm? That you have a walking head case living next to you?"

She turns to look at me, wiping tears from her cheeks with her palms. "You're not a head case, Kacey. But you do need help. Thank you for telling me. It means a lot. One day it will get easier. One day this hatred won't imprison you anymore. You'll be free. You'll be able to forgive."

I subtly feel my head nodding. I don't believe her. Not a word.

The atmosphere of the Jeep has dropped seven levels below

unpleasant. I've bared more to Storm than I ever have to anyone else and it's left me drained. "Look at you—Stripper Acrobat by night, Deep Thought Provoker by . . . later night."

Storm snorts. "I prefer just 'Acrobat.' My clothes happen to fall off sometimes, unexpectedly." She nudges my arm. "Come on. That's enough exposing for one night. For both of us."

Now that I've survived the conversation with Storm, my thoughts move back to Trent with a vengeance. My need to feel his intoxicating presence around me trumps all my other desires. I didn't answer him. I *should* have answered him. I need to tell him that I'm better than okay. That I think I might need him.

The faint sound of laughter carries through the commons as Storm and I walk through the darkness. Some of the college students in the building are still up, partying. I wonder what that would be like—hanging out with friends, drinking, having a normal life—as we round the corner to our apartments.

A silhouette moves past the curtain in 1D.

I stumble, my pulse quickening. Then, without thinking, I walk up to the door and stand in front of it.

"See you tomorrow," I hear Storm call out as she continues on, and I can tell she's smiling.

Inhaling deeply, gathering all the courage I can muster, I lift my hand to knock, but the door flies opens before my knuckles make contact. Trent steps into the doorway, shirtless and expressionless, and my mouth instantly dries. I'm sure he's going to tell me to go to hell. I wait for it. I'm terrified to hear it.

But he doesn't. He doesn't say anything. He's waiting for me, I realize. There's just one word I need to give him. *Yes.* It might make this all better. *Yes, Trent. Yes, it's okay.* I open my mouth and find that I can't. I can't form a single word that will impress upon him the gravity of the situation.

Tense, I step forward. He doesn't back away. He just watches me, his bare sculpted chest and the pants hanging low off his hips taunting me. He's as hot as ever. I could spend days with that body. For once, I hope that I will.

But that's not what I need right now.

I cautiously reach out, my stomach muscles coiled into a tight ball, suddenly panicked that whatever I felt earlier might be temporary, that I've lost it again. When my fingertips graze his and warmth spreads through me, that dread evaporates.

His warmth. His life.

Closing my eyes, I slide my hand farther in, slipping my fingers between his and curling them around. My lips part in a small gasp when his grip tightens over mine. He doesn't move closer, though. He doesn't try anything or say anything. We stand like that, in the doorway, our hands entwined, for what feels like forever.

"Yes," I finally whisper breathlessly.

"Yes?"

I'm vaguely aware that my head is bobbing. So intense is this high that I'm feeling that nothing else matters. I let him gently pull me in. The door clicks closed behind me and he smoothly guides me into his dark apartment with a hand pressed against the small of my back. Down the hall, and into his bed, his sheets cool and crisp and smelling of fabric softener. I sense, rather than see, Trent's body slide in behind me, pressing up against me from toes to shoulder, never once letting go of my hand. Not once. I snuggle against him, reveling in his warmth.

And in that heavenly peace, I fall asleep.

■ ■ ■

A hissing sound . . .
   Bright lights . . .
   Blood . . .
   I'm gasping.

Slow, rhythmic breathing next to me helps regulate my heart rate as I wake up from my nightmare. At first, I assume it's Livie, but then I feel my hand wound into someone's large, hot hand—not Livie's hand.

I roll my head to see Trent's perfect form, the peaks and ripples of his chest, his face relaxed and boyish. I could lie here and stare at him forever. I don't want to let go. Ever.

That's why I have to.

I slip my hand out carefully and slide from the comfort of Trent's bed, closing the door softly behind me as I exit his apartment.

■ ■ ■

Livie is waiting for me in the kitchen, getting breakfast before heading off to school, her eyes wide with worry. "You stayed at Trent's?" Her tone is half accusatory, half astonished.

"Nothing happened, Livie."

"*Nothing?*" She glares at me. That's one thing Livie can do well. Glare until you squirm when you've lied.

"I held his hand," I whisper finally. To anyone outside listening in, we'd sound like a couple of nine-year-olds. But to Livie, who understands the impact of this, this is huge.

She's speechless for a moment, sputtering gurgles and half-words. "Is this . . . do you think this could be something more?" she finally asks.

I shrug indifferently but heat creeps to my cheeks, giving away my excitement.

"You're blushing!"

I pick up a Cheerio and toss it at her head.

She dodges it deftly, smiling. "I think this could be it. I think Trent could finally bring Kacey back to me."

I wonder if she's right. But I just snuck out of his apartment without a word or a note. He might not appreciate that. A twinge of worry jabs me, but I suppress it. I had no choice. If I had stayed, I know exactly what we'd be doing right now and it isn't thinking. I need time to think and adjust to this new reality.

I feel Livie's excitement right down to my bones. For three years, my baby sister has begged me to let go of Billy and move on. The thing is, my issue hasn't been about moving on from my feelings for Billy. Of course, I cared about him. Did I think he was "the one"? I'll never know. At sixteen, everyone is "the one."

No, my issue has been that, because of those last moments with Billy, the very idea of my hands wrapped in someone else's has plagued me, making my heart stop, my stomach drop, my vision blurry, my muscles spasm, and sweat pour down my back all at once.

Until now.

This is different. This feels . . . right again.

EIGHT

"You look fabulous!" Mia drawls, impersonating her mother and making us all laugh. Storm is making veal Parmesan and I'm modeling my new outfits. I'd exhausted Storm's closet and needed a few things of my own, so we spent the afternoon at the mall, buying me new clothes. I let Storm coordinate the outfits. I don't have the first clue how to dress appropriately for a job at a strip club, even after weeks working there. In any case, the ordeal gave me a good distraction from Trent.

"I think I'll wear this tonight," I announce, coming out in a short emerald-green tunic dress that falls off one shoulder, and nude heels.

"Good choice! Can you set the table, Kace?" Storm asks as she bends down to check the oven.

"You know you're going to have to let me cook one day, right?" We've had dinner at Storm's apartment every night for weeks.

"I like to cook."

"Maybe I do too," I throw back, placing the plates on the table, earning a derisive snort from Livie.

"You're short one setting," Storm says with a peek at the table.

I frown. "Uh, no? Four people, four places."

"We need five," she says without making eye contact.

"Storm?"

Someone knocks on the door.

"*Storm?*"

Mia hops to her feet and runs to the door, throwing it open with a dramatic bow.

I take a deep breath as Trent steps in, and I can't help but gawk. He's in dark blue jeans again, but he's wearing a button-down white shirt, untucked. I manage to peel my eyes from him long enough to flash a look of "you're going to pay for this" at Storm before turning back to him. Nervousness and excitement and guilt are churning inside me. I don't know why. Trent and I held hands while watching my friend dance naked. Trent rescued me in the apartment building's now infamous snake attack, and then I jumped him. I spent a night in his bed with him. Eating dinner with him—and my sister and neighbors—hardly qualifies as an intimate encounter that justifies thrashing butterflies. And yet here I am, ready to pass out.

Mia bows dramatically. "Welcome, kind sir. Princess Mia has been awaiting your presence."

Even Mia knew! That little devil.

From behind his back, Trent produces a bunch of five pink roses. He kneels on one knee to present them to her. I hear the collective sigh from all the grown women in the group, including myself.

"Thank you for inviting me," he says. She clutches the flowers in both her tiny hands, and then gazes at Trent with wide, starry eyes that remain unblinking for far too long. Her cheeks flush, and I can tell this is the moment when Mia falls in love with him. This tall stranger has just become her lifelong prince.

Mia turns around and runs toward Storm. "Mommy! Mommy! Look what that man gave me!"

Trent winks as he shuts the door behind him, closing the distance between us. "You disappeared this morning," he whispers.

This is so awkward. Thanks, Storm. "I . . . I know . . . I'm . . ." I'm about to say I'm sorry, but he winks.

"It's okay. I figured it was all a bit too much, too fast." One finger hooks into mine, buckling my knees with waves of excitement.

I think I'm going to fall in love with this man.

Trent's gaze drifts over my outfit and I feel the heat in it. Probably the exact same heat emanating from mine when I gaze at him. "You look . . . nice."

We're still staring awkwardly at each other, when Livie clears her throat. "Dinner's ready."

Storm's tiny apartment pulses with a warm current as the five of us devour her cooking. Somehow the snake fiasco comes up, and I become the butt of everyone's jokes. Even Mia joins in, nibbling on my shoulder like a mock monster. Except she has no front teeth, so it's more like gumming. And through it all, I can't help but frequently look at Trent's face, only to find him looking at me.

By the time dinner is done, and we're saying our goodbyes so Storm and I can head off to work, every fiber of my being craves Trent and I have no interest in pretending otherwise.

■ ■ ■

"Who's Penny? Clearly someone important." I gesture to the sign as we pull up in front of the club.

Storm's fingers tap her steering wheel and her perma-smile falters. "Penny was a really nice girl who met a really bad guy." She turns to look at me. "Five years ago, Cain ran a club downtown. It was a dive compared to this place. Penny was his star attraction. I hear she brought guys in from all over the state and even from Alabama. She started dating this guy, and things got serious. He proposed. Everyone was happy for her. He'd come watch her dance sometimes. He'd give her little kisses and hugs throughout the night. Watch over her a bit. You know, really sweet stuff. Of course, he said once they were married, she'd have to quit. She was fine with that." Storm's voice turns somber.

"Then something happened. No one knows what exactly. One second this guy has his arm around Penny, the next, he's dragging her to the back room by her throat. Nate couldn't get there in time. He found her on the ground with a cracked skull."

I clutch my throat.

"I know. Terrible, right? Cain shut down that place. There was a whole murder investigation. The guy was convicted and went to jail. Cain bought this location and opened under the new name, in honor of her." We exit the car and head toward the back door. "That's why the bouncers are so strict about patrons touching the staff. It doesn't matter if the guy's your husband. If he touches you, he's out. More than once, and he's barred for life."

"Huh . . ." My thoughts drift back to last night, when Nate kicked Trent out for holding my hand. I thought he was being an asshole. Now, I want to hug him. Or a part of him, given that I'd need a ladder and extendable arms to reach around his mammoth size.

I follow Storm's black-clad silhouette to the door. Just before she knocks, she turns and smiles, as though she can read my mind. "They're genuinely good guys, Kacey. I know it's hard to believe, but it's true. Cain's been nothing but amazing with me. He lets me bartend, he sets the stage and equipment up for me to do my act once in a while, and that's all. No rounds, no lap dances, no private stuff. The bouncers collect my tips from my show so I don't have to crawl around on the ground, collecting them myself. They'll take care of you. You'll see."

■ ■ ■

When Trent shows up at half past eleven and takes a seat at the bar, my brain instantly scatters. The fact that I slept in his bed last night, and had dinner with him earlier, doesn't help me relax around him. I think it has actually made me more nervous. *One . . . two . . . three . . . Ugh!* As usual, my mother's advice doesn't help.

I stroll over, trying to regulate my heart rate as I take in his beautiful features. They really are beautiful. He could grace the cover of any magazine. And that mouth . . . I bite my lip, trying not to get all flustered. "Triple scotch on the rocks?" I quirk my brow.

He flashes those disarming dimples at me. "Hold the scotch and add some soda to the rocks, and you've got a deal."

I smile as I throw together his drink and slide it toward him, our fingertips brushing for a millisecond. With a nervous glance over at Nate, I see his focus is elsewhere, and I sigh in relief.

"Don't worry, I know the rules at these places."

"Frequent much?" I ask dryly.

He shakes his head with a wry grin. "Standard protocol. Some places are more strict than others, but they're all the same. I have no interest in getting kicked out again. Once was enough."

I feel a twinge of guilt over that, knowing it was my fault. But Trent's wink dissolves it instantly. I want to stay and talk to him but there's a gaggle of customers waiting. I'm forced to leave him with a disappointed shrug. I spend the next hour pouring drinks for customers while my nerves prickle under Trent's undivided attention.

"Too bad it's so busy here," he says when I get back to where he's sitting.

"Yeah well, some of us have to work to survive," I quip, and I realize I have no clue what he does. I know nothing about him.

"And when are you off next?" he asks casually, sliding a coaster around under his index finger.

"Monday."

Trent gets to his feet and throws a twenty on the counter. "So are you free Monday, say around four?"

"Maybe."

His grin widens. "Great." With a wink, he turns around. I watch him leave the bar, frustration that he's gone weighing me down.

Storm leans in. "What was that about?"

I shrug, the lingering feel of his eyes still on my body. "I'm not sure. I think he just asked me on a date." A rush of adrenaline bursts through me. That sure as hell had better be what he just did or I'm going to lose my shit tomorrow.

Storm gives my shoulder an affectionate squeeze, and I don't flinch. I smile at her. I smile at the guy across the bar waiting for his drink. Heck, I even give Nate a goofy wide grin. I'm not sure, but I think I catch the corner of his mouth twitch upward for a second.

■ ■ ■

I feel like a lightning bolt struck me the second I wake up Monday morning. Not because I had another nightmare.

Because I didn't.

In the last four years, that has *never* happened. I don't know what to make of it, but I feel . . . free.

Then I remember that I have a date tonight with Trent and all else is forgotten.

■ ■ ■

"Nice nails," Livie comments two seconds after stepping through the door. She drops her backpack on the couch, her eyes widening with surprise for just a second. I spread my fingers out in front of me, admiring the black polish. "Where'd you get that done?" Her voice is slightly higher than normal and she's trying not to make a big deal, I can tell.

But it *is* a big deal.

Today, I let a complete stranger touch my hands. And I didn't flinch.

It's as if Trent has broken my curse.

"A spa down the street. They have a two-for-one manicure special on Thursdays. We should go together next time."

"Uh-huh, and what's the occasion?" Livie strolls toward the cupboard to grab a glass, pacing her steps as if she's a bridesmaid walking down a church aisle. I want to laugh. She's trying so hard not to freak out.

"Oh, nothing." I wait until she tips the Brita pitcher to her glass. "I'm going out with Trent tonight."

Her head shoots up to meet my eyes and she misses the cup, spilling water all over the floor. "Like . . . on a date?"

I tuck my hair behind my ear. "Maybe. I guess you could . . ."

Livie's eyes flash with delight. "Where are you guys going?"

I shrug. "Probably the beach. Isn't that what people do on first dates?" I have no idea. It's been so long since I've done anything remotely datelike.

There's a long pause as Livie likely tries to process this new Kacey, the one who goes on dates and gets manicures. And cares. "You know, we don't know much about Trent, do we?" Her head tilts to the side curiously. "What does he do for a living?"

I shrug. "No idea."

A darkness passes over Livie's pretty face. I wait patiently for her to bite her lip for all of two seconds before she blurts out, "What if he's a psychopath who tries to stuff kittens in ATMs?"

"A *hot* psychopath," I correct her, and she scowls at me. "Come on, Livie. I didn't get you away from Darla soon enough."

"Maybe you should find out more about Trent before agreeing to go out with him."

"I didn't agree to go out with him."

"What?" She pauses. "Well, then . . ."

I cut her off. "We know nothing about each other. More important, he knows nothing about *me*. Just the way I like it."

Her lips press together tightly.

"Oh, Livie, stop acting like the mature one here."

"Someone needs to." She stoops to wipe up the water with a dish towel. "I'll be at Storm's for dinner. Can you at least phone her later to let us know he didn't stuff *you* into an ATM? And we need to get cell phones if you're going to start going out with strange men."

I chuckle and nod.

She stops and appraises me with a small smile. "It's nice to see you like this . . . again. What time do you think you'll be home?"

I wink.

"Oh, Kacey," she mutters, tossing the dish towel into the sink.

■ ■ ■

By the time four rolls around, I'm pacing in my living room like a caged bear, counting to ten under my breath, over and over. Waves of excitement, nervousness, and fear chuck my insides back and forth, until I'm sure I'll toss the contents of my lunch onto the hideous carpet.

Right on cue, a soft knock sounds on the door. I open it to find Trent standing outside in jeans and a blue-and-white checkered shirt and aviator sunglasses, leaning against the door frame with one arm above his head. My entire body breaks out in a light sweat.

"Nice door," he says, sliding off his sunglasses. I catch myself staring into those gorgeous blue eyes a tad too long before I make a sound.

He's being playful. I like playful. "Thanks. It's new. We had to replace it after a crazed maniac busted through." I smirk.

He laughs as he reaches toward me to hook his index finger around mine. Electricity streams through my limbs with that small amount of contact. He pulls me out into the open, into his chest, so that he towers over me, and I have to tilt my head back to meet his face. "I heard about that. Terrible situation. Did they finally catch that madman?" he murmurs, smirking.

I pause to inhale. He smells likes the ocean and the woods. And raw desire. "The last I heard he was lurking around a gentlemen's establishment. Clearly he has deep-seated issues. I think they're closing in." I add breathlessly, "I think they'll catch him tonight."

Trent's head tips back and he laughs. "Maybe they will." He drapes his arm around my shoulder as he leads me out toward the parking lot. "That color looks incredible on you," he says, gazing down at my emerald-green shirt. "Complements your hair nicely."

"Thanks." I smile, silently praising myself for buying it today, for the very reason that I know it looks nice against my dark red hair and ivory skin. People think I dye my hair to make it so dark and rich, but I don't. That's one way in which I'm lucky, I guess.

Trent leads me to a red and orange Harley in the parking lot. "Have you ever ridden on one of these?" He holds out a helmet and a black leather jacket. *So Trent's a bike guy.* Inspecting the thing, I'm not sure how I feel about that. I think he may have just climbed a few notches in the hot bad-boy department.

I shake my head as I look down at the bike with hesitation. "Not a lot of protection between me and three tons of moving metal when I'm on this," I say. *Who am I kidding?* I'm not safe riding *in* three tons of metal. I've learned that firsthand.

A gentle fingertip pushes my chin up until I'm looking at Trent's earnest eyes. "I'll keep you safe, Kacey. Just hold on to me. Tight." I let him place the helmet on my head and gently fasten the strap around my chin, his deft fingers brushing my skin in a way that sends shivers through my body. A ghost of a smile passes his lips. "Or are you too scared?"

Now he's challenging me. Like he knows I'll react to that. I can't help but react. I'm like one of those idiots in the movies who slam on their gas pedal and attempt to sail over a two-hundred-foot gap in the road because someone said the word *dare*. My dad got hours of entertainment at my expense for that reason.

"I'm not scared of anything," I lie smoothly as I slide my arms into the jacket that Trent holds open for me. I climb on behind him and shimmy up until my thighs hug his hips. Heat explodes through the lower half of my body, but I do my best to ignore it, wrapping my arms around his torso.

"Nothing at all? Not even a bit nervous?" His brow raises as he glances over his shoulder at me. "It's okay. You can admit it. Most girls are nervous about riding on bikes."

A flash of jealousy sparks inside me at the thought of him with another girl. I quickly quell it. "Do I seem like most girls?" My hands slide around his chest, running along the contours of his body, my fingers slipping through the seam of his shirt to graze the smooth ridges of his muscles underneath. For added effect, I lean forward and press my teeth against his shoulder.

Trent's chest rises with a quick inhale as his hands lift to grab mine and pull them out, placing them with a pat on the outside of his shirt. "Okay, you win. But don't do that while I'm driving or we'll end up in a ditch." He looks over his shoulder again, adding in a soft, solemn tone, "I'm serious, Kacey. I can't handle it."

Another burst of warmth erupts through my thighs but I take his warning to heart and lace my fingers around each other at his waist, pressing my body against his. "Where're we going?"

The low rumble of Trent's bike is the only answer I get and then we're moving.

Without thought, I hug his body tight as we weave in and out of traffic. Trent turns out to be a cautious driver, giving everyone a wide berth, following all the laws. I like that. I feel safe with him. And that scares the shit out of me. It makes me want to jump off this moving bike and run home to hide under my covers because he's just too damn perfect. I squeeze him tightly instead.

It's not until Trent turns onto the interstate and heads south that I realize we're not going to the beach. He's taking me away, somewhere far.

In so many ways, I think he already has.

■ ■ ■

"My sister thinks you like to shove kittens in ATMs," I say as Trent cuts the engine in an Everglades National Park parking lot. "You know, like from *American Psycho*."

His forehead creases. "Really? I thought she liked me."

"Oh, she does, I can tell." I make sure my voice sounds casual as I slide off the bike and take off my helmet. "But that doesn't mean you can't be crazy."

"Huh." Trent's long leg swings around the seat. "How old is Livie again?"

"Fifteen."

"She's smart, that one." I catch his sly smile as he grabs a little cooler bag from a compartment on the bike. "Come on. Let me lead you into the dark, secluded wilderness over there." He jerks his head toward a bunch of hiking signs, flashing me a set of baby blue eyes and deep dimples. The signs include warnings of wildlife dangers. I can't help but wonder if they should also have warnings for idiot girls who follow guys they hardly know into the swamp.

The sun is beginning to sink toward the horizon as we walk down the paved pathway. The trail looks well maintained, but it's quiet. As we move farther and farther in, as the eeriness closes in around us and the air grows thick and heady with the unknown, I can't help but wonder what Trent's plan is. "So why are we in the Everglades?"

He shrugs, looking over his shoulder. "I've never been. Have you?"

I shake my head.

"Well, we live in Miami, so I figured we should go."

"I guess that's a good reason," I mumble as we edge along the trail, lined with tall grass wrapped in shadows from the late-day sun. The perfect place to get rid of a body. "So is this going to be a reenactment of a *CSI: Miami* episode?" I blurt out. *Damn you for freaking me out, Livie!*

Trent stops and turns to study me with a furrowed brow and an amused smile. "Are you seriously worried?"

I shrug. "I'm sure I've seen this episode before. Guy takes girl to remote shack in the Everglades, has his way with her for a few days, and then leaves her body to the alligators so there's no evidence."

He opens his mouth to answer, but then pauses as if in thought. "Well, probably only twenty-four hours. I have a dead-line for work tomorrow."

I cock my head.

"Come on, Kacey!" he bursts out with amazed laughter. "I have never, nor will I ever, stuff a kitten into an ATM! I'm more of a dog person, anyway."

My arms fold over my chest, my brow arching. "You know I can handle myself pretty well, right?"

He chuckles, blue eyes sliding over my body, shooting trem-ors through me. "Oh, believe me. I know you can. You could probably have me flat on my back in under five seconds." *I wish.* "Come on." He grabs hold of my elbow and pulls me forward so we're walking side by side. I impulsively unfold my arms and grab his hand, pulling it up to my mouth to kiss his knuckles.

Pleasant surprise flickers in his eyes. With a lopsided grin, he switches hands so he can haul me toward his body, tossing his arm around my shoulder. He lifts my hand and holds it against his chest. We walk like that in silence, allowing me to feel his heartbeat. It's fast and hard and so damn alive.

"So what do you wanna know?"

"What?" I frown.

"Well, you said Livie thinks you should know more about me, so what do you wanna know?" His tone softens, his face somber, as he stares forward, and I sense a shift in his demeanor. He seems a bit tense, suggesting we're encroaching on a topic he's not comfortable with either.

"Umm . . ." The less we talk about each other's lives, the better. But secretly, I have to admit I want to know everything about him. Right down to the type of soap he uses in the shower. "Well, you already know what I do for a living. What do you do?"

His shoulders slump a little as if relieved by the topic. "Graphic design."

"Really? A computer geek? Never would have guessed." Seriously, I look at his perfect body and I *never* would have guessed. He smiles at my jibe. "And who do you work for?"

"Myself. It's great. I don't have to go anywhere or report to anyone except my clients. I can pick up and move if I want, which is what I did. I can design naked in my living room all day and no one has a clue."

"That's . . . uh . . ." Trent catches my shoulder and hand to keep me upright as I trip over my own two feet. Swirls of light and dark fill my vision from the mental image Trent has just painted. *Dammit!* By the smirk on his face, he knows what saying things like that does to me. I decide I'll be breaking down his front door one day soon, alligator or not. I also decide I need to change the topic before my body drops to the ground and flops around like a fish out of water.

"Where'd you learn how to hit a bag?"

He laughs again. "I was into sports a lot, back in high school and college. It's a good stress reliever, that's all." His thumb rubs my shoulder as we walk on and my heart swells.

"Are both of your parents in Rochester?" I ask, shocking even myself. Now that I've started prying, I can't seem to stop. Worse, I'm asking all the questions I can't answer about myself. "Sorry," I shake my head. "I . . . it's none of my—"

Trent's soft chuckle stops my sputtering. "My dad's in Manhattan, my mom's in Rochester. Divorced, obviously." He offers the information freely, but I can't help notice his shoulders tense, implying it's not something he's comfortable talking about.

I bite my tongue and we continue in silence.

"What else do you want to know, Kace?" He looks down at me. "Ask me whatever you want."

"What do you want to tell me?"

"Everything."

I'm shaking my head. "I'm sure there are things you want to keep to yourself."

"Yes, some things are hard to talk about. But I'll tell you." His hand squeezes mine. "I want you to know me."

"Okay." My voice is soft and weak now and I feel that I have to lay my cards out on the table. "So you know, I'm not big on talking about some things."

I hear him softly exhale. "I've noticed. Can you at least tell me what's off-limits?"

"My past. My family."

Trent's jaw tenses but, after a moment, he nods. "That's a big part of you, Kacey. But, okay. We won't talk about that stuff until you're ready."

I look up and see Trent's blue eyes crinkle with sincerity, and I'm filled with sadness. I'll never be ready to talk about those things. Ever. I don't say that, though. I just nod and say, "Thank you."

He pulls me closer to him, his lips parting as he lays an intimate kiss on my forehead.

■ ■ ■

After touring the lengthy boardwalk that stretches out over the water—along the way, bumping into a small group of park rangers patrolling the area—we find a seat on a stone wall. Trent unzips the cooler bag and hands me a cold bottle of water. It's only then that I realize how parched I am, having been distracted by Trent. "I just really want to see a gator. Then we can grab a bite to eat," he promises.

"This is perfect, Trent. Really." And it is. Absolutely perfect. We're overlooking the marshlands as a golden sun sinks into the horizon, painting the sky in hues of pink and purple. The sounds of soft water ripples and strange bird squawks float through the air. It's just about the most peaceful place I've ever been. Of course, anywhere would be perfect with Trent.

"Yeah?" He rests his hand on the back of my neck, his fingers lingering along the collar of my shirt, slipping under to graze along my bare skin. I shiver in response.

"Cold?" he teases.

I give him a crooked smile. "No. Distracted. You're going to make me choke on my water."

He dips his head in assent as he pulls his hand away, evoking a blip of disappointment inside me. It quickly shifts to concern.

"Look! Do you see that?" Trent's voice rises an octave and his hand moves back to my shoulder as he leans in. He stretches his other arm out to point out the long, narrow head peeking out from the water's surface no more than twenty feet from us.

My appetite vanishes instantly. "Ohmigod. Is he watching us?"

"Maybe. Hard to tell."

"Don't those things move ridiculously fast?" I swallow repeatedly, more than a little freaked out. Gators in enclosures at a zoo are one thing. There aren't any walls separating us here.

"Don't worry. I did some research before we came. This trail is popular for seeing alligators up close. The park rangers are just down that way, in any case."

"If you say so," I murmur, noting how close Trent's mouth is to mine. So close, I could just lean in and . . .

My lips graze the corner of his mouth, catching him off guard. Turning to face me, he regards me with a momentary flicker of surprise. But it lasts only a moment, and then he leans in to cover my lips with his. He kisses me tenderly, his hand finding its way to my chin to turn my head, his thumb gripping my jaw as he pulls my knees close to him with his other hand. My breath hitches as his tongue runs along the edge of my lips before sweeping into my mouth, sending a shock through my entire body. I can't help but reach for him, my fingers settling on the curves of his chest.

He releases the lightest growl as he breaks free. His biceps flex as he scoops my body up onto his lap and burrows his head into my neck, taking my earlobe into his mouth, nipping it painlessly. My hand skates over his throat, reveling in the thickness of it, of its muscles. As my thumb slides over his Adam's apple and his mouth trails kisses all along my neck, I close my eyes and let my head rest against his, weightless and floating in his presence, under his control. Under his touch.

"Kace," he whispers.

I make a strange half-moan, half-gurgle noise in response.

"Are you afraid?"

Afraid? Peeking out of one eye, I check the marsh to see our observer in the same spot. "He hasn't moved yet, but I have to tell you, I doubt I can drive that bike back if you lose a leg tonight."

Trent bursts out laughing and I feel the vibrations right down into my nipples, he's so close. "I'll be fine for tonight. I still need to have my way with you. The shack's back that way." His head jerks behind us.

"I hope you've put fresh sheets down at least."

With another chuckle, he settles his head against my shoulder as I sit in anxious silence, watching the alligator drift away to join its friends. With little effort, within weeks, Trent has torn down my defenses and fear, quickly earning himself a vital place in my life. And then it dawns on me what he was asking. Am I afraid of *this*.

"I'm terrified," I whisper. At first I don't think he heard me. But then he turns to study the contours of my face, his brows drawn together, and I know that he did. "I . . . um . . . I . . . it's been a while since I've done this," I go on to say. *I've never done this. Ever. Nothing close to this.* "And this . . ." I hold up my hand in his. "Just this alone is kind of a big deal for me."

He lifts my hand to press against his lips. Then he clears his throat. "Look, Kacey. What happened in your room that day . . ."

I feel my brow furrow, searching. *My room?*

"The snake in your shower?"

Oh, yeah. My heart jolts like a thousand-watt current just zapped it.

"I'm . . . uh." He stretches his long legs out in front of him but holds me tight on his lap. "I'm trying hard not to let that happen again. For now."

He must be able to read the disappointment that smashes into me because he quickly explains himself, his eyes wide and earnest. "It's not that I don't want it or you." His Adam's apple bobs up and down as he swallows. "Believe me, I'm sure you know exactly how much I do want that right now."

I smile, wiggling in his lap.

He chuckles, my actions softening his serious tone. But it returns quickly. "I have a hard time—a really hard time—controlling myself around you, Kacey. You're unbelievably attractive and I'm a guy. It doesn't take much for you to dissolve my willpower. But

I think we need to move slow. Take our time." He gives me a meaningful look, suggesting he understands more about me than I've told him. "I think that's important, for both of us."

I open my mouth to speak, but I'm not sure how to respond yet. He's right. Slow is good. Slow is safe. But right now, with his fingertips back on my collar, feeling his excitement digging into me, I don't want slow. I want a sudsy hot mess.

I allow myself a moment for a deep breath to try and regulate my spastic heart. "Who says I want *anything* with you? You assume a lot."

"Maybe I do." With a crooked smile, his hand slips up under the back of my shirt, moving painstakingly slowly up along my spine, eliciting a small gasp from me.

"Yeah, that's slow all right," I croak.

"Am I assuming too much right now?"

I shake my head lightly to let him know that he's not assuming anything. I'll happily take anything from Trent that I can get. Slow or fast.

His fingers fan out as they skate over my bare skin, sliding to my rib cage to graze along the various scar ridges. His thumb strokes back and forth. "Couldn't help but notice you have a few of these."

I'm used to people questioning my scars. I've learned to shrug them off smoothly. "Oh yeah? When'd you see those?"

He gives me a wry smile.

"Pervert." I try to push off my embarrassment, but I feel my cheeks flush anyway.

He turns serious. "Is that part of the past you don't want to talk about?"

"Man-eating snake attack in a shower. It's a reoccurring problem for me."

He chuckles softly, but the mirth never reaches his eyes. Sliding his hand out from under my shirt, he pushes my sleeve up to expose the thin white line on my shoulder. Leaning in, his bottom lip grazes over it. "Sometimes it helps to talk, Kace."

"Can we please just stick to the here and now?" I beg softly, confused by the conflicting reaction in my body, both tensing and liquefying under his attention. "I don't want to spoil this."

"Yeah, for now." He lifts his head to look at me again, tucking a strand of my hair back behind my ear. "You don't smile enough."

"I smile tons. From eight p.m. until one a.m. from Tuesday until Sunday. Wouldn't you know? It doubles my tips."

His dimples are in full force now. "I want to make you smile. For real. Always. We're going to go for dinners, and see movies, and walk on the beach. We'll go hang gliding, or bungee jumping, or whatever you want to do. Whatever makes you smile and laugh more." His fingers toy with my bottom lip. "Let me make you smile."

■ ■ ■

Trent doesn't have his way with me that night. In fact, he handles me like I'm a porcelain doll that is two seconds from shattering. Instead, he talks. He talks and talks and talks. I listen, mostly. He talks about the Everglades, and about how a human can hold an alligator's jaws closed with his bare hands, and I ask him if he's one of those *Jeopardy!* freaks. He talks about how Tanner isn't such a bad guy and our apartment building kind of has a *Melrose Place* feel to it, and I laugh. I don't remember rusted hibachis and shriveled weeds in *Melrose Place*. He smiles when he mentions Mia's name and how cute she is.

He talks and I listen to the low, seductive hum of his voice and, although my hormones are planning a full assault to hijack my brain and take over all rational thought, I can't help but get distracted by the shred of life flowing through my soul again.

■ ■ ■

I revel in the feel of my arms around Trent's warm, strong body for the entire ride home, feeling no need to speak, wishing the night would last forever. When he walks me to my apartment door, I'm bowled over by the sudden tornado of emotion inside me—bliss and disappointment, excitement and fear, all converging, ready to knock me off my feet. I also sense a growing awkwardness between us. Maybe because I'm silently wishing he'd invite me back to his apartment and disheartened that I know he won't.

"So, thanks for showing me my first alligator and not having your way with me." I busy myself with searching my purse for my keys. "I'm glad I still have all my limbs and—"

Trent's soft lips cut my rambling short. His arms wrap around me, one hand skimming the small of my back while the other cups the back of my neck. He pulls me close against him, his mouth working slowly against mine, his movements controlled, as if he's restraining himself from doing what he wants to do. Sensing this shoots jittery waves of heat through me. My arms lose all strength and drop to my sides, my purse and keys tumbling to the ground along with them.

Trent breaks free and crouches down in front of me to pick my things up. When he's standing again, he hands everything to me with a challenging smirk. "You going to survive?"

I hate that he can level me so completely and joke about it. *Bastard!* But I do love a challenge. I step forward and press my full body against his, chest to knees, hooking my hand around his back so I can jerk him forward against me, close enough that I can feel him through his jeans. He's not unaffected. I look up into that perfect face and smile sweetly. "Nothing a long, hot shower can't fix."

That did it. I feel him getting harder.

Trent smirks, no doubt fully aware of what I'm up to. What I would do to know what he's thinking right now!

"Do you have a cell phone?" he asks abruptly.

I frown at the sudden change in conversation. "No, why?"

He breaks away from me and takes five giant steps back to get himself to his apartment door. He slides his key into his lock. "Because I don't trust myself around you for more than a minute sometimes." When he turns to size me up, it's with a smoldering look. "Texting is good. It's safer."

"I'll get right on it," I purr, adding with mock innocence, "Leaving so soon? You okay?"

"I will be," he calls over his shoulder as he disappears into his apartment, leaving my mouth dry and my body on fire.

stage five

■ ■ ■

DEPENDENCE

NINE

I'm at the mall at nine o'clock on Tuesday morning to buy two cell phones—one for Livie and one for me. They're nothing fancy but I can text easily, and that's all I care about after lying wide-eyed in bed all night, contemplating Trent.

At noon, as I'm heading out of my apartment door with my gym gear, I bump into him. With a grin, I decide that I really do love living next door to him. I really do.

"How'd you sleep?" he asks, stepping just inside my personal space. I note that I don't mind a bit. In fact, I thrive on Trent Emerson being in my personal space.

"Like someone slipped Rohypnol into my drink," I lie, giving him my full-tooth smile. "I'm on my way to the gym. You interested?"

Blue eyes take in my black tank top shamelessly. "I could burn some energy."

My heart skips three beats. "Then go get your things," I say, and bite my tongue before I offer him a better way to burn energy.

With a smile, he leans in to kiss my cheek. "Give me two minutes."

I wait in the common area, no doubt with a stupid grin on my face, while Trent runs into his apartment. When he comes out, he's in track pants and a fitted white T-shirt. I may not be able to see his tattoo, but I can see every ridge of his sculpted chest and flat abdomen. *How the hell am I going to get through my rounds with that to look at?*

"I'll drive?" he offers with a smile, as if he can read my mind. I can only muster a nod.

■ ■ ■

"You need a hand with the bag?" Trent asks.

"This way, Jeeves." I stroll over to a free spot and toss my stuff against the wall behind it. I begin to stretch my body, feeling each muscle expand and loosen. I always marvel at how far I've come every time I'm about to work out. It took me so long to even move my foot after the accident. At one point, my muscles had deteriorated to nothing, and I was sure I'd never walk again. At the time, I didn't really care.

Trent mimics my stretches, his arms lifting over his head, one arm bent and pulling against the other to stretch his triceps. His shirt rises, exposing the contours of his abdomen and the dark trail of hair running down below his navel.

"Holy fuck," I mutter under my breath, turning around to finish my stretching in blissful ignorance of the god behind me.

"Okay. Ready?" I hear Trent call out. He swings his arms back and forth, clapping when they connect in front of him. "Let's show 'em what we've got!"

"Do you have any idea how to hold a kick bag?"

"Of course." He leans against it, his arms circling the entire circumference.

I don't think Trent has ever held a kick bag. "I said 'hold,' not 'hump.' You want your ribs cracked?"

His arms drop and he moves away from the bag, gesturing at it. "All right then, smart-ass. Teach me."

I grin as I tie my hair back into a ponytail, aware of the small crowd that's formed behind us. Ben is with them and he's wearing that smirk. I still want to slap it away, even though he's turning out to be an all-right guy.

"Okay, what you need to do . . ." I step in front of Trent and slip my hands into his. I start explaining how he needs to distribute his weight and the best height to position his hands, all while still in awe that holding his hands doesn't bother me. In fact, I'd happily hold them through movies, long walks on the beach, and anything else that involves hand-holding. And touching in general. "Put this leg here . . ." My fingers slide to his thigh to reposition his leg, and I feel the corded muscle as he shifts. Hot, strong legs. "And turn your body this way." Now my hands are on his waist, gripping his sides as I turn him slightly. I notice my breathing is speeding up. *Damn, how the hell am I going to work out with him here?* "Most important is your balance. Got it?"

He nods as I begrudgingly drop my hands and step over to my side, getting ready for a kick. "Seriously? You've never done this for your friends before?"

Trent shrugs. He manages to stay straight-faced for another three seconds before a sly smile betrays him. "Yeah, tons of times. But I liked letting you feel me up."

A loud chorus of snickers and laughter erupts. They all knew he was playing me. How did they all know while I had no clue? Probably because I was too busy drooling over his body to notice his practiced movements. Suddenly feeling the fool, I give the bag a soft kick. Okay, maybe not so soft. It flies back under the impact and hits Trent, eliciting a low grunt as he stumbles backward and hunches over, balancing himself with his hands just above his knees.

"I thought you knew how to hold a bag?" I murmur, walking over. I get no answer. With a bit of hesitation, I rest my hand on his back as I bite my lip. "You okay?"

"Kace! You really have a thing against balls, don't you!" Ben hollers through cupped hands so the entire place can hear.

I flush, shooting daggers at Ben as I apologize to Trent. "Shit, I'm sorry. I figured I'd get your shoulder."

He cranes his neck to look up at me while still hunched over. "If you're not interested in me, just tell me. You don't have to ruin me for all women."

"I'm more about action than words." I'm glad he's making jokes, but I still wince. I drop to a crouch in front of Trent and ask in a low voice, "Are you okay? Seriously?"

"Yeah, I'll live. And by live, I mean curl up in the fetal position on my couch with a bag of ice on my nuts for the rest of the night."

"I'll hold the ice," I offer in a soft whisper.

When he turns his head, I see fire in his eyes, and I can't help but smile at his frustration, which matches mine. The smile is quickly followed by a wince. "Just give me a minute. I'll be over there, healing."

Trent leans against the wall, protecting his injured body parts while watching me run through a set of kicks and punches, not fully into it. As I'm finishing, I sense him approach behind me. I squeal in surprise as he grips either side of my hips, pulling me back into him, into all of him. "When you said hold the ice . . ."

"I thought you were near death over there," I answer, breathless. "*That* doesn't feel fatal."

"I was, but you are one hot chick when you pound on the right bag." He jerks me back against him hard and I yelp. Not in pain. No, definitely not pain.

"Didn't you say you wanted to take it slow?" I remind him.

He chuckles darkly. "Yeah, and I also said I have a hard time doing that when you're around." He leans forward and whispers in my ear, "So what do you say? I'm ready to go a few more rounds with you."

Nothing but a strangled sound escapes my lips. I don't know where this side of Trent is coming from. It has to be all the testosterone in the air. Or maybe this is the real Trent and he's been adept at restraining himself. Or it's his way of claiming his territory as the flock of guys watch me every so often, including Ben. Whatever it is, I'd willingly hand over full possession of my body to this Trent to do with it what he will.

I swallow, trying to focus on the bag of sand taunting me as all that bottled-up fighting anger deflates and a new emotion rises. Desire. Raw, uninhibited desire for Trent. I'm two seconds from dragging him into the women's locker room and ripping that shirt off. Hell, I'm ready to take him right here, on the pad, spectators be damned.

His hands slide from my hips, but not before one hand squeezes my ass and then he strolls over to take his position on the other side of the bag. His dark gaze leaves me unnerved. "Okay. I'm ready for you this time."

■ ■ ■

Trent hands my phone back to me with his number programmed into it as we stand in front of my apartment again, the sun's afternoon rays beating down on us. Whatever heat scorched the air back at the gym has evaporated with a mysterious phone call on our way out of the gym. Fun, forceful Trent is gone. This Trent looks agitated and distracted. I soon learn why.

"I've gotta head out tonight, Kace. Work and mom stuff. I don't have a choice. If I don't show up, she'll know I'm not in New York." His voice fades and I catch his eyes widen momentarily, as if surprised.

I frown. *Why would that matter?* Before I have a chance to ask, he rushes to continue on. "I'll be gone until Friday, but you'll hear from me, okay?"

I nod, hoping for another one of his blazing kisses. That, or for him to throw me over his shoulder caveman style and carry me to his bed. Either one would work. But I get a peck on my forehead instead. With a lazy salute and a frown, he spins on his heels and takes off for his apartment.

TEN

Serve drinks.

Smile.

Take money.

I repeat that mantra all night at Penny's. The place is as packed and sordid as ever, and yet it feels empty and boring without Trent there.

It isn't until I'm back home at three a.m. that my phone vibrates in my pocket, sending a thrill through my body. There are only two people who could be calling, and one of them is unconscious next door.

In New York. Surrounded by skyscrapers. Miss you. How was your night?

My heart surges with joy as I type back.

Full of bare flesh and indecent propositions.

I can't bring myself to add one last little piece. That I miss him like crazy. That I can't believe I've wasted weeks keeping him away.

A full minute, I receive his response:

Was any of that bare flesh yours?

Not yet.

I crawl into bed and rest my phone on my chest, waiting for his response. It's a while before I get one.

A cold shower is calling. Sweet dreams. Good night. xox

I cover my mouth as I laugh out loud, afraid I'll wake up Livie or Mia, who's staying at our place tonight. Setting my phone on my nightstand, it's a while before I fall asleep, my mind racing with thoughts of Trent.

■ ■ ■

Three days without Trent is unpredictably tough. We exchange a few messages in the late evenings. Whatever work and family stuff he's doing during the day must keep him busy, because the texts don't start coming until after midnight. When they do, when I feel the vibration in my pocket, it's like Christmas has come.

They're all fairly innocuous: "Hi, how are you?" and "I miss you," and "Bagged any guys at the gym, lately?" messages. Several times, I catch myself typing something a little more provocative only to delete it before hitting "Send." Something tells me it's too soon for sexts, especially given that we haven't gotten past first base.

God, I can't wait until we get past first base!

■ ■ ■

Trent comes back today. That's the first thought that enters my mind when I wake up on Friday. Not carnage, not blood, not the miserable scraps left of my life. For once, the first thought that comes to my mind is the future and what it may bring.

But for such a perfect wake-up, the day sure ends like shit.

I have no idea what time Trent is arriving in Miami. I've sent him a few messages to find out, but I haven't heard back. It's making me incredibly anxious. Awful visuals of planes crashing plague my thoughts all day and into my shift at Penny's.

So when Nate tugs me from the bar and into the back office where Cain holds a phone up for me, my stomach plummets to the ground. "It's urgent" is all he says, his brows pulled together tightly. I stand and stare at Cain and the black receiver, unable to bring myself to face it. It isn't until I hear a child's cry on the other end that I snap out of my daze and grab it from his hands. "Hello?" my voice wobbles.

"Kacey! I tried your cell but you didn't answer!" I can barely understand Livie between her sobs and Mia's wails. "Please come home! Some crazy man is trying to break down the door! He's screaming Mia's name! I think he's on drugs. I called the police!" That's all I get out of her. That's all I need.

"Lock yourselves in the bathroom. I'm coming, Livie. Stay there!" I hang up the phone. My words tumble out in short, clipped fragments and they don't sound like me. To Cain I say, "There's an emergency. It's Mia. Storm's Mia. And my sister."

Cain is already grabbing his car keys and a jacket. "Nate—get Storm off the stage. Now. And have Georgia and Lily cover the bar." He hooks his arm around me, pulling me gently. "Let's get to the bottom of this, okay, Kacey?"

I feel as though someone has kicked me in the gut. My head bobs up and down, while an internal torrent of screams and wails assaults my senses. Storm and I are in Cain's Navigator and on the freeway in under thirty seconds. Nate's hulking body fills up the passenger seat. Storm, in nothing but her silver bikini from her acrobat act, drills me with the same questions over and over again and all I can do is shake my head. *Breathe,* I hear my mother's voice say. *Ten tiny breaths.* Over and over again. It doesn't help. It never fucking helps, dammit! I'm shaking all over as I sink farther and farther into the dark abyss where I go when people I care about die. I can't seem to get out of it. I'm drowning.

I can't bear to lose Livie. Or Mia.

Finally, Storm stops asking me questions. Instead she grabs my hand and holds it to her chest. And I let her, finding solace in her racing heartbeat. It signals that I'm not alone in this.

A circus of police and ambulance lights greet us when we arrive at the apartment. The four of us run past the opened gate, past an anxious Tanner, who's talking to a police officer, past the crowd of curious neighbors, all the way to Storm's apartment to find the door half-hanging off its hinges, split in two by someone's fist or head or both. Three police officers hover over a hunched male form. I can't see his face. All I see are tattoos and handcuffs.

"I live here," Storm announces as she breezes past them and through the door, not batting an eye at the guy. I follow her to find a puffy-eyed Livie sitting on the couch with Mia curled up on her lap, sucking her thumb and choking on ragged sobs, well past the point of hysterical crying. An officer stands over them, reviewing notes. The table lamp that sits next to the door is in pieces and Storm's giant stainless-steel frying pan rests on the floor beside Livie.

Storm is on her knees in front of Mia in a second. "Oh, baby girl!"

"Mama!" Two scrawny arms fly out to wrap around Storm's neck. Storm scoops Mia up and into her arms and begins to sway. Tears run down her cheeks as she hums a song.

"She's unharmed," the police officer assures us, his words releasing the lung's worth of air I've been holding. I rush to Livie, throwing my arms around her.

"I'm sorry. I didn't mean to panic you. It was so scary!" she cries. Her words hardly register. I'm too busy fumbling with her arms and legs, grabbing her chin, rotating her head this way and that, checking for wounds.

Livie laughs, grabbing my hands and holding them together in hers. "I'm fine. I got him good."

"What . . . What do you mean, you 'got him good'?" I shake my head in disbelief.

Livie shrugs. "He got his head through the door so I slammed Storm's gargantuan frying pan over it. That slowed him down."

What? I look at the pan lying on the floor. I look at my dainty fifteen-year-old sister. I look at the pan again. And then, whether in relief, fear, or madness—likely all three—I burst out laughing. Suddenly we're both doubled over, falling against each other as we laugh and snort hysterically. I clutch my middle in pain, the muscles tested in a way they haven't been for too long.

"Who's the crazy in handcuffs?" I whisper between fits.

Livie's laughter cuts short, her eyes widening expressively. "Mia's dad."

I gasp as I glance back at the busted door and then over at Mia and Storm, my imagination running wild. He wanted to get to his daughter. "What was he doing here?" I can't keep the horror from my voice, my desire to laugh disappearing. Dread ripples through me like an aftershock. Just the thought of something bad happening to Mia sends me reeling. Or Storm, for that matter.

Because I love them.

Mia's not just that gap-toothed kid whom Livie babysits. Storm's not just my stripper neighbor who got me a job. As hard as I've tried to keep everyone at arm's length, just like Trent, those two have found a way in. A different way, but one that has inevitably led to a place in a heart I thought long since frozen and incapable of feeling.

Livie wraps her arms around her body as she watches Mia and Storm, and I see fear in her eyes. "I'm just so glad Trent came when he did."

Another gasp. "Trent?" I jump to my feet and spin around, my heart leaping into my throat as I scan the apartment. "Where? Where is he?"

"Here." I turn to find him passing through the entryway. I'm on my feet and colliding into him in seconds. His arms tighten around me, protecting me with their strength. He buries his face in my hair and we stay like that for a long time before he pulls back to rest his forehead against mine. My hands slip around his sides to his back, my fingers crawling up to dig into his shoulder blades and yank him back close to me. His muscles tense beneath me. All the fear and nerves and terror of the day are suddenly morphing into some animalistic need. I *need* to hold him. I *need* Trent. We stay like that, as I press my nose against his chest, inhaling the wonderful mix of woodsy and ocean scents.

"I missed you," I hear myself whisper, surprising even me. Kacey Cleary doesn't admit to missing people out loud. But Trent feels like something valuable misplaced and then found, and I'm overwhelmed with relief.

Trent leans in and kisses my jawline, near my earlobe. "Missed you too, babe," he whispers into my ear, sending shivers through my core.

"Excuse me, sir. Are you sure you don't want to press charges?" a voice asks.

"I'm sure. It's just a bruise," Trent answers, not releasing me from his grip, as though he's as in need of me as I am of him.

"What bruise?" I pull away and look up to see Trent's bottom lip swelling. My hand flies to it, but he grabs it and holds it away. "I'm fine. Really. It's nothing. Completely worth it."

"I'll need to ask this young lady a few questions. Are you her guardian?" I hear the cop ask, and I assume he's talking to Storm, so I continue staring up at Trent's face, unable to peel my eyes away. He's equally unwavering in his gaze.

"Miss?"

"Yes, she is," I hear Livie say, and I snap out of it. He's talking to me. Turning, I find Officer Stares-a-Lot standing behind me. My frown tells him that I recognize him.

He shrugs noncommittally. "You ladies sure are keeping us busy these days." His gaze drifts over to Storm, ever so quickly taking in her body before averting his eyes to the ground as he pushes a hand through his short blond hair. He's a decent-looking guy in a Ken-doll, mama's-boy sort of way. And he's got the hots for Storm. That much is obvious. Then again, who doesn't?

"No one can accuse us of being boring." I smile to myself. "I'm Kacey. That's Storm, but it looks like you remember her, Officer . . . ?" I watch with morbid fascination as blood rushes up to his hairline.

He clears his throat. "Officer Ryder. Dan."

Storm is oblivious, still holding her daughter tightly as she sways her hips, her eyes half-closed and dreamy.

Another throat clears. We turn to find a second officer poking his head into the doorway. "If there's nothing else, we should get this guy to the station for booking." His attention turns to Storm and lingers.

"Then get him to the car. Now!"

The officer catches Officer Dan's lethal glare and growl and ducks out. To Storm, Officer Dan says in a soft voice, "I'd find another place to stay for the night until you can get this door fixed. My shift will be over in a few hours. I can come back and watch over the place until morning if you want?"

Storm breaks free of her spell and turns to look at Officer Dan as if she's seeing him for the first time, her eyes twinkling. "Oh, thank you. I don't have much, but I'd feel safer if someone were watching over it."

Officer Dan flushes for the third time and I have to say I'm impressed with him, his eyes locked on her face the entire time when even Gandhi would have a hard time not looking over her barely clad frame.

"I'll watch over the place until you get here," Trent offers.

Officer Dan sizes Trent up, looks at me in his arms, and likely decides Trent isn't competition. He nods. "I'd appreciate it."

"You have somewhere to stay for the night, Angel?" Cain asks, stepping through the doorway. Nate looms behind him.

"She can stay with us," I answer before Storm has a chance to say a word. She nods silently, her hand still cradling Mia's head, whose lids are drooping closed now.

"Okay, then. I've got to get back to the club to close up. I'll put your earnings from tonight in my safe. You can pick them up tomorrow," Cain offers with a sincere smile, adding, "Take tomorrow night off."

"Thanks, Cain," I hear myself say. Storm is right. They really are nice guys. "Thanks, Nate." I get a grunt in return. But then Nate takes three mammoth steps to close the distance between himself and Storm. Like watching a bear paw at a newborn, I cringe as Nate's hand reaches out to cover Mia's head. He's gentle, though, giving her a soft pat. "Sweet dreams, Mia," he rumbles. Sleepy blue eyes look up at him. I'm sure she's two seconds away from screaming. I know I would be. But I watch her little hand lift up to squeeze his one finger, the gesture yanks on my heartstrings. With that, Cain and Nate leave.

"Come on, let's get Mia to bed." Livie puts her arm around Storm and gently ushers her toward the door, just as Tanner steps in. "Not now, Tanner," Livie murmurs, leading them out and next door.

He scratches his head in that Tanner way but nods, stepping aside. I bury my mouth in Trent's chest again, this time to keep from laughing. I never noticed coming in, so zoned in on getting to Livie and Mia, but Tanner's wearing Batman pajamas.

Tanner runs his hand up and down the door frame and I know what he's thinking. "This wasn't Storm's fault, Tanner," I start to say, afraid he's going to throw down his one coveted rule. This would definitely be classified as disturbing thy peace. But he waves my words away, mumbling, "Never seen people with such bad door luck."

Trent peels himself away from me and steps forward, pulling out his wallet and another wad of cash. "This should cover it. Can you get your guy in first thing in the morning?"

"You don't have to do that, Trent," I say as Tanner's meaty paw wraps around the money.

He comes back to grab hold of me again, shaking his head dismissively. "We'll sort it out tomorrow."

Tanner lifts his hand to wave the money in thanks and moves for the doorway.

Officer Dan stops him. "Sir, I suggest you speak to the building owner about replacing those entrance gates immediately and with a better system, given how easily these can be forced open, as demonstrated tonight."

Tanner appraises the cop with shrewd eyes. "I agree, Officer, but the owner of this building is a Scrooge whose purse strings are tighter than a—" He glances at me and ducks his head. "He's cheap, that's all."

"Would it help if he received a formal order from the Miami Police Department and the City of Miami indicating he's liable for a multimillion-dollar lawsuit if he doesn't provide adequate security for his residents?"

Tanner's brow arches in surprise. "You can do that? I mean . . ." He clears his throat and that wry smile stretches over his face. "I do believe that would influence him, Officer."

Officer Dan nods curtly, a thinly concealed smile touching his lips. "Great. I'll come up with something and have it to you first thing tomorrow." Turning to Trent, he says, "I can cut out from my shift early. Can you make it until four?"

"I'll be here."

With that, Officer Dan exits, stooping slightly to pass through the doorway. Tanner and his Batman pajamas follow closely behind, leaving Trent and me alone.

I peer up to admire Trent's gorgeous face. "I feel like I haven't seen you in months," I murmur, rising on my tiptoes to lay a gentle kiss on the uninjured side of his mouth.

His hand lifts to brush my cheek as he smiles down at me. "You've got to be tired. Why don't you get some sleep? I'll stay and watch over things."

I fight to hide the disappointment from my face. Being near him feels so good, so right, so comforting. Adrenaline and attraction rush through my limbs. The last thing I am right now is tired. But I also don't want to appear needy. I give him my best suspicious once-over. "And who's going to watch over you to make sure you don't steal anything?"

"Me? The guy who keeps buying strange girls front doors?"

"Strange girls!" I gasp, my hands flying to cross my chest in mock horror. "I take offense at that. Besides, how do I know you're not some batshit-crazy stiletto-wearing kleptomaniac who'll steal Storm's underwear and drink all the mustard?"

He rolls his eyes. "It was ketchup, and that was only once. It did nothing for me, I swear it." I giggle as Trent's arms lift to settle on my shoulders. He looks down the length of my body before settling on my face. "I do have an appreciation for women's underwear. Just not on me."

I struggle to swallow as my heart leaps into my throat, the blood pulsing against my eardrum as this electric pulse channels between us, rousing every nerve in my body. But then he breaks off, taking three large steps back and exhaling deeply. I smile to myself. At least I'm not the only one who feels it.

"We should do something about this door. The police tape doesn't exactly keep prying eyes out."

Another wave of heat roils through me. *What would prying eyes see?* Trent rifles through the closets until he pulls out an old blanket. "I hope she doesn't mind."

I help Trent secure the blanket against the opening with an array of tape, tacks, and other adhesive things I find in the kitchen drawers. It's after one o'clock in the morning when we finally finish and my adrenaline rush is crashing, leaving me exhausted. I flop down on the sectional. "I haven't been off my feet for more than ten minutes tonight." Trent takes a seat at the end of the couch. Gently lifting my feet, he slides first one heel off and then the other.

"Oh," I moan. "You can stay." He grins, but says nothing as his skilled hands rub the bottom of my feet in smooth, circular motions. Around and around, slowly, deftly. I groan and lay my head back, enjoying his strength, his undivided attention. "Okay, you've earned at least one underwear strut. Go." I fling my arm lazily toward Storm's room. "Pick your weapon. Storm has quite the collection."

Trent chuckles. "Depends on who's strutting."

I open one eye to find heat in his light blue eyes. Again, I see him switch from the cautious, responsible Trent to the one who seems willing to have me on my back, and I don't know what to think of it except that I'm certain I want the latter version right now. His hand begins moving a little faster, a little more ardently, his breathing is heavier. And then his hands are shifting to my calves and he pulls me toward him. As I slide, my dress slips higher up, revealing more leg. Luckily it stops at my thighs, just as my butt reaches the side of his thigh. My bare legs are now stretched over his lap. One of his hands rests on the inside of my thigh, shooting lightning bolts through my entire body. The index finger on his other hand traces along my right outer thigh—up, up, farther . . .

It stops on my tattoo, on the edge of my scar, and strokes back and forth along the ridge. "Did you get the tat to cover this scar?"

"If I did that, my entire right side would be one big tattoo," I lie.

"Why five ravens?" he asks as his fingers trail along the tails.

"Why not?" I pray he'll leave it at that.

But he doesn't. "What does it mean?"

When I don't answer, he says, "Please talk to me, Kacey."

"You said I didn't have to." My voice turns bitter. Trent has effectively tossed a bucket of ice water over my body, dousing the heat from a moment ago.

His hand leaves my leg to rub his forehead. "I know. I know I did say that. I'm sorry. I just want you to trust me, Kace."

"It has nothing to do with trust."

"What does it have to do with, then?"

I stare up at the ceiling. "The past. Stuff I don't want to talk about. Stuff you promised me we wouldn't have to discuss."

His hand finds its way back to my thigh, his eyes focused on it as he gently squeezes. "I know I said that, but I need to know you're okay, Kacey." There's a twinge of something in his voice that I can't quite identify. Worry? Fear? What is it?

"What, are you afraid you'll wake up duct-taped to your mattress?"

"No." I catch a hint of anger in Trent's voice. The first ever. It vanishes with the softness in his next words. "I'm afraid I'll hurt you." The air in the room grows somber as Trent lifts his eyes to my face and I see they're full of grief. He leans over enough that he can reach my cheek, brushing a thumb against it.

His words—or more his tone and the pain in his eyes—stir a need in me to ease whatever is upsetting him.

I *want* to make Trent happy.

And I realize that I *want* him to know me. All of me.

I swallow, my mouth suddenly going bone dry. "I was in a bad car accident a few years ago. A drunk driver hit my dad's car. The right side of my body was crushed. I have dozens of steel pins and rods through my body, holding me together." *Physically. Nothing but ten tiny breaths holds the rest of me together.*

Trent exhales loudly, falling back into the couch. "Did anyone die?"

"Yeah," I manage to say. A sudden explosion of panic inside curls my tongue, preventing me from saying more. My hands start trembling uncontrollably. *Too much, too soon*, my psyche is saying.

"Wow, Kacey. That's . . . that's . . ." His hand smooths over the length of my leg again; however, it's lost that intimate feel. Now it's comforting. I don't want comforting. Nothing he can do will comfort me.

"Kiss me," I demand, glaring at him.

His eyes widen. "What?"

"I gave you what you wanted. Now give me what *I* want." He doesn't move. He just stares at me as though I've set myself on fire. I seize his bicep and squeeze tightly, using it as leverage to pull my body up and onto his, shifting one leg over a stunned Trent's lap to straddle him. "Kiss me. Now," I growl. His jaw clenches and I know my persistence is wearing on him. It's only more obvious a second later when he squeezes his lids shut. "Trent—"

He hunches forward, his head slumping into my shoulder. "You know it's taking every ounce of me to maintain control, right?"

"Don't. Forget control. You don't need it," I whisper into his ear.

He groans, flopping back. "You're making this so hard, Kacey," he murmurs, a pained look on his face.

With my hands on the back of Trent's broad shoulders, I

shimmy forward until I'm right on him, feeling his intense need for me so acutely. I lean in and let my lips brush over his neck. "What exactly am I making hard, Trent?" My voice is intentionally breathless to entice him.

It works.

Trent's hands grab me from behind as he pulls my body flush against his, his mouth devouring mine with a new level of hunger. He forces my mouth open and his tongue slides in, entwining with mine. Gripping the back of my head with one hand, he pushes my mouth closer against his.

I'm no less forceful, my hands fisting his shirt, fumbling with the buttons to expose his smooth, hard chest as I edge closer. His hands push at the bottom of my dress and find their way underneath to clutch my bare hips. I release a small gasp as his fingers skate up and around my thighs to my pelvic bone, fitting under the elastic of my thong and sliding forward and down.

I'm sure this entire "going slow" plan of his is effectively quashed, but then his finger grazes the ridge of another scar and his hand freezes. His lips break free of mine and he pushes my body to the edge of his lap.

"I can't."

"You already are," I mumble, grappling with his hands so I can resume my position against him.

But it's too late. He's already ducking his head, looping his arms around my legs to lift and reposition me, pulling me to him in a protective embrace. We stay silent for a long moment, his forehead pressed against my shoulder. "I'd fix it all for you if I could. You know that, right?" he whispers. I wonder if he's talking about my scars or the last four years of my life.

"Yes" is all I say. Yes to all of it.

ELEVEN

I wake up to silver curtains and an early dawn sun peeking in. I'm in Storm's bed, still wearing my dress. Rolling over, I find Trent lying on his back, bare-chested and in boxers, sound asleep. One arm is tossed over his head while the other rests across his torso. I guess I fell asleep on him last night and he carried me in here.

There's just enough light that I can study Trent's body unabashed and see that it is as gorgeous as I expected. It's long and muscular and flawless, with just a thin line of dark hair trailing down a sculpted abdomen.

"See something you like?" Trent's low, teasing voice startles me and I jump. Grinning, I look up to see a sexy, crooked smile. His mood has switched back to playful.

"Not really," I murmur, but my cheeks flush, giving me away.

His hand cups my face. "You blush a lot. I'd never have taken you for the blushing kind." After a pause, he offers, "Go ahead. I've got nothing to hide."

I feel my eyebrow arch. "Carte blanche?"

His other arm stretches back to nestle under his head. "Like I said . . ."

I decide that Trent really doesn't get the meaning of taking it slow, but I'm not going to argue. "Okay." An idea strikes me. Curiosity, actually. "Roll over."

His eyes narrow slightly, but he obliges, smoothly flipping over so I can admire the ripples in his back, his broad, strong shoulders, and the span of script that stretches from blade to blade.

My finger trails it softly, spiking goose bumps across his skin. "What does it mean?"

He starts to answer, but then he pauses, as if he's hesitant about telling me. That makes me want to know a hundred times more. I wait quietly, tracing the letters back and forth with my fingernail. "*Ignoscentia*. It's Latin," he finally whispers.

"What does it mean?"

"Why do you have five ravens on your leg?" he throws back at me, a rare hint of annoyance in his tone.

Dammit. Of course he'd ask that. I'd do the same if I were in his position. I bite my bottom lip as I weigh my options. Do I shut him down again or do I give him a bit to get a bit? My interest in Trent outweighs my need to keep everything hidden.

"They're for all the important people in my life who I've lost," I finally whisper, hoping to God he doesn't ask me to name them. I don't want to name the one that represents me.

I hear his sharp inhale. "Forgiveness."

"What?" That word hits me like a punch to the chest. Just the sound of it—so impossible—leaves me nauseous. How many times had the counselors pushed me to *forgive* those guys for killing my family?

"My ink. That's what it says."

"Oh." I exhale slowly, my fists balling up to stop my hands from trembling. "Why do you have that on your back?"

Trent rolls over and spends a long moment gazing at me with a grim expression, eyes full of grief. When he answers, his voice is husky. "Because forgiveness has the power to heal."

If only that were true, Trent. I struggle hard to keep from frowning. I wonder how different our pasts must be for him to have a tattoo promoting forgiveness when I'm wearing one symbolizing the very reason why I can't forgive.

There's another long pause and then Trent's sly grin returns, his arms nestling his head again. "Clock's ticking here . . ."

I shake the seriousness away. Propping myself up onto my knees to get a better view, my eyes drift over his lips, his jawline, his Adam's apple. They roll leisurely down his chest, and I make a point of leaning in and parting my lips near his nipple. I hear his breath hitch, and I'm sure he can feel my breath against his skin. I pull back as I continue farther down, checking once to see if he's watching me. He sure is.

A nervous twinge stirs in my stomach. I focus on the feeling for a second and realize that I adore it. It makes me feel alive. And I decide I want more than just a twinge so I push it, sending it into overdrive as I reach up and skim the elastic band of Trent's briefs with my index finger. It's not hard to see that he's aroused. I curl my finger underneath the elastic . . .

And find myself on my back in a split second, with both my arms over my head, my wrists pinned beneath one of Trent's strong hands. He's hovering over me, holding all of his weight up by that one arm, grinning. "My turn."

"I'm not done yet," I fake pout.

He smirks. "Tell you what, if you can last five minutes with the same level of scrutiny—without moving at all—I'll let you finish."

I make a tsking sound but inside I'm screaming. "Five minutes. Easy."

Trent cocks his head, his arched brow signaling that he can see through my bullish exterior to the melting pile of goo beneath. "You think you can handle it?"

"Can you?" I ask, twisting my mouth to fight the stupid nervous grin ready to expose itself. Just seeing those heated blue eyes boring into my face is enough to unravel me. "What if I lose?" I realize this might work to my advantage either way.

Somber eyes flash and I sense a shift between us. "If you lose, you agree to talk to someone about the accident."

Sexual blackmail. That's what Trent has up his sleeve. He's breaking his *going slow* rule in hopes of making me talk. My teeth grind in response. No way in hell am I agreeing to this. "You're a natural at ruining the mood," I force out, squirming beneath him.

But he grips me tightly. He leans forward, his lips grazing mine as he begs, "Please, Kacey?"

I close my eyes, trying not to let that gorgeous face weaken my resolve. *Too late.* "Only if I lose, right?"

"Right," he whispers.

My competitive side answers for me before I can think this through. "Fair enough." *I. Will. Not. Lose.*

I see the wide grin stretch across Trent's beautiful face and my body tenses up. "You're going to play fair, right?"

"Yes. One hundred percent fair." There's a teasing darkness in his stare, and I realize I'm in trouble. I watch as he sits back, towering over me on the bed, those blue eyes leaving my face to drift over the length of my body, in no rush. "This isn't fair yet," he murmurs. Leaning forward, two hands settle on the edges of my dress on my shoulders. He pulls them down.

I gasp as my dress—a stretchy tunic—slides off. His thumb runs along the scar on my shoulder as his hands move down the length of my body, taking my dress with him. I'm left in nothing but my strapless bra and a thong. I hold my breath as Trent soaks up every square inch of my body—every curve, every detail.

He leans forward, his hand sliding beneath my back. "Still not quite fair." I feel his fingers play with my bra hook and I suck in a gasp. *He wouldn't.* The supporting tension in my bra gives way as Trent unhooks it. When his hand moves away, it leaves with the only thing that covered my breasts. "There. That's fair."

I. Will. Not. Lose.

I'm determined not to move, even as I lie all but bared to Trent's prying eyes and evil smirk. I'm mulish enough to believe I can do it, too. But then Trent leans forward, moving his mouth only inches from my breasts as I had done to him, and I'm fighting tooth and nail against the urge to squirm. I gasp as his breath brushes over my skin and my nipples instantly harden. When he peers up at my face, I have to close my eyes. I can't handle the look in his. It's full of heat and desire and intentions. He chuckles softly as his attention shifts farther down. Cool air skates down my abdomen. "You have an incredible body, Kacey. Mind-boggling."

I make an unintelligible sound of acknowledgment.

"I mean, I could just stare at it. And touch it. All day long." I don't know what it is about Trent right now—his smooth voice, his actions, his proximity to my body—but desire is tearing through my willpower and congregating in my lower abdomen, planning an insurgence.

And he hasn't even touched me.

I peek through one eye to see the tops of Trent's shoulders, his muscle straining as he shifts farther down, stopping below my belly button. I struggle to see the clock. *Another three minutes. I can last three minutes. I can . . . I can . . .* Trent runs his index finger along the front of my panties just as I had done to him and I let out a soft moan before I can stop myself. Looking down, I see him watching me now, biting his bottom lip, his arrogant smirk gone.

His eyes stay locked on mine as his index finger curls under the elastic band and begins to slide down.

Like a violent wave crashing into me, I come completely undone. Swirls of haze and light fill my vision and I'm floating on seven layers of clouds, my muscles shift from being rigid as a pole to pliable putty, and I don't ever want to lose this high.

With deep, ragged pants, I faintly notice Trent hovering above me again a moment later. Hot lips touch my collarbone as he grazes it.

"You lose," he whispers in my ear with a soft chuckle. Then he's off the bed and pulling his jeans on.

"No I didn't," I mumble as an afterthought, breathless. How the hell can he call *that* losing?

■ ■ ■

"You okay here alone?" Trent whispers as I sip a glass of orange juice and watch the sweaty man work on the door. When I raise an eyebrow, he chuckles. "Of course you are. I forgot you kicked my ass."

"A bag of sand kicked your ass, remember? Where you off to?"

His hand touches the small of my back and he presses me against his body as he whispers in my ear. "Cold shower." Shivers run down my spine and I'm ready to drag him back into Storm's room, but he makes a beeline out of the apartment before I can get my claws into him.

"Who lost, again?" I call out in a high-pitched voice, smiling.

I quietly watch Sweaty Door Guy work as I flip through a magazine, still glowing from the morning with Trent; enough that this guy's hairy ass crack peeking out from loose faded blue jeans doesn't faze me. Livie has staggered through, half asleep and on her way to school. When I suggest she skip the day, she looks at me as if I'd suggested she marry the repairman. Livie doesn't miss school for anything.

I'm reading an article on "Ten Ways to Say You're Sorry Without Saying the Word" when Storm's soft voice calls out, "Can I please get by?"

Sweaty Door Guy cranes his neck, sees Storm, and fumbles

with his hammer as he clears a path for her curvy frame. She walks through, matching my smile, two tall Starbucks coffees in her hands. "Do I need to change my sheets?" she says with a wink.

"Ohmigod, Storm!" Fire burns my face as I see Sweaty Door Guy's eyes widen. Storm can be inappropriate sometimes after all. I quickly change the topic. "How's Mia?"

The reminder of last night erases her smile and I regret asking. "She'll be fine. I just hope she doesn't remember any of it. She doesn't need to remember her father like that."

"What's going to happen to him?"

"Well, apparently he broke parole. That, added to the 'breaking and entering,' should give him at least five years in prison. That's what Dan thinks, anyway. I hope he'll clean himself up by then." She takes a long sip of her coffee and I notice her hand shaking. She's still rattled by last night. Rightfully so. If I pull my head out of this distractive Trent sex cloud I'm stuck in, I'd realize that last night was still deep under my skin.

"I swear, I wasn't sure Nate wasn't going to throw the cops out of the way and rip his head off," Storm adds, and I nod in agreement.

There's a long pause. "So . . . *Dan*, huh?"

Storm blushes. "I was up early. I couldn't sleep, so I brought him a coffee. Needed to thank him for everything. He's nice."

"A coffee? That's all?" My brow arches.

"Of course that's all. What do you think I'm going to do? Give the guy a blow job outside my apartment door?"

A harsh coughing erupts behind us. Sweaty Door Guy, covering up a gasp.

It's Storm's turn to flush, and I smile with satisfaction. Clearly she forgot we had an audience. "Are you saying you're not interested?"

"No, I didn't say that, but . . ." She toys with the lid of her cup.

"But what?"

"Excuse me," Dan's voice interrupts us, and we both jump.

"Speak of the devil," I murmur, covering my smile with another sip of coffee. Storm's face has turned purple. I know what she's thinking. She's wondering how long he's been listening.

Dan steps over what remains of the door frame. "Sorry to bother you again."

"No bother," I chirp, grinning.

He nods appreciatively, and I'm sure I see a faint blush creep into his cheeks. "Just wanted to let you know that I got that safety order to your landlord. The gates should be fixed shortly."

Storm's eyes widen. "Already?"

He grins. "I know a guy who knows a guy, who knows a guy."

"Thank you so much, Officer Dan," she says, and I'm hit with a weird visual of them in a sex scene with her addressing him in the exact same way. I give my head a shake. *Too many hours at the club.*

They stare at each other for an awkward moment, until Dan scratches the back of his head, his cheeks flushing. "So, um, unless there's something else I can do for you, I'm going to grab some sleep."

"Oh, okay," Storm nods.

I roll my eyes. *Utterly clueless.* "Dan." Devious little plot hands rub together inside my head. "Are you free tonight?"

Dan looks from me to Storm. "Yes, I am."

I catch the side "what the hell are you doing" dagger glare from Storm, but I ignore it. "Good. Storm was just saying that she'd love to go out to dinner with you." Dan's face lights up. Going out with Storm is exactly the *something else* Dan would like to do. "How about around seven?" I suggest. "That works for you, right, Storm?"

Her pretty head bobs up and down dumbly, looking like she may have swallowed her tongue.

Dan looks at her warily. "Are you sure, Storm?"

It takes her a minute to pull her tongue back out to operational mode. "It's perfect." She even manages a tight smile.

"Okay. See you then."

He walks out, his pace picking up as I holler, "Can't wait!"

I turn back to find Storm glaring at me. "You enjoyed tormenting that poor man, didn't you?"

"Oh, I think he's okay with a little torment if the end result is a date with you."

"I have to work tonight though."

"Nice try. Cain gave you the night off. Come on, what else you got?"

Storm's shoulders sag. "This is a bad idea, Kacey."

"Why?"

"Why? Well . . ." Storm sputters, struggling for a valid excuse. "Look at the last guy I brought home." She gestures at the broken door.

"Storm, I don't think you can compare Officer Dan to that strung-out asshat of an ex-husband. They're kind of on opposite ends of the spectrum. I'm not sure that guy last night was even human." My brow quirks. "Do they need to make a 'So I Married an Alien' movie starring you?"

She rolls her eyes. "Oh, come on, Kacey. Don't be naïve. He's a guy. He knows what I do for a living. There's only one thing he's interested in and it's not my cooking."

I shrug. "I don't know about that. I might do you for more of that veal Parmesan."

Sweaty Door Guy breaks out into another coughing fit, harsh enough that I think he may hack up a lung. Storm's hand flies to her mouth, trying not to laugh. She tosses a pillow at my head, but I duck, sending us into an explosion of titters as we scurry to her bedroom and close the door.

"So what are you gonna wear tonight?" I mock in a bubbly Valley girl voice.

She sighs. "I don't know, Kace. What if he only wants me for . . . this?" Her hands gesture to her body.

"Then he's the biggest idiot on the face of the earth, because you're so much more than a pair of giant boobs and a pretty face."

A tiny smile blossoms to dissolve her worry. "I hope you're right, Kacey."

"You also have a killer ass."

She tosses another pillow at my head.

"All kidding aside, Storm. I see how he looks at you. Trust me, that's not it."

She scrunches her bottom lip as if she wants to believe me, but can't.

"And if that's all he's looking for, then we'll set fire to his balls."

"*What?*" Storm's face twists in a mixture of shock and amusement.

I shrug. "What can I say, Storm? I'm into some weird shit."

Storm's head falls back as she howls with laughter. "You're crazy but I love you, Kacey Cleary!" she shrieks, throwing her arms around my neck. I can only imagine what Sweaty Door Man is thinking right about now.

■ ■ ■

Trent shows up to my door at noon in his leather jacket. "Ready?"

"For what?" I ask, memories of the morning, of what he's capable of doing to me with barely a touch, still fresh in my mind. Part of me wonders if he's here to continue where we left off earlier. That part is extremely excited.

He smirks, holding up a helmet. "Nice try." Walking over, he grabs my hand and pulls me from my chair. "We made a deal and you lost." A sinking feeling settles in the pit of my stomach as he leads me toward the door. "There's a support group nearby. I figured I'd take you."

Support group. My legs freeze. Trent turns around and studies my expression. By the way my insides are reacting, it can't be a pretty one.

"You promised, Kacey," he whispers softly, stepping forward to cup my elbows. "You don't have to talk. Just listen. Please. It'll be good for you, Kace."

"So now you're a computer geek *and* a shrink?" I bite my tongue, not meaning to be that harsh. Gritting my teeth against the urge to scream, I close my eyes. *One . . . two . . . three . . . four . . .* I don't know why I keep following my mom's stupid advice. It never brings me relief. I guess it's become more like a security blanket that I've dragged from my old life into my new. Useless, but comforting.

Trent waits patiently, his hand never leaving my elbow.

"Fine," I hiss, shaking away from him. I grab my purse from the couch and stalk out the door. "But if they break out in a fucking round of 'Kumbaya,' I'm so gone."

■ ■ ■

The group therapy session is in a church basement, complete with ugly yellow walls and dark gray school-grade carpet. The smell of burnt coffee permeates the air. There's a small table set up in the back with cups and tea biscuits. I'm not interested in any of that. I'm not interested in the group sitting in a circle in the center of the room, participating in idle chatter, or the skinny middle-aged man with faded blue jeans and feathered hair standing in the center.

None of it.

With a hand against my back, Trent gently prods my stiff body forward and I feel the air shift as I move closer. It thickens in my lungs, until I have to work to draw it in and push it out.

When the man standing in the center looks up at me and smiles, the air grows even thicker. It's a warm enough smile, but I don't return it. I can't. I don't want to. I don't know how.

"Welcome," he says, offering two empty chairs to our right.

"Thanks," Trent murmurs behind me, shaking the guy's hand as I somehow get my body to bend into the chair frame. I nudge it back a bit and stare straight ahead, distancing myself from the circle. And I avoid all eye contact. People think they're allowed to talk to you and ask who died when you make eye contact.

Outside the circle is a sign that reads "Post-Traumatic Stress Disorder—therapy session." I sigh. Good ol' PTSD. It's not the first time I've heard that term. The doctors in the hospital warned my aunt and uncle about it, saying they thought I suffered from it. Saying it would likely work itself out with time and counseling. I never understood how they believed that night could ever possibly *work itself out* of my thoughts, my memories, and my nightmares.

The man leading the group claps his hands. "Everyone, let's get started. For those of you who don't know me, my name is Mark. I'm sharing my name, but there's no need for you to share yours. Names are not important. What's important is that you all know you're not alone in the world with your grief, and that talking about it, when you're ready, will help you heal."

Heal. There's another word I never understood as it related to the accident.

I can't help but peer around the group now, careful that I don't seem interested as I study their faces. Luckily, all eyes are focused on Mark, watching him with fascination, as if he's a god with curative powers. There's a mix of people—old, young, female, male, well-dressed, disheveled. Suffering knows no boundaries.

"I'll share my story," Mark begins, pulling his chair forward as he sits down. "Ten years ago I was driving home from work with my girlfriend. It was raining hard and we got T-boned in an intersection. Beth died in my arms before the ambulance came."

My lungs suddenly constrict. I see, rather than feel, Trent's hand on my knee, squeezing gently. I can't feel anything.

Mark continues, but I struggle to focus on his words, my heart rate climbing like it's on its way to Mount Everest. I fight the urge to stand and run, to leave Trent here. Let *him* listen to this horror. Let him see the kind of pain these people have experienced. I have enough of my own to deal with.

Maybe he has some sick fascination with this shit.

I barely hear Mark as he talks about drugs and rehab, as words like "depression" and "suicide" are spoken. He's so calm and collected as he lists the aftereffects. How? How is he so calm? How can he throw out his own personal tragedy in front of these people as though he's talking about the weather?

". . . Tonya and I just celebrated our second wedding anniversary, but I still think about Beth every day. I still suffer through moments of sadness. But I've learned to cherish the happy memories. I've learned to move on. Beth would have wanted me to live my life."

One by one, the people go around the circle, airing their dirty laundry to all as if it requires no effort. I inhale short, hard breaths through the second tale: a man lost his four-year-old son to a freak farming accident. By the fourth, the coils around my insides have stopped tightening. By the fifth, all the emotions that Trent has managed to coax out from hiding over the last few weeks have fled back as tragedy upon tragedy beats me over the head. All I can do to avoid reliving the pain of that night four years ago, right here in this church basement, is to bottle up everything human inside of me.

I'm dead inside.

Not all the group members share their stories, but most do. No one pressures me to speak. I don't offer, even when Mark asks if anyone else wants to share and Trent squeezes my knee. I make not a sound. I stare straight forward, anesthetized.

I hear murmurs of "goodbye" and I stand. With robotic movements, I climb the stairs and walk out to the street.

"Hey," Trent calls out from behind me. I don't answer. I don't stop. I just start walking down the street toward my apartment.

"Hey! Wait up!" Trent jumps in front of me, forcing me to stop. "Look at me, Kacey!"

I follow his order and look up at him. "You're scaring me, Kace. Please talk to me."

"I'm scaring you?" The protective numbing coat I pulled over my body for the session falls away as rage suddenly fires through it. "Why would you do that to me, Trent? Why? Why do I have to sit and listen to people recant their horror stories? How does that help?"

Trent's hands push through his hair. "Calm down, Kace. I just thought—"

"What? What did you think? You don't know the first thing about what I've gone through and you . . . what, think you can swoop in, give me an orgasm, and follow it up with a survivor's group full of fucking cyborgs who talk about their supposed loved ones like everything's all right?" I scream on the side of the street and I don't care.

Trent's hands move to touch my arms as he shushes me, glancing around. "You think that wasn't hard for them, Kacey? Can't you see the torture in their faces as they relive their stories?"

I'm not listening to him anymore. I throw his hands away with a shove and take a step back. "You think you can fix me? What am I to you, some pet project?"

He flinches as if I'd slapped him across the face and I grit my teeth. He has no right to be hurt. He made me sit through that. *He* hurt *me*. "Stay away from me." I spin around and quickly walk down the sidewalk.

I don't look back.

Trent doesn't chase me.

TWELVE

Storm's hands fidget with a beaded bracelet as seven o'clock rolls around. It's bizarre that she's so nervous, considering she can swing over a stage topless in front of a room full of strangers. I don't remind her of that, though. I just help her pick out a classy yellow dress that flatters her skin tone and accentuates her curves, but not too much. I help her clasp her necklace and pin her hair back on one side. Mainly, I try my damndest to smile when all I want to do is curl up into a ball and hide under my covers, alone.

"Ten tiny breaths," I murmur.

She frowns into her mirror. "What?"

"Take ten tiny breaths. Seize them. Feel them. Love them." My mother's voice rings in my ear as I repeat her words and fight off a choke. That stupid session today has left me bothered, my defenses wavering, my ability to bury the pain challenged.

Storm's frown dips further.

I shrug. "I dunno. That's what my mom always used to say. If you figure it out, let me know, okay?"

She nods slowly and then I watch as she breathes in and out slowly, and I imagine she's counting in her head. That makes me smile. Like I'm passing on a little bit of my mother to Storm.

We hear the knock on the new front door and, a moment

later, Mia's little hands fumbling with the lock. All is quiet, and then Mia approaches, her bare feet slapping hard against the floor as she runs down the hall, yelling, "Mommy! The police officer is here to take you away!"

I snort and shove Storm toward the door. "Stop fussing. You look great."

Officer Dan is in the living room, putting his hands into his jean pockets and pulling them out, and then putting one in and taking it out. I can't help but smile a bit as I watch him. He's as uneasy as Storm. Though when he sees her, his face brightens.

"Hi, Nora."

Nora? His blond hair is styled in that messy, spiky way. He's wearing a fitted black golf shirt that shows off a solid body. I catch a faint whiff of men's cologne. Not too much. Just enough. All in all, Officer Dan cleans up *really* well.

She smiles back politely. "Hi, Officer Dan."

He clears his throat. "Just Dan is fine."

"Okay, Just Dan," she repeats, and then the room fills with awkward silence.

"Officer Dan brought you flowers, Mommy! Tigers!" Mia runs to the kitchen where Livie is arranging a beautiful bouquet of deep red tiger lilies in a milk jug. Mia reaches up to grab one and knocks the jug over. Water and flowers splash everywhere. "Shit!" she exclaims.

"Mia!" Storm and Livie scold at the same time through gasps.

Mia's eyes turn big and round as she looks between the two of them, realizing what she's done. "I get one. Right, Kacey?"

My hand flies to my mouth to contain my laughter as Livie's eyes shoot daggers at me.

"They're beautiful, Dan." Storm rushes over and scrambles to pick them all up. I use this moment to catch his attention. "She's really nervous," I mouth.

Surprise flashes in his eyes. He knows what she does for a living. He's likely made the same wrong assumption as I have—that Storm is made of steel. That's not the case, though. Far from it.

He nods and gives me a wink. Clearing his throat, he says, "I've made reservations for seven thirty." Stepping forward, he offers Storm his arm. "We should head out now, Nora. The place is down by the water. It'll take a while to get there with traffic."

She looks up at him and smiles, all fuss over the flowers vanishing.

Good. Take the lead. Smart, Dan. Two points.

"Have fun. We won't wait up!" I catch a flash of Storm's crimson cheeks before the door is shut and locked, signaling my dour mood to return.

■ ■ ■

I end up working that night without Storm. I need the distraction. When last call sounds and Trent doesn't show up or text, my disappointment is paralyzing. Why would he come, though, I remind myself. I screamed like a lunatic at him on the sidewalk and told him to stay away.

Trent doesn't come visit me at Penny's the next night, either. Or the night after that. Three days later, I think I might lose my mind. Whatever rage coursed through me the day of the grief session is overshadowed by a new void. A Trent void. It throbs like a deep ache through every fiber of my being. I crave his presence, his body, his voice, his laugh, his touch, his everything.

I need him.

I need Trent.

■ ■ ■

On Thursday at noon, I sit at our kitchenette in my short shorts and tank, shoveling Cheerios into my mouth and staring at my phone as if willing a text to come through. Finally, I suck back a mouth's worth of air and force my thumbs to work out a message.

Any interest in a matinee?

I sit at my table and gawk at the stupid thing, wondering if he's already deleted my text, or if he's even bothered to read it. I consider pressing my ear up against the wall between our apartments to see if I can catch any "crazy bitch" comments out of him. But that doesn't sound like something Trent would say, even if it were true. Which it is.

A whole five minutes later, after sinking every last one of my Cheerios into my milk, my phone beeps. I drop everything and grab it.

What do you have in mind?

Flutters stir in my chest. Damn flutters! I hadn't thought that far ahead. I have no idea what's playing. I decide to be lighthearted.

Depends. You okay with nudity?

This time, Trent responds immediately.

Define nudity.

Okay, good. He's playing along.

Well . . . first I take my top off . . .

I nibble on my fingernail, waiting to see what he comes back with. I don't get a response. Maybe I went too far, too soon. Maybe he's still annoyed with me. Maybe . . . I hear a door slam shut. A shadow passes by our window and a second later, someone is pounding on my apartment door.

It has to be Trent.

I run to the door and throw it open, struggling to conceal my eagerness. There he is, in a pair of jeans and a loose T-shirt, his hair slightly mussed, bright blue eyes spilling over my body, settling on my chest for a long moment. I'm not wearing a bra and there's no doubt he can see my nipples' reaction to him. When that gaze lifts back to my face . . . *whoa* . . . it has just the right mixture of anger, frustration, and smoldering heat to make me bite my bottom lip. And that's all it takes to push him over the brink.

"God, Kacey," he growls, and takes two quick steps in to slam against my body, his hands seizing my biceps as his mouth claims mine. Dipping my head back, he forces his tongue into my mouth, demolishing me with a depth of need I've never experienced before. *This is the real Trent.*

Unleashed.

I struggle to stay upright as my body slackens under his intensity. Leading me backward, Trent sandwiches me between himself and the back of the couch and I quickly become aware of how turned on he is.

Suddenly I'm off my feet and perched on the headrest, Trent's hips fitting snug between my thighs. His arms fold around me. One hand clutches the back of my neck, while the other sweeps my hair to the side to expose my neck. His lips slide first to my throat and then along my jawline, up to my ear.

"You enjoy torturing me, sending mixed messages, don't you, Kacey?" His growl pulsates through every single one of my nerves. Then his mouth is back on mine, this time even hungrier, more insistent, and it's all I can do to take a breath. He presses harder against me as a hand slips under the hem of my shirt and climbs to cup the swell of my breast, his thumb stroking my nipple, shooting a current through to the depths of my body.

This sudden Trent onslaught throws me completely off my game—all my senses are assaulted. But I finally catch a handle on my wits, enough to will my hands to his chest, my fingers raking along his abs to hook tight around his belt buckle. I yank him hard against me until his erection digs into me. "Is this clear enough?" I growl back. "I'm not the one who wants to take things slow."

Trent breaks free, a wild, dark look in his eyes, as if he's shocked. He pulls me down off the couch and then, spinning on his heels, he storms out of my apartment, yelling, "Don't send any more fucking texts like that!"

I'm left standing there, shocked, speechless, and turned on as hell. *He's angry? He's angry! He's fucking angry!* I stomp over to the table and snatch my phone.

What the hell was that?

It takes two minutes, but my phone beeps with a message:

You enjoy testing my willpower. Stop torturing me.

What? *Me* torturing *him*? He's the one with this stupid, "thou shalt go slow" crap!

One little text hardly qualifies as torture.

It's not just the one text.

Well then come back here.

No, I told you we're taking this slow.

I think that ship sailed with your little stare-down game the other morning. According to the very wise Bible, we're an old married couple.

I smirk. Aunt Darla would have a coronary if she knew how I was using the Bible to my advantage. The smile is torn clean off my face when my phone chimes again.

You need help.

I stare at those three words for a long moment, gritting my teeth. It's not a surprise to me that he says it. He's said it before. Somehow, though, seeing it in a twelve-point font feels different. Official. I don't respond.

A minute later . . .

You've been through a terrible ordeal and you've bottled everything up. You're going to explode one day.

Here we go. I rub my forehead with frustration. Persistent fool.

What? You want the gory details about how I lost my parents, best friend AND boyfriend, all in one night? Does that kind of thing get you off?

That fire inside me rages again, the same one from three days ago when he forced me into that therapy session. I put the phone down and inhale deeply, trying to douse it before it takes control.

I can't stop myself from reading his next text when the phone chimes.

I want you to trust me enough to tell me about it. Or someone, at least.

This isn't about trust! I've told you that already! My past is my past and I need to bury it where it belongs—In. The. Past.

You're vulnerable and I'm taking advantage of you by letting things like what just happened, happen.

I groan in exasperation.

Please, take advantage of me! I'm giving you permission!

Trent doesn't answer. I sigh, deciding to respond seriously.

I'm fine, Trent. Believe me. I'm better than I've been in a long time.

No. You just think you are. I think you're suffering from a serious case of PTSD.

I fling the phone against the wall that adjoins our apartment, seething. Metal and plastic sail through the air as the thing shatters. Everyone wants to be my personal fucking shrink.

■ ■ ■

I'm astonished when Trent shows up at Penny's that night. More so, I can't keep my mouth from hanging open as I watch him sit down by the bar, just like he did before, acting as if we hadn't just had a nuclear-sized fight. I raise my chin a notch. I'm not going to apologize. No damn way.

A box with a red bow magically appears in front of him. He slides it forward, his dimples forcing a smile on my face whether I like it or not. *Dammit!* Of course I go over and open it. Who doesn't love presents?

Inside is a brand-new iPhone.

"Wasn't hard to figure out what that loud bang was against my wall when you didn't answer my next text," Trent murmurs, an amused smirk on his face.

"Oh yeah?" I slide my tongue over my teeth, acting all cool and unaffected. But inside I'm *so* not unaffected by Trent. "What'd the text say?"

He shrugs, now feigning indifference as well. That twinkle in his eye is his only tell. "I guess you'll never know." He exhales deeply as he holds my stare. It's as though the afternoon's tension doesn't exist anymore, and I don't see how that's possible because

I still feel it. He's up to something. I can't figure out what, though.

"Just think, our afternoon could have gone a completely different direction had you not smashed your phone to smithereens," he says, sliding a straw into his mouth. His eyes blaze with not so pure intentions.

Inside, I want to leap over the bar and into Trent's lap. That's inside. Outside, I'm cool as a November chill. "What can I say? I have anger management issues."

His mouth twists as if in thought. "You need to find a way to deal with those issues."

"I have. It's called pounding on a bag of sand."

His brow arches playfully. "Clearly it's not working well."

I lean over the bar, resting my body on my elbows. "And what would you suggest I pound on instead?"

"Jeez! Would you two just give in already?" Storm calls out with mock exasperation, a martini shaker in her hand.

I hadn't realized how loud we were. Glancing to my other side, I see Nate's smirk, and I instantly flush. I don't know why, but I do. I'm always flushing lately.

Trent doesn't answer Storm or me, taking a long sip of his soda instead, and I delude myself into thinking that maybe he's finally given up on pushing me to deal with things long since buried. Maybe this can work.

■ ■ ■

Over the next few weeks, Trent holds true to his word about making me smile. Unfortunately, he also holds true to his word about taking things slow. Only this time, he actually does. After those few short and hot slipups, the unrestrained Trent is chained and the one who occupies my time offers nothing more than guarded kisses and hand-holding.

It's enough to drive me insane.

Each day, I hop onto Trent's bike, wrap my arms around his chest, and let him whisk me off. We always start off with the gym, likely because he doesn't want to see me smash my phone against the wall again. I'm finding now, though, that I don't have as much desire and focus to run through my drills with him around. Those take attention and determination and, let's face it, bottled-up rage. Trent has a dousing effect on my rage. We end up goofing off and play fighting until we get dirty looks and decide to leave. By that point, I'm usually so hot and bothered by Trent that I need to jump into the shower. I keep hoping he'll lose his way and stumble in there. He never does.

The rest of the days are busy. Paintball fighting, bike riding along the Miami boardwalk, a Dolphins game, restaurants, cafés, ice-cream shops, a Frisbee league. It's as though Trent's got a "Make Kacey Smile" itinerary and it's jam-packed. By the time I get to work each night, my face hurts from so much smiling.

"Don't you ever work?" I ask him one day as we walk down the sidewalk.

He shrugs, squeezing my hand. "I'm between contracts."

"Huh. Well, aren't you worried about paying bills? You're blowing all your money on me."

"Nope."

"Must be nice," I mutter dryly, but I don't press any further. I just walk down the sidewalk, hand in hand with Trent.

And I smile.

■ ■ ■

"Why don't you stay until close?" I murmur quietly.

Trent's hand slides across his mouth as if considering how to answer me. "Because then I'll have to walk you home."

I frown, slightly taken aback. "Yeah, I can see how that would be horrific."

"No, you don't get it." His gaze slides to my mouth before lifting back to my eyes. "What do you think will happen when I walk you to your door?"

I shrug, catching his drift but playing dumb, just so I can see what he says. He stands up and leans in, reaching to grab an olive. When he looks at me again, his eyes have that smoldering quality to them that he can't hide from me completely, the one that makes my knees wobble.

"At home, we don't have Godzilla chaperoning us." His head jerks toward Nate, who's ever watchful of Trent's proximity.

I put on my best confused look. "Well, Nate's not there when you walk me to my door during the day."

He chuckles softly. Yup, there they are. Those deep dimples that I want to run my tongue against. "You know you're shit at playing dumb."

I press my lips together to keep from smiling.

Trent leans farther against the bar, close enough that I'm the only one who can hear him. "I have a hard enough time keeping my hands off you all day. I wouldn't stand a chance, knowing you're about to get undressed and climb into bed."

I brace myself against the counter as I watch him slide an olive into his mouth, his tongue curling around it.

So he wants to play dirty . . .

■ ■ ■

For the next week, I scavenge Storm's closet, picking the shortest, tightest outfits I can find. I almost take one of her sequined stage outfits. I then make a point of leaning over in front of Trent often throughout the night, swaying my hips to the music. When Ben makes a snide comment about me getting ready for my first stage performance, I nail him in the solar plexus and continue on my way, eliciting a deep roar of laughter from Nate.

But I can't seem to break Trent's resolve to keep his hands off me. He only watches, resting on his elbows with his hands folded in front of me. Watching me move. Watching me flirt with him. Watching me turn myself into a hot mess over him.

Finally, one night, I lose it.

"Dammit, Trent!" I snap, slamming his club soda on the counter in front of him. He looks taken aback. "What the hell do I have to do to get your attention? Do I need to get up there?" I throw an arm toward the stage.

His eyes widen for just a second, in shock. He reaches forward to hold my hands, but he catches himself in time and instead folds them across his chest. "Believe me, you have my full attention." He gives me a heated look that makes my mouth go dry. "You always have my attention. It takes every ounce of self-control not to show you how much attention you have." As quickly as that look appeared, it slides away. "I want you to get help, Kace," he says softly. "I'm here for you, every day. Always. I'll stand by you the entire time, but you need to get help. No human can bury their past indefinitely. It's only a matter of time before you crack."

"This is sexual blackmail!" I hiss. First, he tried to force me into talking with that galactic hands-free orgasm and that backfired. Now he's withholding completely as a means of forcing me. Bastard! I stalk away, refusing to look at him for the rest of the night.

The next shift at Penny's, Trent is proven right.

THIRTEEN

Storm is doing her acrobat thing onstage and I'm watching her, while stealing frequent glances at my new phone for a text from Trent. Nothing. He's not here tonight. It's the first night he hasn't been here in a long time and I feel his absence like a missing limb. Maybe he's finally given up on me. Maybe he realized I'm a lost cause and that he won't be getting laid anytime this century if he waits for me to break down and seek out therapy.

Storm's feet touch down on the stage to a raucous round of applause. She bends down to pick up her top, covering her breasts as best she can with an arm. I've seen Storm topless so many times by now, I don't bat an eye. In fact, I'm getting used to naked females all around me. I'm starting to feel like the weirdo in the trench coat in the middle of a nudist beach.

Storm is amazing, I think for the hundredth time, as the entire place claps and hoots. Everyone except a scrawny guy in the corner. I see him there, shouting at her, waving a fist full of money. He refuses to give it to the bouncer collecting for her. I get the impression that Nate is about to toss him out on his skinny ass.

And then I don't know how it happens, but the guy somehow scampers past the bouncers and onto the stage, screaming, "Bitch!" A blade appears. I watch in horror as he grabs hold of Storm's hair and yanks her head back. Even though I'm standing at a distance, I see his dilated dark pupils. This guy's on something.

My jaw drops to scream, but nothing comes out. Not a sound. With a swing of my arm to clear all the glasses off the bar, I spring over it and run, shoving people out of the way, kicking and kneeing and punching as I clear a path through to the stage. Blood rushes to my head and my feet pound the floor with each heartbeat and all I can think is that I'm going to lose her. Another friend, dead. Mia will grow up without her mother.

This can't be happening again.

I reach the stage to find a cluster of tight black shirts hovering. I can't see Storm. I can't see anything. I push and shove and claw, but I can't get past the wall. My hands fly to my throat, assuming the worst possible outcome hidden beneath this horde of bodies.

And I pray.

I pray to whoever decided to keep me alive that they grant the same grace for Storm, who deserves it far more than I ever did.

A giant erupts from the crowd of bouncers.

Nate.

And he has the guy within his grasp.

He stalks past me with a menacing look, the guy dangling by the neck from one of his fists. I hope he squeezes too tight and crushes the man's larynx. But that hope hasn't calmed my nerves a bit because Storm is somewhere in there and I still don't know if she's alive.

"Storm!" I scream.

Finally the wall of bouncers breaks apart. Ben guides me through with a hand on my back to find Storm huddled awkwardly on the floor, her limbs folded into themselves. A pang of alarm stabs me. She looks so much like Jenny did in the car.

I dive to her side.

"Oh, Kacey!" she cries, and throws herself on my shoulder. "All I could think of was Mia."

I'm shaking. "You're alive. You're alive. Thank God you're alive," I mumble over and over as my hands grope her arms, her neck, her shoulders. No blood. No wounds.

"I'm okay, Kacey. I'm okay." Her cheeks are red and tearstained, her makeup smeared all over her face, but she's smiling now.

"Yes," I confirm, swallowing the painful ball in my throat. "You're not going to die. You're okay. I haven't lost you." I'm too close to Storm. Too close to getting hurt the way I did when I lost Jenny. An avalanche of memories crushes any sense of relief I should feel right now. Suddenly, I'm trapped in the past, with a best friend whom I'd known since we were two, with whom I shared days and nights filled with laughter and tears, anger and excitement. An acute ache blossoms in my chest as I realize they're all the memories I hope to create with Storm, too.

All the things that man just tried to steal from me.

With a hint of trepidation, Storm reaches forward and takes my hand in hers. I hadn't breathed since I leapt over the bar. Now I exhale. And something snaps inside me. It's as if the little needle on my moral compass breaks in half.

As if a hate bomb detonates inside me.

He tried to steal my second chance from me. He needs to pay.

Fluorescent lights illuminate the inside of Penny's, casting an unpleasant glow over the spilled drinks, empty bottles, and garbage as bouncers usher patrons out. I catch sight of Nate's broad shoulders as he rounds the corner toward the back exit, the guy still within his grip. My teeth grind against each other.

I'm faintly aware of Trent standing near the front entrance. He's pointing toward the stage and arguing with a bouncer to let him pass. My attention lingers over him for a split second, but nothing really registers; all my thoughts are driven back to the hall where that vile creature, the one who tried to rob me of my new life, left.

I'm up and running.

I'm shoving grown men out of the way as I tear down the hall after Nate. I round a corner in time to see his enormous frame pass through the back door. As I speed to catch up, my heart-beat racing, blood rushing to my head, I sense my hand grab an empty glass bottle sitting on a crate. Without thinking about it, my hand smashes the bottle against the wall, sending shards of glass flying in all directions.

My fist squeezes the neck tightly, imagining how sharp the broken edges are.

How effective they must be.

When I plow through the back door, I find Storm's attacker standing in the parking lot. Alone.

Perfect.

Without a sound, I charge forward, my arm drawn behind my back as I ready my aim. The Weasel turns to see me and his beady little eyes widen. *Six feet, five feet, four feet* . . . My hand is about to catapult the broken glass deep into his chest, to let him feel the level of pain I would have had to endure had he success-fully attacked Storm, when two giant trunks sweep in and lift me off the ground, securing my arms tightly against me.

"No!" I scream. I'm kicking and screaming with everything I'm made of. My teeth clamp down on Nate's arms and I taste copper. He grunts, but doesn't stop, carrying me back inside the doorway. He drops me on the ground and leans forward to meet me eye to eye, his hands still securing my arms.

"Let the police take care of it, Kacey!" The rumble in his voice vibrates through me.

"Police?" I frown and peer past him. The Weasel isn't alone. Four cruisers with flashing lights line the parking lot and a dozen officers mill about, scratching notes down as witnesses recount the turn of events. Somehow I hadn't seen them.

"Ohmigod." I stumble back, vomit rising into my throat, the bottle slipping from my fingers and tumbling to the floor as I clutch my middle.

"I got you before they saw what you were about to do. No one saw anything, and if they did, they'll let it go," Nate promises, his dark gaze searing deep into my face as if looking for something. For a demon lurking, perhaps.

"Kacey!" A breathless Trent yells as he catches up with me. I'm now hyperventilating, my chest heaving as though I'm fighting for my last breath. The one I can never seem to catch. His attention falls to the broken bottle lying by my feet. "God, Kacey. What were you about to do?"

I'm swallowing and struggling for air and shaking my head and trembling. "I don't know, I don't know. I don't know," I mutter over and over again. But I know. I know what I almost did.

I almost killed a man.

■ ■ ■

Streetlights pass by in a blur as Dan drives us home in his police car. I know Trent is somewhere behind us on his bike, and all I can think of is the look of horror on his face when he asked. *What were you about to do?* And he knew. No doubt he knew.

Storm helps me out of the car as if it were me who was attacked. How is she acting so calm?

One step forward. One step forward. One step forward.

"Kacey, I'm okay. I promise," I just barely hear Storm say as she leads me hand in hand toward the apartment.

I know she's fine and I'm thankful. But I'm struggling. I'm struggling to keep myself from crumbling into pieces on the sidewalk.

I almost killed a man tonight.

Aunt Darla's counselors were right all along . . . *One step forward. One step forward. One step—*

Fingers snap in front of my face and break my trance. I look over to see an ocean of worry in Storm's blue eyes. "I think she's in shock," she says to someone else, clearly not me.

"No, good. I'm good. Good," I mumble, and suddenly I'm grasping for Storm's biceps and squeezing, panic surging through me. "Don't tell Livie. Please?" She can't find out what I almost did.

Storm nods. I see her exchange worried looks with Trent and Dan.

"Come on." The ground disappears as a set of strong arms scoops me up. In seconds Trent has me lying on my bed and he's pulling the covers over me.

"No, I'm not tired," I mumble, struggling weakly to get up.

"Just . . . rest. Please?" Trent says softly. His hand smooths over my cheek and I grab it, holding it tight, pressing my lips against his palm.

"Stay." I hear the desperation in my voice.

"Of course, Kacey," he whispers. He kicks off his shoes and climbs into bed next to me.

I close my eyes and nuzzle into his chest, reveling in the warmth of his body, the steady rhythm of his heartbeat, the smell of him. "You hate me, don't you? You must hate me. I can't help it. I'm broken."

Trent squeezes me close to him. "I don't hate you. I could never hate you. Give me your heart, Kacey. I'll take everything that comes with it."

I start to cry. Uncontrollably, for the first time in four years.

■ ■ ■

"Pull my finger."

Jenny giggles hysterically. She giggles every time Billy says that.

And I roll my eyes, just like I do every time he says that. "So hot, Billy. Take me now."

"Kacey," my mother admonishes, overhearing me.

Billy winks and squeezes my hand tight and I squeeze back. Mom and Dad are in the front, talking about next week's game and how I need to get my license soon so they don't have to cart my ass around anymore. Of course I know they're joking. They'd never miss one of my rugby games.

"Would you stop being so cheap and just buy me that damn Porsche already, Dad?"

"Language, Kacey," my dad scolds, but he looks over his shoulder to throw me a smile. I know he's beaming inside. I scored the winning try at tonight's game, after all.

Everything that happens next happens in a fog. My body jerks violently. Something smacks into it. A weight presses down hard against my right side. I feel myself tossed and turned. And then it all just . . . stops.

And I'm vaguely aware that something is very wrong.

"Mom? Dad?" There's no answer.

It's hard to breathe. Something squeezes my ribs. My right side feels numb. And I hear a strange gurgle. I listen closely. It sounds like someone taking his last breath.

I bolt upright, my body drenched in sweat, my heart pounding against its confines, racing so fast I don't know where one beat ends and the next begins. For a moment, I curl up into a tight ball and rock, trying to shake the dreaded knowledge that I had caused the accident. If I hadn't distracted my dad, he would have seen the car coming and could have avoided it. But I know I can't change it now anyway. I can't change anything.

I'm relieved to find Trent lying next to me, his bare chest rising and falling slowly. He hasn't abandoned me yet. The streetlight outside casts a pleasant glow over his body and I sit quietly and take his form in, wanting to mold myself to it. I fight against the urge to touch it, to trace my fingers along its perfectly sculpted curves.

With a sigh, I stand and walk over to my dresser on wobbly legs, wondering how long before this new life falls apart, too. Before I lose Trent, and Storm, and Mia. This new life was almost dismantled tonight. Just like that. I should just walk away, I tell myself. Disappear and end all of these relationships and spare everyone more heartache. But I know that's not possible. I'm in too deep. I've somehow made room for all of them in my life and my heart. That, or they've made room for me in theirs. Either way, I won't survive the void that will be left when they're gone.

With my back to Trent, I take off my soaked dress and let it drop to the floor. I unsnap my bra and toss it alongside the dress. My panties follow next. While lifting a tank top and shorts from my top drawer, I consider hopping in the shower to cool off when a soft voice says, "You have the prettiest red hair."

I freeze, my cheeks flaming, acutely aware that I am standing completely naked in front of a guy that can make me climax just by looking at me the right way. I hear the bed creak and footsteps approach slowly, but I don't move. Trent edges up behind me and the air in the room grows thicker. I can't turn around. I can't face him and I don't know why.

I can feel his existence as if it's wrapping its hand around my soul, cradling it, trying to protect it from harm, and I'm terrified. Terrified because I don't ever want the feeling to end.

Every nerve in my body short-circuits. I stiffen as his hand grazes my shoulder before shifting my hair over to one side, exposing one side of my neck the way he likes to do. A cool breeze tickles there as he leans down close.

"You're so very beautiful. All of you."

He yanks my PJs out of my grasp and lets them drop to the ground as he takes my hand in his. His mouth trails off to my right shoulder and he begins to sweep tiny kisses across my scar line, sending shivers everywhere. Pushing my arm up so my hand rests on my head, I sense him shifting his body. Down, down, he continues, his mouth moving gently along my rib cage, over my hip, all the way to my outer thigh, kissing each line marking my tragic past. The entire time, my left hand holds his while my other one rests on my head. And my body trembles with anticipation.

Trent's hands move to grip the outsides of my thighs securely as he lays a final kiss on my tailbone and I wobble slightly from weakened knees. I sense him standing behind me again, his hands skating back up and around to my belly, pulling my body firmly against him, letting me feel him hard against my back.

My head falls back against his chest with a mixture of excitement and frustration—excited that Trent is allowing me close after weeks of keeping me away, frustrated that this will end all too abruptly.

But he shows no signs of ending this as his hands continue to move up over the contours of my breasts, cupping their fullness. I hear him sharply inhale. Slowly, he turns me around and pins my arms behind my back.

I don't know why, but I can't bring myself to look at him, so I stare at his collarbone instead and feel his chest rise and fall against mine, my nipples hardening as they graze against his skin. I exhale in short pants as he leans down and whispers, "Look at me, Kacey."

I do. I look up and let myself sink into those blue eyes, so full of worry and pain and desire.

"I'll make you whole again, Kacey. I promise you, I will," he whispers. And then his mouth covers mine.

I'm aware of the wall now flattening against my back, of his boxers dropping to the ground, of strong arms lifting me up, of my legs wrapping around his hips, of feeling him against me.

Pushing inside me.

Making me whole.

■ ■ ■

It's still dark outside when I wake again. This time my head rests on Trent's chest, my body entwined with his. His fingers doodling over my back tells me he's awake. It's not a nightmare that's woken me up this time. It's Storm and Dan's raised voices through the wall.

"He could have killed you, Nora!" Dan yells. "Forget the money. You don't need the money."

Storm's voice isn't nearly as loud or booming, but I manage to hear it all the same.

"You think I spent all those years training with a place like Penny's as my goal? I screwed up, Dan. I made bad choices and I have to live with them. For now. For Mia."

"Mia is who I'm thinking about. What if that guy killed you tonight? Who would take care of her? Her father? From prison?" There's a quiet moment and then Dan starts yelling again. "I don't know if I can do this, Nora. I can't be afraid you're going to die every time you go to work."

I snort. "Look who's talking," I mutter to myself, but then I bite my tongue. This is between them.

"Well, I'm not making decisions based on what some man wants because when you're gone and I'm still here, I have to live with the outcome." I hear her voice crack at the end and I know she's crying. The yelling dies down and I'm glad. I don't want to hear Dan and Storm break up.

"Can I ask you something without you getting angry, Kacey?" Trent asks.

"Uh-huh," I agree without thinking.

"What do you know about the driver who hit your car?"

My body instantly tenses. "He was drunk."

"And?"

"And nothing."

"Nothing at all? No name, face, anything?"

I pause, deciding if I want to answer. "Name. That's it."

"Do you remember it?"

I inhale sharply. I'll never forget. "Sasha Daniels."

"What happened to him?"

"He died."

There's a long pause as Trent continues drawing swirls on my back and I start to believe the conversation is over. *Stupid girl.* "Was he alone?"

I hesitate but decide to answer. "He had two friends. Derek Maynard and Cole Reynolds. Derek and Sasha weren't wearing seat belts. They were both thrown from their vehicle."

My head rises and lowers with Trent's deep breath. "Has the survivor—this Cole guy—made contact with you?"

I close my eyes and enjoy the warmth of Trent's chest, fighting the dread as he drags me back into that deep, dark place. "His family tried. I filed restraining orders and told the police that if any of them so much as approach me or Livie, I'd kill them all." At the time, I was bound to a bed and unable to move, let alone murder. Still, the cops came through with passing the message along.

Now, though—now I know I'm capable of anything.

Of murder.

"I do not want to see, or talk to, or know *Cole Reynolds.*" The name twists my mouth with disdain. "It was his car that plowed into ours. He handed his keys to his friend who then shattered my life to smithereens. I hope wherever he is, he is suffering. I hope everyone he loves has abandoned him. I hope he doesn't have a dime and has to eat cat food and maggots. I hope he goes to sleep every night and wakes up reliving that terrible night. Reliving what *he* did to me. To Livie." I let out a vacuous sigh and lie back down on Trent's chest, as if unloading that sheer magnitude of hatred was somehow liberating. "And then I hope his balls catch on fire." My voice is cold and hard. I don't bother to conceal the hatred of my words. I unleash fullheartedly. I revel in it. Hatred good. Forgiveness bad.

Silence takes over as Trent's arms tighten around me, his chin resting on the top of my head. I feel a new tension in him and I'm not surprised. I wonder what Trent thinks of his pretty little fucked-up redhead now.

■ ■ ■

I wake up to an empty room and a note on my pillow. Five words.

Had to go. I'm sorry.

I assume Trent has a new work contract. Still, I'm disappointed. I could use another dose of his body if he's willing to administer it. I roll out of bed and stretch, the horror of last night at Penny's pushed aside in favor of my memories of a night with Trent. It's been so long since I felt that. Scratch that. I *never* felt that. Sex was never like that with Billy. I cared deeply about him, but we were young and inexperienced. Trent's not inexperienced. Trent knows exactly what he's doing and he does it very well. And something's just different with Trent. He's like ripe watermelon after a lifetime of thirst. He's like air after years underwater.

He's like life.

stage six

. . .

WITHDRAWAL

FOURTEEN

I walk into Storm's apartment to find Mia waiting expectantly like a wide-mouth bass while Dan, in striped boxers no less, tosses Cheerios into her mouth. I'm relieved that Storm and Dan made up. I like seeing Storm with him.

He stops the game to look me over. He seems worried. "How are you feeling today?"

"Good." I smile as I pop a Cheerio into my mouth. Dan doesn't know me. He doesn't know how skilled I am at blocking out horrid memories. I'm a master. In only hours, the incident is all but forgotten and, as long as no one brings it up, it will stay that way. I walk over to Storm, who's mixing batter in a big glass bowl. "Pancakes?" She holds up a ladle.

I nod, patting my stomach. "Did you see Livie this morning?"

"She left for school not long ago." She drops a spoonful of pancake mix onto the griddle and it makes a sizzling sound. She fixes me with the same worried look that Dan just gave me. "How are you feeling, really?"

"I'm . . . good. I'm better."

"You sure? Dan knows a guy you can talk to if it'll help."

I shake my head. "I'm good. Seeing you here, alive and well, and serving me pancakes is all I need." I rub her back with one hand as I grab a plate of food with the other. Yup, this is exactly what I need. Storm and Mia, and Livie and Trent. Even Dan. This is all I need right now.

■ ■ ■

I have the night off. You coming over?

I wait and wait, but I get no text response from Trent. Impatient, I walk over to his apartment and knock. No answer. His place is pitch black. Then I wander out to the commons on a fake mission to inspect the hibachi. Really, I want to see if Trent's bike is there. It is. I go and knock on his door again and wait. Still no response.

Cain won't let either of us work that night. In fact, he's forced Storm to take an entire week with danger pay. I'll bet Dan is happy about that. By the light bounce in Storm's step, I think she's okay with it, too. I would be happy also. If Trent were here.

I don't hear from Trent the next day.

Or the next.

No text. No call. It's as though he's dropped off the face of the Earth.

I go back to Penny's on the third night with a sinking feeling in the pit of my stomach. The music is dull, the lights are blinding, the customers are annoying. It's not the same without Trent and Storm there and I'm miserable. I can't even force a smile. I know Storm will be back in a few days. Trent, though—I feel his absence like a knife in the center of my back. It's painful, I can't reach it to pull it out, and I'm sure it will be my demise if it persists.

Trent being gone eats at me all week. It makes me grouchy and snappy and generally unpleasant to be around. I'm well aware of it, but I don't care. It makes me start fights with Livie on my one night off over what to watch on television. It makes her start to cry and call me a bitch. Livie never does that. It makes me lurk through the commons every night, casting furtive glances at 1D. Wherever he went, Trent's not back.

What if he's never coming back?

■ ■ ■

Day Five.

I scream in horror as I watch my parents' Audi sink into the river, my eyes locked on the person trapped behind the wheel.

Trent.

I'm a sweaty tangled mess in my sheets when I come to, gasping. *It was just a dream! Oh, thank God!* It takes me a good fifteen minutes to shake the image scalding my mind. But I can't shake the idea. What if Trent did get into an accident? No one would call me. I'm nobody. I haven't had a chance to be anybody yet.

I harass Storm to give me Dan's number. Then I harass him to check the police reports for a Trent Emerson being in an accident. He tells me he can't abuse his position like that. I snap and slam my phone against the counter. Then I call him back and apologize, and he agrees to bring his laptop so I can search the news, the obits, anything.

It's well into the night before I accept that Trent is probably alive and well. He's just not with me.

■ ■ ■

Day Nine.

Wandering past Trent's apartment door on my way to the gym, I freeze. I'm sure I just caught a whiff of something funky.

Ohmigod.

Trent is dead.

I run to Tanner's door and hammer on it until it flies open. Tanner is standing there in his standard Batman pajama pants and deer-caught-in-the-headlights eyes. "Come on!" I grab his arm and yank him out. "You need to open 1D right now!"

Tanner uses his weight to resist me. "Wait a minute. I can't just open—"

"I think Trent's dead!" I shriek.

That gets him moving. I wait behind him with itchy feet as he fumbles with his giant key ring, his hands shaking. He's bothered by this. *Of course he is.*

When he opens the door, I shove past him, not even considering what I'm rushing in to see. It's dim and tidy inside. Sparse, even. I wouldn't know someone lived there had it not been for a laptop sitting on the desk, Trent's navy sweater hanging over the back of the couch, and the smell of his cologne lingering in the air.

Tanner moves past me and does a quick sweep of the bedrooms and bathroom. He even opens the closet door. When he comes back to face me, it's with a glower. "Why exactly did you tell me Trent was dead?"

I swallow, averting my gaze. "Oops."

"Okay, get out of here." He ushers me toward the door none too gently with a hand on my shoulder. I hear him grumbling something about drugs and hormones as he lumbers away.

■ ■ ■

Day Thirteen.

Kick. Punch. Spin. Kick.

The bag takes my punishment without complaint. I slam and pound against it, all my anger and anxiety coming to a head. Trent has another life in Rochester. That has to be it. With a tanned, blond, unbroken woman. They probably have two perfect little kids together who say "please" and "thank you" and haven't learned to swear like sailors because of their mother's incessant profanity. He must have come to Miami to have a quarter-life-crisis affair. I am nothing but someone's quarter-life crisis, and I fell for it like a mindless sap.

Kick Pivot. Spin. Kick.

This feels good.

I feel like I'm gaining control again.

Later, at Storm's house, I sit on the couch and watch an episode of *SpongeBob* with Mia. Lying next to me on the cushion is a dark-haired Ken doll. It kind of reminds me of Trent. I give serious consideration to stealing it, painting "Trent" over its chest, and taking a lighter to where its man parts should be.

■ ■ ■

Day Seventeen.

"Was he real?" I mumble, staring at the phone in my hand. *I didn't buy this for myself, did I?*

"What?" Livie asks, looking up at me in surprise.

"Trent, was he real? I mean, I could understand if he wasn't real. Who could be that beautiful and sweet and perfect and want someone as fucked up as me?"

There's a long pause and when I look over at Livie, she's staring at me as if I'd swallowed a bag of broken glass. I can tell she's worried about me. Storm's worried about me, too. I think even Nate is worried.

■ ■ ■

Day Twenty.

Kick. Punch. Punch. Kick.

I'm raging against the bag.

Trent used me. To what sick end, I can't decide. He obviously has a twisted fetish. He found a damaged woman and targeted her weakness with his dimples and his charm. He broke through my shell, wormed his way in to melt the ice over my heart. Then he abandoned me after discovering just how fucked up I really am. But not before getting laid, of course.

And I let him in. It's my fault! I'm the idiot.

I pound away on the twenty-pound bag of sand. I love the sand. It absorbs all my emotions without disapproval and lets me use it without expectation.

"Angry about something?"

I whip around to find Ben standing behind me with his arms folded over his chest and a knowing smirk on his face. I turn back and execute a perfect kick. "Not at all."

Ben walks around to catch the bag. He gestures for me to continue while he holds it. "Where's your boyfriend?"

I hoof the bag extra hard, and in a way I know Ben isn't expecting. I hope it hits him square in the balls, just for bringing up Trent. It doesn't, but it does earn a grunt. "What boyfriend?"

"The one who's always at the bar."

"Have you seen him at the bar lately?" *Punch.*

There's a long pause. "No, suppose I haven't."

"Well, then, Lawyer Boy, what would you deduce from that? Or are you not able to? You're not going to make a very good lawyer if that's the case."

Another kick to the bag. Another grunt from Ben.

"So you're unattached again?"

"I've always been unattached."

"Right. Well, then, how about we go out tonight?"

"I'm working."

"So am I. Let's grab an early dinner and head over together."

"Sure, fine. Whatever," I say without thinking. I don't want to think.

Ben's brow arches. "Seriously?"

I stop kicking now and wipe the layer of sweat from my forehead with my forearm. "Isn't that what you wanted to hear?"

"Well, yeah, but I was expecting a 'drop dead' answer."

"I'm good for that, too."

"No, no!" Ben quickly answers, backing away from me. "I'll come get you at six?"

"Fine," I say, flying through the air with a perfect roundhouse.

■ ■ ■

"What did I agree to?" I ask myself as I stand under the hot water, staring up at the showerhead, imagining another serpent there to scare the daylights out of me. If I screamed loud enough, would Trent magically appear? Would he break down the door again? I wouldn't let him leave this time. Not a chance.

I run into Livie in the kitchen. We've hardly talked since our fight. "I'm sorry, Livie," is all I say.

She ropes her arm around my waist. "He's a jerk, Kacey."

"A stupid jerk," I mumble.

"A big stupid jerk," she answers. It's a game we used to play when we were younger. It drove our parents batty.

"A big stupid smelly jerk."

"A big stupid smelly jerk with hemorrhoids."

I slap my forehead. "Oh! And she pulls out the 'roids for the win!"

Livie giggles. "Where are you going?"

I slide out from her grip to put my shoes on. "Out."

"Like on a date?" Livie's face lights up.

I hold my hand up to forestall her excitement. "Ben's a meathead from work. We're grabbing a bite and then he's driving me to work, and I'll smash his nuts if he tries anything."

There's a knock on the door. "One meathead, coming right up!" I joke as I throw open the door, expecting to find Ben's giant frame and obnoxious grin filling the doorway.

I stumble back two steps as the air is knocked out of my lungs.

It's Trent.

FIFTEEN

"Hey," he offers, sliding his aviator glasses off to show me those beautiful two-toned blue eyes that I could lose myself in.

I stare into them, feeling the blood drain from my body as I watch a full gamut of emotions play across his face—relief, guilt, grief, bitterness, and then guilt again. I'm sure there's an array of reactions showing on my own face, too, as I simply stand there, mouth agape, having lost all ability to speak.

Livie hasn't, though. Far from it. "You! Stay away from her!" she shrieks, charging forward. She breaks my trance, and I just manage to grab her before she rakes ten layers of Trent's skin off with flailing claws.

"Give us a minute, Livie," I manage to say calmly. But inside, a torrent of sensations threatens to sweep me off my feet. The door beside me sways and I fight harder to pull air into my lungs as my heart speeds up. *Trent is back*. It's as much a punch to the gut as a swell inside my chest. Like a bad addiction, I know it's wrong, but, damn, does it leave me satisfied.

Livie turns and stomps toward her room, but not before throwing one last icy glare Trent's way. "Hemorrhoids! Remember that, Kacey!"

Her sudden outburst ruptures my panic attack like a needle to a balloon, and I find myself chuckling. *God, I love that girl!*

Maybe it's my laughter that eases Trent and prompts him to touch me—I don't know. "Let me explain," he begins, his hands moving to mine.

I recoil, angry again. "Don't you dare touch me," I hiss.

He holds his hands out in front of him—palms outward—in a sign of peace. "Fair enough, Kace. But give me a chance to explain."

My arms cross my chest and I hug myself tightly to keep from collapsing. Or reaching out to him. "Go ahead. Explain," I growl, fighting the overwhelming urge to throw myself at his body, to not listen to any excuse because none of it really matters. It's the past, and the way he makes me feel when I'm near him is all that matters right now. But I can't do that. I can't be weak.

His lips part to speak and my knees go wobbly. *Oh God.* If I have to stand in front of him for one more second, I am going to lose all my fight.

Ben appears around the corner like a knight in shining armor.

"Time's up," I declare a little too loud. I shoulder past Trent, slamming the apartment door shut behind him. "Hey, Ben!" It's obvious to anyone who knows me that this is all an act. I'm never this cheery. I'm never cheery, period.

Ben looks at me, and then at Trent, and I see the wheels turning. He knows he just interrupted something. He's a smart meathead. "Do you want me to—" He gestures toward the exit, suggesting he could leave.

"Nope!" I hook my arm through his and tug him forward, holding my head high and Ben's arm close, letting my anger fuel me forward.

Inside, I feel the walls caving in.

■ ■ ■

"You've hardly touched your pasta," Ben notes. We're at an Italian restaurant five minutes away from Penny's.

"I've touched it plenty," I grumble as I stab it with my fork. "I've touched it so much that your pasta is jealous. I hear talk of a spaghetti smackdown."

"You've hardly *eaten* your pasta," Ben rephrases, and smirks.

"I'm not hungry."

"Is it because of that guy?"

We've been sitting at this restaurant for forty-five minutes and this is the first question Ben has asked me. The rest of the time, I've listened to him drone on about the shot knee that kept him from a football scholarship, and about how he wants to be a criminal lawyer in Vegas because that's where all the rich crooks live. I don't know whether he doesn't ask me anything because he's a narcissist or because he realizes I don't like answering questions. Either way, it has suited me just fine.

I sigh as I pull a twenty out of my purse and toss it on the table. "We should probably get going soon."

He frowns as he hands the money back. "My treat."

"I'm not having sex with you."

"Whoa! Who said anything about sex? I'm just here for the meal and the pleasant company." He acts all offended, but the glimmer in his eyes tells me he's teasing. An unattractive snort escapes me.

"Okay, fine. Mediocre company." He shoves a piece of bread into his mouth and adds with a smile, "Hot piece of ass."

"And that's the Ben we know and love," I confirm with an exaggerated nod and a sugar packet to his forehead.

"Seriously, though," Ben starts as he scrapes the last mound of pasta from his plate. I wait patiently for him to finish chewing and swallow. "Why'd you agree to come out with me? You're obviously not over that other guy and, even if you were, I'm no idiot. I don't know what that day in the gym was . . ."

Dammit. I am that obvious. I hope I'm not to Trent, though. I don't want him to see through me so easily. I shrug. "You don't want me, Ben. I'm seven layers of fucked up with a side of batshit crazy."

He grins, but I catch the sadness in his eyes as he throws down a few bills to cover the meal. "I already knew that."

"Well, then, why'd you ask me out? *Especially* after what I did to you that day in the gym?"

He shrugs. "Waiting for your next moment of full-on crazy? I'll be faster next time. In and out."

I burst out laughing. Ben's shameless honesty is a welcome relief.

"I don't know, Kace. I'm around a lot of sluts and airheads. You're different. You're smart and funny. And you can shrink a guy's confidence like no other girl I've met."

"I didn't think anyone could shrink that swelled head of yours, Ben."

He grins arrogantly. "Depends which head you're talking about."

■ ■ ■

"I hear Trent's back in town?" Storm whispers to me as I pour shots of Patrón for a bachelor party.

"Oh yeah?" I mutter, pursing my lips. I don't know what else to say. I haven't forgotten. I can't get through a minute without his name popping into my mind, without remembering how incredible his touch feels against my skin, without wanting it all back the way it was for that short, magical period of time before he ripped my heart out of my chest and tossed it to the curb.

I hate him for making me feel like this. For giving me hope, only to yank it all away. For pulling me above the water, helping me breathe again, before shoving my head back under.

So when I find him staring down at me from the other side of the bar near last call, I have to brace myself against the counter, anger and grief slamming into me with such force that I struggle to stay upright.

"What do you want?" I hiss.

"I need to talk to you."

"No."

"Please, Kacey." That tone, that voice. I feel it probing for my weak spot, a place to wiggle in and win me over. I won't let it. Not this time.

"You had three weeks to talk to me and . . . oh wait!" I smack my forehead for effect. "You disappeared off the face of the fucking Earth. That's right. I almost forgot."

"Just give me five minutes," he pleads, leaning forward.

"Fine! Go ahead. This is the perfect time and place to talk." My arms fly out, exaggerating how much this is *not* the perfect time and place to talk.

Trent's jaw tenses. "I mean it, Kacey. Five minutes, in private. I need to explain something. I need . . . you."

"Oh, you *need* me? Interesting." I force the words through clenched teeth. Inside, the glue that holds me together strains against that word. *Need.* Trent *needs* me. "Fine." I slap my towel down onto the bar and holler, "Back in five, Storm!"

She looks over, sees Trent, glances at me with concern, but then nods.

"Come with me." I stomp past him. I'm acutely aware that Nate and Ben are following close, but I continue. I march past Jeff and Bryan, the two bulldog bouncers who watch over the private rooms. They don't try to stop me. I'm sure my stiff spine and scowl that says "back the fuck away before I choke you with your own tongue" have something to do with that.

My leg flies forward to kick open the door to an available room.

Spinning on my heels, I stand with arms folded across my chest, watching Trent's lean body and his apprehensive face approach me. Jerking my head toward the room, I command, "Get in."

"Kacey . . ."

"You said private. How much more private can you get than a private room?" I ask, my tone coated with ice.

With a defeated sigh and a small nod, Trent passes through. Behind him, I see Ben lean in to say something to Nate. It seems to keep the beast at bay. Ben heads toward me with a look of concern. "You okay, Kacey?"

"What do you think, Ben?"

His brow furrows in thought. "I think I'll stand guard out here. I won't come in. Not unless I hear something that sounds bad—deal?"

"Deal." I offer him a small nod of appreciation. I think, after our sordid past, Ben and I have come to an understanding. I may even call him a friend.

I storm into the room, slamming the door behind me. Inside is a small, dimly lit space with a black lounge chair and mood music, different from what plays out in the main club area. Storm says staff thoroughly cleans and sanitizes the rooms after each client leaves. Even if that's not true, right now I don't care.

I stalk over to where Trent stands and I shove him backward into the lounge chair. Then my hand fumbles with the side zipper of my skirt.

"What are you . . ." Trent begins to ask, but his words die as I unzip my skirt and let it drop to the ground. I step out of the skirt as my hands move to unbutton my gauzy blouse, starting at the top.

"Kacey, no." Trent leans forward.

My three-inch heel slamming into his chest forces him back into his seat.

"This is what you came for, isn't it? This is what you *need*?" My tone is as cold as a deep freeze. "What you've always wanted?" I toss my shirt on the floor and glower at him in nothing but my bra, panties, and heels. "This is the part where you tell me I'm so beautiful. So say it. Say it so we can get this over with, and you can disappear again." My voice wavers a bit at the end and I clam up, not trusting it right now.

"No, Kacey. Jeez." Trent slides off the chair onto his knees, his hands finding their way to my thighs to hold them delicately.

"No touching the girls. Did you forget the rules already?" I sneer at him.

His eyes haven't left mine, and in them I see a torrent of indescribable emotion that threatens to melt all of my defenses. I have to break his gaze and look away. A lump is forming in my throat that I can't seem to shove down.

"I'm sorry. I never wanted to cause you more pain than you've had to endure."

"Really? Leaving me a vague note the morning after Storm's attack—after we have sex for the first time—and then disappearing for almost three weeks is your way of *not* causing me more pain?" My voice cracks and I grit my teeth. I hate my voice.

His head bows forward against my belly as his hands slide up to my hips before moving back down to my thighs again. They feel so good. I don't want them to feel good. Damn, traitorous thighs. *Fight it, Kacey. Fight it.*

"Kacey, I was wrong."

I swallow. "About?"

"About pushing you like I did. I thought if you opened up about your past, I could somehow fix it for you. I shouldn't have kept pushing you like that." I gasp as I feel a set of warm lips trail my belly. He knows that will melt my defenses. He's not playing fair. Worse, I don't want him to play any other way. "I should have just focused on making you happy. And I will. From now on, Kacey. I will. I will devote every day for the rest of our lives to making you happy. I promise."

Will not buy it. Will not buy it. "You've said that before. And then you vanished." I don't like the way my tone falters, as if I'm about to cry. *One . . . two . . . three . . . four . . .*

Fuck. Useless.

He leans back on his heels and his hands slide down my thighs again. He doesn't meet my eyes, though, choosing instead to stare at the floor between us. When he speaks, his jaw is tense with a hint of anger. "Kacey, you're not the only one with issues. I'm fucked up, okay? There are things about my past that I don't know how to tell you. That I *can't* tell you."

His admission catches me off guard. *Trent with a dark past?* I've never once contemplated that. Why have I not contemplated that? I've been so wrapped up in my own issues that I haven't even thought of his, that's why. But how dark could anything from his past really be? With a shaky finger, I reach out and gently push his chin up so his head tilts back, so those beautiful blue eyes can pull me in. He seems so level-headed, so well-adjusted, so perfect.

"I've never once pushed you to divulge your skeletons," I say, my tone softer, without bitterness.

"I know. I know, Kace." Trent's grip on my thighs tightens as he draws me closer to him. His fingertips slide up to grasp my hips in their entirety, his thumbs sliding along my pelvic bone, lighting a tiny spark of need mixed among these emotional flames already burning bright. My hands instinctively slide down to cover his.

He continues. "After that night, I . . . I thought I'd pushed you too hard. I thought I caused what happened the night Storm was attacked."

I shudder from the reminder. My dark side. My murderous

side. "You didn't cause that, Trent. That was me, finally coming unhinged."

"I know, babe. I know that now. But I had to get away and think. I had to walk away for a while and—"

"You could have sent me a message."

"I know. I fucked up. I'm sorry. I just didn't know how to explain why I ran off. I was scared." I look down and see the tears welling in his eyes. All my rage is extinguished; all my defenses shatter.

I can't handle seeing Trent like this.

"No, it's okay." My hand strokes the back of his head with nothing but compassion while my other one wipes the tear away. *Who is this person talking?* She's not the one who ran around the apartment in a tirade, stalking the news and ready to mutilate Ken dolls.

"I'm so sorry, Kacey. I'll stop pushing you. No more talk of the past. None. Just the future. Please? I need you."

Again, that *need* word. I can't even speak. I only nod.

But that's enough for Trent. Strong fingers flexed at my hips tug me down. I willingly drop to my knees. Trent pulls me to him so our bodies hold tight against each other. Warm hands find their way across my bare back to unclasp my bra. He casts it aside and reaches forward to cup my breasts at the same time that his mouth finally finds mine.

The feel of his lips sends a wave of irrepressible hunger through my body in a shudder. Three weeks without this. I don't know how I survived. I reach down and fumble with his shirt. I want it off. Now. I want my bare skin against his. Now.

As if sensing the urgency, he breaks from my mouth long enough to yank his shirt off over his head and then dives back in, his chest pressing against mine as I slide close to him. "Kace," he whispers, his lips shifting greedily to my neck as one hand moves up my inner thigh to slip under my panties. I gasp as his deft fingers touch me. "I'm never letting you go again. Never."

My heart races as I rock back and forth against his hand, as I whisper his name, as I fumble with his zipper, letting the last three weeks disappear into the well of the past.

SIXTEEN

"Did I do that?" I frown as my finger touches the side of Trent's face, where a red welt has formed.

He winces. "Livie's got a mean left hook."

"Seriously?" I prop myself up to get a better look at it. And at Trent, in general. At his entire naked body, lying on the carpeted floor of the dimly lit V.I.P. room. I don't hear the steady pulse of music in the club anymore. That must mean the place is closing up. I don't know how long we've been in here. Ben hasn't bothered us, though. Not that I noticed, anyway.

Trent starts to speak and stalls several times. "When you left your place with that goon, Livie stormed out and chased me around the commons, screaming at me that I broke your heart. Then she hauled back and punched me, and told me I'd better go and make you happy again. Forever."

My head flops down on Trent's bare chest as I laugh. "I think my temper may finally be rubbing off on her." I replay her words in my head as I nuzzle against him, inhaling his scent. "Forever's a long time."

Trent's arms squeeze around me. "Forever's not long enough with you."

■ ■ ■

"Do you think if I go out there right now, Livie will hit me again?"

"Anything's possible. But I do feel pretty happy right about now," I murmur, stretching out in my bed.

Trent's arms extend back to cradle his head, a cocky grin curving his lips. "I sure hope so. I tried my best. Five times last night, I think? If that didn't fix you . . ."

I lift myself up and throw one leg over his body to straddle him, arching my brow. "Oh, you fixed me last night. Today's a different story."

Hungry eyes graze the length of my body and then settle on my face. "Seriously?"

I shrug and then wink suggestively.

He chuckles as his hands comb through his hair, sending it into wilder disarray. "I've heard redheads were crazy, but man, no one warned me that you were sex fiends."

I playfully flick his nose. With a roar, he rolls and pins me down on my back, holding himself up to linger over me, high enough to give me a full view of his entire body. With a wry smile, I throw my legs around his waist and pull him down to me.

■ ■ ■

The weeks fly by, and Trent stays. He sleeps in our apartment most nights now. He's usually at the club late in the evening, sitting and watching me quietly with that intense, teasing stare that makes my knees buckle because I know what's waiting for me when I get home. He stays, and he makes me happy. Happier than I've been in a long time. In many ways, happier than I've ever been. He makes me laugh. He makes me giggle. He makes me *feel* again. And at night, he takes my nightmares away. Not all of them, but they're not on daily repeat anymore. And when I do wake up, drenched in sweat and gasping for air, Trent is there to hold me and stroke my hair, to promise me that it's over, and that what he and I have is real.

Each day, tiny pieces of Before Kacey fall into place. Or come out from hiding. Maybe Kacey Cleary has been buried somewhere deep inside all this time, just waiting for the right person to pull her from the deep, dark waters.

To save her from drowning.

I don't notice the pieces at first, but Livie sure does. I catch her watching me all the time—when I'm fixing myself a sandwich, when I'm cleaning, when I'm shopping—a small smile touching her beautiful lips. When I ask her what's up, she just shakes her head and says, "Kacey's back." And she's happy.

Storm and Dan are going strong. I think Storm might be in love, though she won't admit to it for fear of jinxing their relationship. I can tell that Dan is head-over-heels in love with her, and with Mia, by the way he watches them, a tiny smile always touching his lips.

And how is Mia? Well, one morning, Trent and I wake up to her hovering over our bed with a gapped-tooth grin and two quarters in the palm of her hand. "Look, Trent! I sold my teeth last night!" All I could do is laugh. Laugh, and remind myself to get a lock for the door so she doesn't learn more than cuss words from me. She's the happiest kid I've ever seen because she's surrounded by people who love her.

True to Storm's promise, I'm making more money at Penny's than I could ever dream of making elsewhere. My bank balance grows considerably each week. Two more years of this, and maybe I'll be able to pay for Livie's tuition. Livie's so smart and so good. And so deserving.

Everything is perfect.

■ ■ ■

"Why do we have to be at Penny's three hours early?" I moan, pulling my jacket against my body, feeling the light December chill. There's an unusually cool weather front coming through Miami for this time of year, I hear. It's still balmy compared to Michigan but, all the same, goose bumps cover my skin.

"Liquor license training. We do it every year. Anyone who serves needs to go through the course," Storm explains.

"Three hours of how to pour a drink? Seriously?"

"Don't worry," she says as she bangs on Penny's back door. "They let you sample, too."

"Great. I'll be slurring before our shift starts," I grumble with a quick nod to Nate as I pass through. It's dark and quiet inside. I've never been at Penny's when it's this quiet. "Where is everyone? This is creeping me out."

"By the bar," Nate rumbles behind me, his hand prodding me forward. I peer over my shoulder and his mouth splits open to reveal gleaming white teeth. *I can't believe I used to be afraid of this giant teddy bear.*

We round the corner into the dimly lit main club area.

"Surprise! Happy birthday!"

I jump back and slam into Nate, who wraps his trunk-of-an-arm loosely around me while his deep laughter reverberates off the ceiling. Everyone's there, standing on the stage, under the spotlights. Trent, Livie, Dan, Cain, Ben. Even Tanner.

And Mia! She's off to the side, dancing around in circles with Ginger and a bunch of other fully clothed dancers I don't recognize.

"Are you surprised?" Storm giggles as she grabs my arm and tugs me forward. "Livie told us you turn twenty-one tomorrow and we wanted to surprise you. Cain offered to throw you a little party here."

As if on cue, Cain wanders over and tosses his arm around

my shoulder. "Hope you're okay with a birthday party at Penny's. We figured this would be a guaranteed surprise."

I find myself struggling to speak, not sure how to respond as I take in all the people. "Of course I am. Thank you."

He hands me an envelope. "Twenty-one only comes once, sweetheart. You're a hard worker and you take care of my Storm. Here's a little something from everyone. Enjoy the food, the wine. Everything. Take the night off." He pinches my cheek and then turns to Storm. "Keep that little princess of yours away from the stage, you hear me? Don't want her getting any ideas."

She rolls her eyes. "Of course, Cain."

I shake my head as I watch him walk away. He's an odd duck. Hearing him say that, given this place is his life and he employs all these dancers to do just that—be on the stage—his words are unexpected.

I see Trent finding his way over to me with a seductive grin and two champagne flutes in his hands. "You know I don't drink, Trent," I say as I take one.

We smile at each other as he curls his free arm around my waist and pulls me in to him, kissing my neck. "Has my plan worked? Have I made you happy?" he whispers into my ear.

My breath hitches. It always does when Trent is near. "I can't even begin to describe how much."

His cool nose grazes my cheek. "Try."

"Well . . ." I lean forward, pressing myself against him. I don't know how it's possible, but those electric sparks zap me every time I touch him as if it's the first time. "Better yet, how about I show you when we get back home?"

I feel his response dig into my stomach and I giggle, still in shock that this gorgeous, sweet, devilish guy is all mine. He clinks our glasses. "Here's to the next eighty years," he murmurs, and then tips his glass back and takes a sip.

"Eighty? God, you're optimistic. I figured you're good for another ten, and then I'll have to trade you in for a younger model."

He leans down and kisses my mouth, and I taste the champagne's sweetness on his tongue. "Good luck with that. I'm not going anywhere."

■ ■ ■

My fingers weave together as I ride back with Trent, the evening breeze nipping at my cheeks. As tempted as I am to let my hands wander, I know better than to distract him while he's driving. I can wait until we get home, but just barely. Livie and Mia are in Dan's car, following behind us with the dress I changed out of as soon as I realized I wasn't working tonight. Thankfully, Livie brought me a change of clothes so that I could ride home with Trent. Storm decided to work. She promised we'd do a girls' day tomorrow.

Trent parks the bike and I climb off. I don't get very far, though, before he grabs the front of my jeans at the zipper and yanks me back to him. "Stay in or go out tonight?" His teeth lightly nip my neck.

"How about both? First go out, and then stay in."

"That makes no sense." The sound of his chuckle against my ear sends shivers through my body.

I giggle. Then I shove him hard and he tumbles to the grass. I start running. "If you can catch me, you get to choose." I manage to get the key into the lock before he reaches me. I'm running through the commons toward our apartments, squealing with anticipation, expecting to feel strong hands grab hold of me any second.

When they don't, I slow down and glance back. Trent is standing in the middle of the commons, frozen, his face ashen as if he's seen a corpse.

"Trent?" I walk back toward him. Following his riveted gaze, I discover a well-dressed older couple standing ten feet away, watching us. In my mad dash, I'd missed them.

The man's appearance strikes me as familiar and I quickly realize he has Trent's eyes and mouth. Looking to the woman, her hair pulled into a sophisticated bun, I recognize Trent's narrow nose.

"Trent, are these your parents?"

No answer.

I've secretly been dying to meet his parents. His father is a big-shot lawyer in Manhattan; his mother runs a creative agency. She funnels a lot of contract work through to Trent. That's how he gets his clients. I know that they're divorced and yet here they are. Together. A spike of fear channels through me. There must be bad news if they both traveled all the way here.

Trent still hasn't moved, and this is now beyond awkward. I don't know why he's acting the way he is. It didn't sound like there was bad blood between them. Someone needs to do something. I step forward with a polite smile and extend my hand. "Hi, I'm Kacey."

I feel my smile slide off as Trent's mother's face lightens five shades. She closes her eyes and squeezes them shut as if she's in pain. When they open again, they're glistening with tears. She turns to Trent and swallows, her words barely above a whisper and full of anguish. "How could you, Cole!"

That name.

My heart stops beating altogether.

When it starts up again, it's a slow, pounding, irregular rhythm. "*What?*" I croak. I turn to find Trent's face twisted with dread and guilt, but I still don't get it. "What . . . why did she call you that, Trent?"

His eyes shine as his lips part to whisper, "I just wanted to make you happy again, Kacey. It's the only way I can fix it."

stage seven

. . .

BREAKDOWN

SEVENTEEN

I'm falling.

Falling backward into the deep, dark water. It's pouring over me, into me, through my mouth, up my nose, filling my lungs, seizing my will to breathe, to live.

I accept it. I welcome it.

In the distance, I hear voices. I hear people calling my name, but I can't find them. They're safe, above water. In another world. The world of the living.

There's no place for me there.

$$\blacksquare\ \blacksquare\ \blacksquare$$

"When will she wake up?" I hear Livie ask above the soft rhythmic beeping. I'd heard enough of those machines in my day to recognize it for what it is—a hospital IV. If that doesn't clue me in to where I am, the sickly sterile hospital odor sure does.

"When her mind is ready," an unfamiliar male voice explains. "Kacey has gone into severe psychological shock. Physically, she's fine. We're just ensuring her body stays hydrated and nourished. Now we have to wait."

"Is this normal?"

"From what I understand, your sister suffered a traumatic

experience four years ago and has never recovered emotionally from that."

The voices stop long enough that I dare crack open my lids. White and yellow walls fill my hazy vision.

"Kacey!" Livie's face appears suddenly. Her eyes are puffy and lined with dark rings, as though she hasn't slept in days, her cheeks red and blotchy from crying.

"Where am I?" I ask, my voice coming out raspy.

"A hospital."

"How? Why?"

Livie's mouth falls open for a second before she pulls it closed again, trying to act calm. For my benefit. I know that. I know my Livie. Always so selfless. Always so caring. "You're going to be fine, Kacey." Her hands fumble with my blankets to find my fingers. She squeezes. "You're going to get help. I'll never let Trent hurt you again."

Trent. That name attacks my body like a thousand pinpricks. I jolt in response.

Trent is Cole.

Trent destroyed my life. Twice.

Suddenly, I'm gasping for air, the reality squeezing my lungs like a vise. "How . . ." I start to say, but I can't speak because I can't breathe. *How is Trent, Cole? How did he find me?* Why *did he find me?*

"Breathe, Kacey." Livie tightens her grip on me, crawling in to lie down beside me, and I realize I'm hyperventilating.

"I can't, Livie!" I cry out, tears burning my cheeks. "I'm drowning."

Her sobs fill the room.

He knew. All that time he pretended to be caring and sympathetic and unaware of my past, he was the cause of my past. It was his car, his friend, his drunken night that stole my life from me.

"It's okay, Kacey. You're safe." Livie's arms hug my body to hers, her weight resting against me to stop my body from shaking.

We stay like that for minutes. Hours. A lifetime. I don't know. Until Storm crashes into the hospital room, panting as if she's just run a marathon, a wildness in her eyes like I'd never seen before. "I know, Kacey. I know what happened to you. I know everything, now." Tears spill out over her cheeks. She climbs into the other side of my bed and grabs hold of my hands. The three of us lie there like sardines.

Tangled, sobbing sardines.

■ ■ ■

A hissing sound . . .

Bright lights . . .

Blood . . .

Trent's beautiful face, his hands on the steering wheel.

Pointing at me.

Laughing.

"Kacey!" Something sharp smacks my face. "Wake up!"

I'm still screaming, even as Livie's bulging eyes come into focus in front of me. A sharp sting bites my cheek.

"I'm sorry I had to slap you, but you wouldn't stop screaming," Livie explains through her tears.

The nightmares are back, only they're worse. A million times worse.

"You won't stop screaming, Kacey. You need to stop." Livie sobs as she curls up in my bed beside me and begins to rock, muttering to herself, "Please help her. God, please help her."

■ ■ ■

"Which hospital is this, again?" I've been here two days now, and Storm and Livie haven't left my bedside except to use the bathroom or get water and food.

Storm and Livie share a long, edgy glance. "A specialized one," Livie says slowly.

"In Chicago," Storm adds, setting her chin up a notch.

"*What?*" My voice gathers more strength behind it than I thought possible. I struggle to sit up in bed. I feel like I've been run over by a truck.

Livie rushes to add, "There's a PTSD clinic nearby. It's supposed to be the best in the country."

"Well . . . what . . . how . . ." I finally pull myself upright with the help of the bed rails. "Since when does public health cover the best PTSD clinic in the country?"

"Calm down, Kacey." Storm gently pushes me back down into a lying position. I don't have the strength to fight her.

"Uh, no, I can't calm down. We can't pay for this . . ." I fumble with my IV, cursing to myself.

"What're you doing?" Livie asks, panic in her voice.

"Ripping this damn thing out of my arm and getting the hell out of this swanky cuckoo's nest." I swat her hand away as she tries to stop me. "What's it costing, huh? Five thousand per night? Ten?"

"Shhh—don't worry about that, Kace." Storm smooths my hair.

It's her turn to get a hand swat. "*Someone* has to worry about it! What the hell am I going to do? Take up permanent residence at Penny's V.I.P. room wearing nothing but knee pads so I can pay the bill?"

"I see our patient is awake?" The unfamiliar soft voice from before interrupts my fit. I turn to see a decent-looking older man with a receding hairline and kind charcoal eyes hold his hand out toward me. I hadn't even heard him come in. "Hello, I'm Dr. Stayner." I glare at that hand like it's covered in spots and oozing pus until he pulls it back. "Yes, that's right. Your issue with hands."

My issue with hands? I scowl at Livie and she averts her gaze.

If any of this bothers the doctor, I can't tell. "Kacey. Your case was brought to me by—"

"Dan," Storm cuts in, her eyes shifting between the doctor's and Livie's.

"Right. Dan." He clears his throat. "I think I can help you. I think you can live a normal life again. But I can't help if you don't want to be helped. Understand?" I'm left gaping at this man who calls himself a doctor but so clearly can't be. What kind of doctor walks into a room and says that?

When I don't answer, he strolls over to look out the barred window. "Do you want to be happy again, Kacey?"

Happy. There's that word. I thought I *was* happy. And then Trent destroyed me. Again. I fell in love with my family's murderer. I spent night after night with him next to me, inside me, dreaming of a future with him. Bile rises to my throat at the thought.

"A requirement of my therapy session is that my patients talk, Kacey," Dr. Stayner explains without a hint of sarcasm or annoyance in his voice. "So I'll ask you again. Do you want to be happy?"

God, this guy's pushy! And he's going to force me to talk. That's what this is about. Why does everyone insist on dredging up the past? It's done. It's over. No amount of talking will ever change it, will ever bring anyone back. Why am I the only one who sees this?

That comforting numbness is back and it's taking over my limbs and chest, forming a hard, icy coating over my heart. My body's natural defense. Numbness to take away the pain. "There's no such thing as being happy for me." My voice is cold and hard.

He turns to me again, those kind eyes tinged with pity. "Oh, there is, Miss Cleary. It will be an uphill battle, and I will test you every step of the way. I can be unconventional with my methods.

With you, I will do things that are questionable. You may hate me at times, but you and I will get there together. You just have to want to. I will not move you into my clinic until you willingly agree to it all."

"No," I growl defiantly. The very idea of going anywhere with this quack is outrageous.

I hear a choking sound beside me. It's Livie, struggling to stay calm. "Kacey, please," she pleads.

I set my jaw stubbornly, even though it pains me to see her like this.

But suddenly a rare fury flashes in her eyes. "You are not the only one who lost her parents, Kacey. This isn't just about you anymore." She jumps out of my bed and hovers over me, her fists balled up. And then she rages like I've never seen before. "I can't take it! The nightmares, the fighting, the distance. I've had to deal with this for four years, Kacey!" Livie is hysterical now, tears pouring freely, screaming, and I expect security to burst in any second. "Four years of watching you come and go in my life, wondering if today's the day I'm going to find you hanging in a closet or floating in a river. I get that you were in that car. I get that you had to see *everything*. But what about me?" she chokes, the fury deflating, leaving her drained and miserable. "I keep losing you over and over again and I can't take it anymore!"

Her words hit me over the head like a sledgehammer.

I thought my heart was already broken, but it wasn't.

Not completely.

Not until now.

"I know what happened the night Storm was attacked, Kacey. I know," Livie says, watching me under a meaningful gaze. *Storm.* I shoot a glare her way, and Livie scolds me with a waggling finger. "Don't you dare give Storm grief over telling me, Kacey Delyn Cleary. Don't you dare. Storm told me because she cares about you, and she wants you to get help. You almost attacked a man with a broken beer bottle. We're not going to help you avoid your shit anymore, understand?" Livie gracelessly wipes the tears away. "I'm not doing it anymore."

I've told myself time and time again that this is all for Livie. Everything I've done was to protect Livie. Watching her now, looking at what she has had to deal with, I wonder if it's all been about protecting myself. I know Livie lost her parents. I know she lost me, too, in a way. But have I ever *really* considered what she feels like? Tried to put myself in *her* shoes? I figured no one's shoes were half as bad as the ones dragging me down like cement blocks. And Livie never let on. She's always been so strong and level-headed. She's always been Livie—with or without our parents. I just thought . . .

I didn't think . . . My God! I never *really* weighed my actions, all my reactions, and what they do to Livie. I just figured that if I was upright and breathing, I was here for her. For Livie. But in a way, I never really have been.

I feel my head bob up and down, all my resistance vanishing. All I've ever told myself is that I want to protect my little sister from pain, but it hasn't been about protecting her. It's been about protecting me. All I keep doing is causing pain for her. For everyone in my life.

"Good." Dr. Stayner takes that as an agreement. "I will have your room prepared. The first part of your therapy will begin now." I'm reeling over how quickly he's moving ahead. He's efficient and businesslike, but at the same time like a tornado, swooping in to wreak havoc. He smoothly walks over to the door and motions someone in.

No. I cower in my bed and squeeze Livie's hands until she whimpers slightly. *Good God, please . . . no! He wouldn't.*

An older version of Trent turns the corner and steps into my room, sorrow marring his handsome features.

Trent's father.

Cole's father.

Fuck. I don't even know what to call him anymore.

"I want you to listen to what Mr. Reynolds has to say. Nothing more. Just listen. Can you manage that?" Dr. Stayner asks me.

I think I nod, but I'm not sure. I'm too busy staring at this man's face. It reminds me so much of *his* face. *His* eyes that I fell into day after day. Happy. In love. Yes. In love. I was in love with Trent. With my life's murderer.

"We'll be here with you the whole time," Storm says, gripping my free hand.

Trent/Cole's father clears his throat. "Hello, Kacey."

I don't respond. I watch him slide his hands into his pockets and hold them there. Just like his son does. "My name is Carter Reynolds. You can call me Carter."

A shiver runs through my body at the sound of that family name.

"I want to apologize to you for all that my son has put you and your sister through. I tried to do so four years ago, but the police issued the restraining orders. My family and I respected your privacy. Unfortunately, Cole . . . Trent has since harmed you again."

He takes a few steps farther into the room until he's at the foot of my bed, casting a furtive look at Dr. Stayner, who smiles at him. "It was our car . . . my car . . . that Sasha drove the night of the accident." A frown flashes across his face. "I think you knew that, though, right? Insurance papers would have indicated that."

He pauses as if he's waiting for me to acknowledge what he's said. I don't.

"We lost Cole after the accident. He ceased to exist. He dropped out of Michigan State, quit football, cut off all contact with his friends. He left his girlfriend of four years and stopped drinking altogether. He changed his name from Cole Reynolds to

Trent Emerson—his middle name and his mother's maiden name."

Carter pauses, his lips pressing together in a slight scowl. "That accident tore our family apart. His mother and I divorced a year later." He waves his hand dismissively. "That doesn't matter. What I do want you to know is that Cole . . . er . . . Trent is a troubled young man. Two years after the accident, I found him in my garage with the car running and a hose connected to the tailpipe. We thought we lost him for good that night." Carter's voice cracks with emotion and I feel an unwelcome spike of pain from the image. "Soon after that, we admitted him to Dr. Stayner's inpatient program for post-traumatic stress disorder." Again, Carter looks to the doctor to see him smiling and nodding him on. "When they released Trent, it was with a seal of approval. We were sure he had recovered. He laughed and smiled again. He began calling us regularly. He enrolled in a graphic design school in Rochester. He seemed to have moved on. He even attended outpatient programs and therapy groups to help others get through their grief.

"Then, six weeks ago, it looked like he was having a relapse. He appeared on his mother's doorstep, mumbling something about you and how you'll never forgive him. We brought him here and admitted him to Dr. Stayner."

I fight hard to school the shock from my face. So all the time that Trent was missing, he was here, in Chicago. In a hospital for PTSD, the thing of which he was insistent on curing me.

"A few days after his release, Trent was ecstatic again. We couldn't figure it out. We thought maybe he was manic or on drugs. Dr. Stayner said no to both. He couldn't tell us what was going on, because of patient–doctor privilege.

"And I didn't know what was going on, to be clear. Trent hid critical information during his sessions with me, knowing I wouldn't approve," Dr. Stayner interrupts.

"Right," Carter dips his head in assent. "We figured it out

three days ago, when his mother ran into the receptionist here and she asked if Trent and Kacey had worked things out. She didn't think anything of it, given that Trent had mentioned to her he had a girlfriend named Kacey and they were having trouble. I guess he felt telling the receptionist was low risk."

Carter sighs. "When my son left the inpatient program two years ago, he did so with the belief that if he could fix your life, he would be forgiven for all the pain that he had caused." He looks down at the floor now, as a shadow of shame crosses his face. "My son has been watching you from a distance for two years, Kacey. Biding his time until he approached you."

I hardly notice Livie's fingers dig into my forearm. Trent has been following me? *Stalking* me? All because he wants to fix what he broke? *I want to make you happy. Make you smile.* His words play back in my head. It all makes sense now. He truly did. He was on a mission to fix me.

"His mother and I had no idea, Kacey. Honestly. But Trent has watched over you for the past two years. He knew someone from school who could hack into your email. That's how he found out you were moving to Miami. We had no clue that he up and left New York. But he did, leaving his condo and his life to come to follow you with this notion that if he could fix your life, he would be forgiven. We talked daily over email and voice mail. He even came to visit his mother once."

"So I was a project," I mutter to myself. A peace project.

Nausea. That's all I feel right now. Thick bile rises up my throat as this realization hits. He never cared about me. I was a step in a fucked-up twelve-step program he created in his head. "It doesn't matter." My voice is hollow. It really doesn't matter.

All the good that Trent brought to my life is dead. This person was never really alive.

Storm speaks up now, for the first time since Carter stepped in. "Kacey, Dan wants you to press charges against Trent. What he did is wrong and illegal and fucked up on so many levels. He deserves to go to jail."

I smirk to myself. Storm never swears. She must be really mad.

"But I made him wait to report it until you were feeling better and you could make the call. I thought that should be your call." She adds with a low growl, "Even though I want to shoot the bastard in the head."

I nod slowly. *Report Trent. Charge Trent. Trent goes to jail.*

"His mother and I understand if you want to press charges," Carter says calmly, but I see his shoulders droop from the thought of losing his only son.

"No." The word surprises me as it leaves my lips.

Carter's brow raises, surprised. "No?"

"Kacey, are you sure?" Livie asks, her hand squeezing mine.

I look at her and I nod. I have no idea why, but I know that I don't want to do that. I'm sure I hate Trent. I'm sure I have to hate him because he's Cole, and hatred for Cole is all that I know.

I look up at Carter, imagining this man pulling his son's limp body from his car, and it's not hatred that I feel right now; it's pity. For him, and for Trent, because I'm intimately familiar with the level of pain that would drive a person to do that. It's an end that has danced through my own thoughts once or twice over the years.

"No. No charges. No police. It won't change anything."

Carter squeezes his eyelids shut for a moment. "Thank you." The words are hoarse and full of emotion. He clears his throat. With a look at Livie, he adds, "I understand there is a matter of Livie's custody."

"No, there's no matter. She's under my custody." I turn to glare at Livie. Why did she tell him?

"I called Aunt Darla," she explained softly. "I didn't know if you were going to make it for a while. She said she could take me home with her and—"

"No! No! You can't leave me!" I yell suddenly, my heart rate spiking.

"She's not going anywhere, Kacey," Carter promises. "Except back to Miami to go to school. My firm will ensure all the legal custody paperwork is drawn up. Custody may need to go to Ms. Matthews for now, until you're better or Livie is old enough."

I nod numbly. "Th . . . thanks." He's helping us. Why is he helping us?

He gives me a firm smile. "I've also had a conversation with your uncle." His eyes turn cold and hard. "There is still insurance money left, Kacey. He didn't squander it all. I'll see to it that it is all transferred into your and your sister's names." He pulls something from his inside coat pocket. "Here's my business card, should you ever need anything. Ever, Kacey. Livie. Anything. I will help in any way that I can." He places it on a side table.

With a nod to Dr. Stayner, he heads toward the door, his shoulders slouched as if carrying a terrible burden. And I suppose he is, after what his son has done. He stops with a hand on the doorknob. "For what it's worth, I've never seen Trent as happy as he's been while with you. Never."

■ ■ ■

I stare at the clinic's large oak doors. They contrast so greatly to the sterile white stucco exterior. Still, it's a nice building.

My home for the next little while.

A tiny hand slips inside mine and I don't recoil. "Don't worry. It's not so bad and, if you're good, when you get out, we'll go get ice cream," Mia says with a somber face. She and Dan spent their time visiting Chicago's zoos and parks while Storm stayed with me.

Now they're here to see me off. She raises her free hand with two fingers held high. "Three scoops!"

Storm slides up behind her with Dan hanging on to her arm, laughing. "That's right, Mia." She winks at me.

"Ready?" Livie asks, hooking her arm through mine.

Inhaling deeply, I look at the place again. "It looks a little posh."

"Don't worry. I know a guy who knows a guy . . . who knows a guy." Dan grins. For some reason, I don't believe him. I have a feeling that Carter Reynolds's manicured hands are somehow in the mix. Maybe I'm a buy-one-get-one-free offer for Stayner not curing his son. Given Dr. Stayner's track record, I don't know why they think he can help me. For once, though, I don't fight it.

Livie and I walk forward, our steps mirroring each other's. "Thank you for doing this, Kacey," she whispers, wiping away the tear that rolls down her cheek.

A man in a light blue uniform opens the door and reaches forward, offering to take my bag.

"I'll call as often as they let me," Livie calls out, giving my forearm one last squeeze before letting go.

I wink, putting on a brave face for her. "See you above water."

EIGHTEEN

I won't survive this.

I can't survive this.

All they want me to do is talk. Talk and talk and talk. About my feelings, my nightmares, the almost assault on Storm's attacker, my dead parents, Jenny, Billy, Trent. Every time I shove it all back into that dark, cramped closet where it belongs, Dr. Stayner barges in and drags it back out like a madman on a mission, with me kicking and screaming as I hang on to his coattails.

None of this will help me.

Neither will the antianxiety meds. They make me feel tired and nauseated. Dr. Stayner tells me they take time to work.

I tell him I'm going to punch him in the face.

I hate his guts.

And when I close my eyes at night, Trent is there to greet me, laughing. Always laughing.

I tell that to Dr. Stayner one day in his office, during my daily private session. "Do you think he's laughing, Kacey?" he asks.

"That's what I just said, isn't it?"

"No, you told me you had a dream about him laughing at you. But do you believe that he's laughing?"

I shrug. "I don't know."

"Don't you?"

I glare at him. This conversation has gone on far longer than I expected. This is what I get for opening my big mouth. Normally, I stay quiet and give simple "yes" and "no" answers. Those have worked well for me so far. I don't know why I thought this would be an innocuous topic.

"Let's think about this a moment, shall we, Kacey?" He leans back in his chair and he just sits there, watching me. Is he thinking about this? Does he think I'm thinking? This is unnerving. I let my focus roam around his office to distract myself from the awkward silence. It's small and clinical. He has walls upon walls of books, just like any normal shrink should have. But he's not like any other shrink that I've met. I don't know how to describe him. His voice, his mannerisms—they're all unusual.

"Trent is a young college guy who drank too much one night—like most college students. Then he made a horrible, stupid mistake."

My hands clench and I lean forward in my chair, imagining myself spurting acid from my teeth to melt Stayner's skin. "*Mistake?*" I hiss. I hate that word. I hate when they use that word to describe that night. "My parents are dead."

Dr. Stayner's finger pokes the air. "That's the *result* of his horrible, stupid mistake. That's not his horrible, stupid mistake, though, is it?" When I don't answer, too busy glaring at the navy-blue checkered carpet on the floor, I feel something pelt my forehead. I look down to see a paper clip on my lap.

"Did you just throw a paper clip at me?" I ask, shocked.

"Answer the question."

I grit my teeth.

"What was Trent's horrible, stupid, life-altering mistake?" Dr. Stayner pushes.

"He drove home," I grumble.

Another paper clip pelts my forehead as Dr. Stayner shakes his head frantically, his voice rising a notch. "No."

"He gave his keys to his friend to drive home."

"Bingo! He made a choice—in his inebriated state—a choice that he shouldn't ever have made. A very bad and very dangerous choice. And when he sobered up, he learned that that choice killed six people." There's a long pause. "Put yourself in his shoes for a moment, Kacey."

"I will not—"

Dr. Stayner anticipates and cuts my objection off at the kneecaps. "You've been drunk before, right?"

I purse my lips tightly.

"Haven't you?"

A night flashes in my mind without much thought. Six months before the accident, Jenny and I went to a field party and got loaded off Jäger bombs. It was one of the most fun nights I'd ever had. The next morning was another story.

"That's right," Dr. Stayner continues as if he can read my mind. Maybe he can. Maybe he's a super-freak quack. "You probably did a few stupid things, said a few stupid things."

I nod begrudgingly.

"How drunk were you?"

I shrug. "I don't know. I was . . . drunk."

"Yes, but how drunk?"

I level him with a glower. "What is wrong with you? Why are you prying so much?"

He ignores me. "Would you have driven home?"

"Uh, no?"

"And why not?"

"Because I was fifteen at the time, genius!" My fingers are turning white now, gripping on to the chair handles tightly.

"Right," he waves his hand dismissively. "But apparently his point hasn't been made. "What about your friend? Friends? Exactly how drunk were they?"

I shrug. "I don't know. Drunk."

"Was it easy to tell? Was it so obvious that they were drunk?"

I frown as I think back to Jenny dancing and singing on top of a picnic table to Hannah Montana. Exactly how drunk she was, I have no clue. Jenny would do that dead sober. Finally I shrug, the memory bringing a painful lump to the back of my throat.

"What if, at the end of the night, your friends told you they had stopped drinking hours ago and could drive home? Would you believe them?"

"No," I answer quickly.

That finger goes up again, waggling. "Think about that for a minute now, Kacey. We've all been there. Out for a good night, had a few drinks. You know you can't drive, but do you automatically not trust anyone else? I've been there, myself."

"Are you making excuses for drunk driving, Dr. Stayner?"

He's shaking his head furiously. "Absolutely not, Kacey. There's no excuse. Only terrible consequences that people have to live with for the rest of their lives when they make one stupid decision."

We're silent for a moment, the doctor no doubt still waiting for my answer.

I look at my hands. "I guess that could happen," I begrudgingly admit. *Yeah*, thinking back, there may have been one or two times that I climbed into a car, assuming the driver was fine because she said so.

"Yes, it could." Dr. Stayner nods knowingly. "And it did happen. To Cole."

My rage ignites suddenly. "What the hell are you doing? Are you on his side?" I snap.

"I'm on no one's side, Kacey." His voice has returned to being even and calm. "When I hear your story—the tragic *accident*—I can't help but empathize with everyone involved. You. Your family. The boys who died because they didn't do something as simple as buckle their seat belts. And Cole, the guy who handed someone his keys. When I hear his story, I feel—"

I storm out of Dr. Stayner's office then, with his shouts of "empathy!" following me down the hall, into my room, looking for ways to crawl into my soul and torment me.

■ ■ ■

"How's it going there?"

I want to reach into the phone and hug Livie. It's been seven days and I miss her terribly. I've never been away from her for this long. Even while I was in the hospital after the crash, she visited me almost every day.

"Dr. Stayner is definitely unconventional," I mutter.

"Why?"

I sigh, exasperated, and then tell her what I know she doesn't want to hear. "He's a nut job, Livie! He yells, he pushes, he tells me what to think. He's everything that a shrink isn't supposed to be. I don't know what quack school he went to, but I can see why Trent came out of here more fucked up than when he went in."

Trent. My stomach tightens. *Forget about him, Kace. He's gone. Dead to you.*

There's a pause. "But is it working? Are you going to get better?"

"I don't know yet, Livie. I just don't know if anything will ever really get better."

■ ■ ■

Jenny laughs hysterically as a car passes us on the road. "Did you see the look on Raileigh's face when I belted out 'Super Freak'? It was classic."

I laugh along with her. "You sure you're okay to drive?" After I jumped off the hood of George's truck and tackled one of Billy's friends to the ground, I knew there was no way I was in any state to get behind the wheel, so I gave her my keys.

She waves her hand dismissively. "Oh, yeah. I stopped drinking, like, hours ago! I'm—"

A bright flash of lights distracts us both. They're headlights and they're close. Too close.

My body jerks as Dad's Audi crashes into something, my seat belt cutting into my neck from the force as a deafening sound explodes in the air. In seconds it's over and there's nothing left but silence and an eerie feeling, as if all my senses are both paralyzed and working in overdrive.

"What happened?"

Nothing. No answer.

"Jenny?" I look to my side. It's dark now, but I can see enough to know she's not sitting behind the wheel anymore. And I know we're in trouble. "Jenny?" I call again, my voice shaky. I manage to unbuckle my seat belt and open my car door. There's that saying, "scared sober." I know that's what I am now as I walk around the front of the car, keenly aware of the engine's hiss and the smoke rising from the mangled hood. It's totaled. My hands push through my hair as panic rises inside me. "Ohmigod, Dad's going to—"

A pair of sandals on the ground stop me dead.

Jenny's sandals.

"Jenny!" I scream, scrambling over to the patch of grass where she's lying facedown, unmoving. "Jenny!" I shake her. She doesn't respond.

I need to get help. I need to find my phone. I need to . . .

It's then that I notice another hunk of metal.

Another car.

It's in far worse shape than the Audi.

My stomach sinks. I can faintly make out the outline of people *in it. I stand and start waving my arms around frantically, without thought. "Help!" I scream. There's no point. We're on a dark wooded road in the middle of nowhere.*

Finally giving up, I creep over to the car, my heart pounding in my ears. "Hello?" I whisper. I don't know if I'm more terrified to hear something or nothing at all.

I get no answer.

I lean in and squint, trying to get a glimpse through the broken glass. I can't see . . . it's too dark . . .

Snap. Snap. Snap . . . Like stage lights, suddenly a rush of light pours down over the area, illuminating the horrific scene within. An older couple sits hunched over in the front seat and I have to look away, the mess of bloody flesh too gruesome to handle.

It's too late for them. I just know it.

But there's someone in the back, too. I rush over and peer in to see a broken body with raven-dark hair cradled in the contorted door.

"Ohmigod," I gasp, my knees buckling.

It's Livie.

Why the hell is she in this car?

"Kacey." Ice-cold fingers grip my heart at the sound of my name. I peer farther in and find a tall, dark form sitting next to her. Trent. He's hurt. Bad. But he's awake and he's looking at me with an intense stare.

"You murdered my parents, Kacey. You're a murderer."

The night nurse, Sara, rushes into my room just as I'm coming to, screaming at the top of my lungs. "It's okay, Kacey. Shh, it's okay." She rubs my back in slow circular motions as a cold sweat breaks out over my body. She continues to do so even as I curl up in the fetal position, hugging my knees to my chest tightly. "That one was unusually bad, Kacey." She's been in here a few times already, during my nighttime episodes. "What was it about?" I notice she doesn't ask me if I want to talk about it. She assumes I need to, whether I want to or not. That's the thing about this place. All they want you to do is talk. And all I want to do is stay quiet.

"Hmm, Kacey?"

I swallow the prickly lump in my throat. "Empathy."

. . .

"So maybe you're right."

Dr. Stayner's brow curves up in question. "Is this about the dream you had last night?"

My scowl tells him it is.

"Yes, Sara told me. She wanted me to know in case I should be concerned. That's her job. She didn't betray you." He says it like it's a line he's said time and time again. "What happened exactly?"

For whatever reason, I tell him the entire nightmare, from beginning to end, shivers running over my body as I relive it.

"And what made it so horrible?"

I cock my head and glare at the doctor. Clearly he hasn't been listening to me. "What do you mean? Everyone was dead. Jenny was dead, Trent's parents were dead. I killed Livie. It was just . . . so awful!"

"You killed Livie?"

"Well, yes. It's my fault."

"Hmm . . ." He nods, giving nothing away. "How did you feel when you saw Jenny lying there, dead?"

My hands anxiously press against my stomach from the thought.

"So you mourned her," he answered for me.

"Of course I did. She was dead. I'm not a sociopath."

"But she was driving the car that crashed into Trent's family. Into Livie. How can you possibly mourn her?"

I'm rambling faster than I'm thinking. "Because it's Jenny. She'd never want to hurt anyone. She didn't do it on purpose—"

I stop short and glare at him, clueing in. "Sasha is not Jenny. I see what you're doing."

"And what is that?"

"You're trying to make me see Sasha and Trent as people who laugh and cry and have families."

His know-it-all brows rise.

"It's not the same! I hate them! I hate Trent! He's a murderer!"

Dr. Stayner leaps out of his chair and runs over to his bookshelf, pulling out the biggest dictionary I've ever seen. He storms over and throws it into my lap. "There. Look up the word 'murder,' Kacey. Do it! Look it up!" He doesn't wait for me to, likely feeling his asinine point has been made. "You're not a stupid girl, Kacey. You can hide behind that word or you accept it for what it is. Trent is not a murderer, and you don't hate him. You know both are true, so stop lying to me and, more importantly, stop lying to yourself."

"Yes I do hate him," I spit back, my voice losing some of its strength.

I hate Dr. Stayner right now.

I hate him because in the back of my mind, I know he's right.

NINETEEN

Dr. Stayner leads me into a small white room with a window overlooking another small white room. "Is this a one-way mirror?" I knock on it.

"Yes, it is, Kacey. Sit down."

"Okay, Dr. Dictator," I grumble, flopping into the proffered chair.

"Thank you, Patient Pain in the Ass."

I smirk. Sometimes Dr. Stayner's unconventional methods make this less painful. Mostly not, but sometimes.

"What punishment do you have in store for me today?" I ask nonchalantly as the door on the other side of the mirror pushes open. My body goes rigid and I inhale deeply when I see the face walking through.

It's Trent.

Cole.

Trent.

Fuck.

It's been weeks since I saw him last. With that light brown messy hair of his, striding in with those long, lean muscles, he's as beautiful as ever. That much I have to admit. And I hate admitting it. Except now I see no smile on his face. No dimples. Nothing that resembles the charming guy I fell in love with.

In love with. I clench my teeth to fight the ache that comes with that recognition.

He takes the chair positioned directly in front of me. I don't even need to know Trent to recognize the raw agony in his eyes. But because I do know him, or some slice of him, that pain screams out to me.

And it's intolerable. Instinctively, I want to reach out and take it away.

Dr. Stayner's hands push down on my shoulders a second before I can bolt out of the room. "He can't see you, Kacey. He can't hear you."

"What's he doing here?" I whisper, my voice shaky. "Why are you doing this to me?"

"You keep saying you hate Trent and we both know you don't. He's here so you'll admit that to yourself once and for all and move on. There's no room in your recovery to hang on to hatred."

I can't pry my eyes away from Trent, even as I deny Dr. Stayner's words. "You are one fucked-up, twisted doc—"

Dr. Stayner cuts me off. "You know that he's also my patient, Kacey. And he needs as much help as you do. He also suffers from PTSD. He also deluded himself into thinking he could bury his pain instead of deal with it appropriately. He just did it in a less conventional way. We won't talk about that now." I flinch as he pats my shoulder. "Today, I'm cheating a little. This is a two-for-one session."

"I knew it." I shoot an accusatory finger up at him.

Dr. Stayner smiles as if my reaction is funny. I don't find any of this funny. I wonder what the medical board will think of this when I report him.

"This is as much for Trent's healing as it is for yours, Kacey.

You are going to sit, and you are going to listen to what he has to say. After this, you won't see him again. He's leaving after today to go back home. He's doing well, but treating him effectively when he knows you're in this building has been impossible. I can't risk the two of you running into each other. Do you understand?"

An unintelligible grunt is my only answer. Trent has been here this entire time and Dr. Stayner didn't warn me? My stomach spasms with the thought of turning a corner and running face-first into him again, unprepared.

Dr. Stayner leans over to flip a switch beside a speaker. I could bolt right now. I could. I'd probably get away. But I don't. I just sit and stare at this guy whom I know so well, and not at all, and I wonder what he could possibly have to say. And as much as part of me wants to, I can't force myself to look away.

"He can't see you. He wanted it that way. There's a red light to tell him his microphone is now on," Dr. Stayner explains, and I hear a soft click behind me. Glancing back, I see that he's stepped out of the room, leaving me to face the guy who destroyed me twice.

I wait with balled fists and a clenched stomach as Trent shifts in his chair, pulling it toward me until his knees touch the glass. He leans forward and rests his elbows on his thighs, dropping his focus to his fingers, fidgeting. Those fingers, those hands— they were my salvation not long ago. How could things change so quickly?

With slow, almost pained movements, Trent looks up, and he's level with me, boring into my eyes, those light blue irises flecked with turquoise landing on me with such force that I'm sure he can see me. I panic, shifting to the left and right. His pupils don't follow. *Okay, so maybe Stayner isn't lying.*

"Hey, Kacey," Trent says softly.

Hi, I mouth back before I can stop myself, the sound of his voice wrenching at my guts.

Trent clears his voice. "This is a bit weird, talking to myself in a mirror, but it's the only way I knew I could get through saying all that I needed to say, so . . . I'm happy that you're here, with Dr. Stayner. He's a great doctor, Kacey. Trust him. I wish I had trusted him fully. Then maybe I wouldn't have put you through all this." He presses his lips together and looks away. I'm sure his eyes turn glassy, but they're normal when he turns back to face me again.

"What happened that night four years ago was the worse decision I've ever made, and one that I will live to regret for the rest of my life. If I could turn back time, and save your family, save my family, save Sasha and Derek, I would. I'd do it. I'd do anything to change it." His Adam's apple bobs up and down as he swallows. "Sasha—" He dips his head again. I close my eyes at the sound of that name. It still hurts, hearing it, but not as much anymore. Not since Dr. Stayner's lesson on empathy. When I open my eyes, Trent faces me again, tears of hurt and loss spilling down his cheek.

That's all it takes. My body constricts, the sight of him so upset slashing through any defenses I had left. My hands fly to cover my mouth, tears springing to my eyes before I can stop them. I madly brush them away, but they just keep coming. After everything, seeing Trent in pain still burns me.

And it's because I don't hate him. I can't. I loved him. If I'm honest with myself, I may still love him. I don't even care that he basically stalked me. I don't know why I don't but I know that I don't.

There, Dr. Stayner. I admit it. Damn you!

"Sasha was a good guy, Kacey. You won't believe me, but you would have liked him. I grew up with him." Trent smiles sadly now, reminiscing. "He was like a brother to me. He didn't deserve what happened to him but, in a strange way, it's better this way. He wouldn't have lasted ten minutes with that kind of guilt. He—" Trent's voice cracks as he runs his thumb across his cheeks to wipe away his tears. "He was a good guy."

Trent's gaze roams the perimeter of the glass window. "I know you must hate me, Kacey. You hated Cole. So much. But I'm not Cole, Kacey. I'm not that guy anymore." He pauses and inhales deeply. When he speaks again, his voice is steady and even, his eyes brighter, his shoulders held a tiny bit higher. "I can't fix what I did to you. All I can say is that I'm sorry. That, and dedicate my life to letting others out there know how much this mistake can cost. How much it can hurt." His voice drifts off. "That much I can do. For me and for you."

With a slow, cautious movement, he lifts a shaky hand and presses it against the glass. He holds it there.

And I can't help myself.

I match my fingers perfectly to his, imagining what it would be like to feel his skin again, to have those fingers curl over mine, pull me in to him, into his warmth. Into his life.

We stay like that, hand against hand, tears rolling down my cheeks, for a long moment. Then his hand drops back to his lap and his voice turns soft.

"I wanted to tell you in person that, even though my intentions were wrong . . ." He swallows, his voice husky. "I thought that making you fall in love with me would fix everything else I had done to you. I thought I could make you happy, Kacey. Happy enough that if you ever did find out, you'd be okay with it." He dips his head into his hands, holding his face for a moment before he lifts it again. A sad smirk touches his lips. "How fucked up is that?"

There's a long pause, a chance for me to study him, to remember all those days and nights of laughter and happiness. I can't believe it was real. It feels like a lifetime ago. "What I felt for you was real, Kacey." Now he levels the glass with a gaze full of heat and emotion. One of his Trent stares that buckles my knees. "It still is real. I just can't hold on to it anymore. We both need a chance to heal."

My heart leaps into my throat. "It *is* still real," I confirm out loud, softly. It is real.

Fresh tears spill down my cheeks as I realize what's happening. Trent is saying goodbye.

"I hope that one day you can heal from all of this, and someone can make you laugh. You have such a beautiful laugh, Kacey Cleary."

"No," I whisper suddenly, my brow furrowing. "No!" Both of my hands fly to the glass to pound on it. I'm not ready for goodbye, I realize. Not like this. Not yet.

Maybe not ever.

I can't explain it. I sure as hell don't want to feel it. But I do.

I hold my breath as I watch Trent stand and walk out of the room, stiff-backed. The sight of the door closing—of Trent walking out of my life forever—unleashes a torrent of sobs.

TWENTY

I study the titles in Dr. Stayner's library, busying myself so I don't have to look at the fat lip I gave him after yesterday's group session. It complements the black eye I gave him in last week's session. Since the day Trent said goodbye, I've been feeling emptier than ever before. There can be no doubt—Trent or Cole, mistake or murderer—that man had a strong hold on my heart, and he's taken a chunk of it with him.

"So, my sons have taken to calling Wednesdays 'Dad's Ass Whupping Wednesdays,'" Dr. Stayner announces.

Well, now that it's out in the open, I can't very well avoid it. "Sorry," I mumble, hazarding a glance at his face and wincing.

He smiles. "Don't be. I know I pushed you a bit harder than I probably should have. Normally I ease my patients into talking about their trauma. I thought a more aggressive approach might work for you."

"What gave you that brilliant idea?"

"Because you've compartmentalized your emotions and pain so tightly that we might need dynamite to break through," he jokes. "I mean, look at you. You're a trained fighter. You could probably set my sons straight. In fact, I might have you over for dinner to beat the snot out of them soon."

I roll my eyes at my unconventional quack of a doctor. "I wouldn't go that far."

"I would. You've taken all that tragedy and channeled it into one hell of a tough defense mechanism." His voice turns softer. "But all defense mechanisms can be broken. I think you've already learned that."

"Trent—" His name drifts over my tongue.

He nods. "We're not going to talk about the accident today." My shoulders slump with that news. That's usually all Dr. Stayner wants to talk about. I wait as he makes himself comfortable in his chair. "We're going to talk about coping. About all the ways that a person can cope. The good, the bad, and the ugly."

Dr. Stayner goes through a laundry list of coping mechanisms, marking each one off on a finger, cycling through his hands several times. "Drugs, alcohol, sex, anorexia, violence—" I sit and listen, wondering where he's going with this. "An obsession with 'saving' or 'fixing' that which is broken." I know who he's talking about.

I was Trent's coping mechanism.

"All these mechanisms seem like they help at the time, but in the end, they leave you weak and vulnerable. They're not healthy. They're not sustainable. No human can lead a healthy, fulfilling life with lines of cocaine by their bedside. Make sense so far?"

I nod. I'm no good for Trent. That's what Dr. Stayner is saying. That's why Trent said goodbye. The wound inside is still raw from that day, but I don't bury the pain. I'm done burying it. There's no point. Dr. Stayner will drag it right back where it's impossible to avoid, like a buffalo carcass sprawled out on a one-lane highway.

"Good. Now, Kacey, we need to find you a coping method that works for you. Kickboxing is not it. It helps you channel your rage, yes. But let's find a way to permanently extinguish that rage.

I want you to brainstorm with me. What do you think are healthy coping mechanisms?"

"If I knew, I'd be doing them, wouldn't I?"

I get an eye roll. An eye roll from a professional! "Come on now, you're a smart girl. Think back to all the things you've heard. What other people have suggested. I'll get you started. Talking to others about the trauma is one."

Now it's my turn to roll my eyes.

Dr. Stayner waves his hands dismissively. "I know, I know. Believe me, you've made yourself clear. But talking about your pain and sharing it with others is one of the most powerful ways to cope. It helps you release the hurt, not bottle it up until you explode. Other ways to cope include painting, and reading, setting goals, journaling about your feelings."

Hmmm. I could do journaling. It's still a private activity.

"Yoga's fantastic too. It helps clear your mind; it makes you focus on your breathing."

Breathing. "Ten tiny breaths," I murmur more to myself than aloud, feeling my lips curl with the irony.

"What's that?" Dr. Stayner leans forward, pushing his bifocals up with one finger.

I shake my head. "No, nothing. Something my mother used to say. 'Take ten tiny breaths.'"

"When did she say that?"

"Whenever I was sad or upset or nervous."

Dr. Stayner's fingers rub his chin. "I see. And did she say anything else? Do you remember?"

I smirk. Of course I remember. It's firmly emblazoned in my mind. "She would say, 'Just breathe, Kacey. Ten tiny breaths. Seize them. Feel them. Love them.'"

There's a long pause. "And what do you think she meant by that?"

I frown irritably. "She was telling me to breathe."

"Hmmm." He rolls a pen over the surface of his desk as if in deep thought. "And how will tiny breaths help? Why tiny? Why not deep breaths?"

I slap my hands on his desk. "That's what I always wondered. Now you see why it always confused me."

But he doesn't see. By the tiny crook of his lips, he sees something different. Something that I don't see. "Do you think it matters if they're tiny or deep?"

I scowl. I don't like these kinds of games. "What do you think she meant by it?"

"What do *you* think she meant by it?"

I want to punch Dr. Stayner in the mouth again. I *really, really* want to punch him again.

■ ■ ■

Just breathe, Kacey. Ten tiny breaths. Seize them. Feel them. Love them. I play these words over and over in my head the way I have a thousand times before to no avail, as I lie awake in my cell that's not actually a cell. It's a nice small room with a private bath and sunny yellow walls, but I feel confined all the same.

Dr. Stayner knew what my mom meant right away. I could tell by that snotty smirk on his face. I guess you have to be super smart. Dr. Stayner is obviously super smart. I, obviously, am not.

I inhale deeply, jogging my memory of the conversation. What did he say, again? Breathing can be a coping mechanism. And then he questioned the tiny breaths. But he set me up. He already had the answer to it. And the answer is . . .

One . . . two . . . three . . . I count to ten, hoping profound wisdom will strike me. It doesn't.

Do you think it matters if they're tiny or deep? he asked. Well, if they're not tiny breaths and they're not deep breaths, then they're just . . . breaths. Then you're just breathing for the sake of . . . breathing.

. . . *Seize them. Feel them. Love them* . . .

I bolt upright, a weird calming sensation flows through my body as the answer dawns on me.

It's so simple. God, it's so fucking simple.

stage eight

. . .

RECOVERY

TWENTY-ONE

Six weeks later. Group therapy.

One . . . two . . . three . . . four . . . five . . . six . . . seven . . . eight . . . nine . . . ten.

I try not to fidget with my fingers as they sit folded in my lap. "My name is Kacey Cleary. Four years ago, my car was hit by a drunk driver. My mother and father, my best friend, and my boyfriend were all killed. I had to sit in the car, holding my dead boyfriend's hand, listening to my mother take her last breath, until the paramedics could free me." I pause to swallow. *One . . . two . . . three . . .* I take deep breaths this time. Long, deep breaths. They're not tiny. They're huge. They're monumental.

"I used alcohol and drugs to drown out the pain at first. Then I moved on to violence and sex. But now"—I look directly at Dr. Stayner—"I just appreciate the fact that I can hug my sister, and laugh with my friends, and walk, and run. That I am alive. That I can breathe."

I'm above water.

And this time I'm staying where I belong.

■ ■ ■

A loud rush of clapping greets me at Penny's as I turn the corner to find everyone waiting for me. Nate's the first to greet me, stooping down and lifting me up into an enormous bear hug. I don't even flinch from the contact. I've learned to appreciate it fully again.

"I always knew you were batshit crazy!" Ben hollers from somewhere. I whirl around in time for him to scoop me up and hold me tight to his body. "And tough as nails, for surviving all of that," he adds softly in my ear. "I would have cried like a five-year-old girl. You okay?"

I pat his arm as he puts me down. "I'm getting there. I've got a really long road ahead."

"Well, it hasn't been the same without you here, I can tell you that much," he says. His brow furrows. "Hey, so is that your sister over there?" His head nods toward Livie, who's standing with Storm and Dan. "Because, I was thinking of asking her—"

"She's fifteen." I smack him playfully in the stomach. "Have they not taught you the meaning of statutory rape in school yet, Lawyer Boy?"

His eyes widen in surprise, his hands rise up in a sign of surrender. "Dammit," I hear him mutter under his breath, shaking his head as he gives Livie another quick once-over.

It's just before opening and the girls are in their outfits—or lack thereof—so Mia has stayed home with a sitter. Livie's eyes stick to Storm and Dan, afraid to wander anywhere. Tanner's there, too, his jaw hanging open shamelessly.

The biggest surprise though? My unconventional quack is there.

"I'm not sure this constitutes healthy patient–doctor protocol," I joke, poking him in the ribs.

He chuckles as he throws his arm around me in a side hug.

"Neither does punching your doctor in the face . . . twice, but I let that slide, so do me a solid."

Livie and Storm's mouths drop open while Dan and Ben double over, laughing.

"Champagne, anyone?" Cain sweeps through with a pat on my back and a tray of tall, filled flutes. A twinge of familiarity saddens the moment as I remember the last time someone handed me a champagne flute. I was with Trent.

I miss him. I miss his eyes, his touch, the way he made me feel.

That's right. I can admit it to myself now without guilt or anger or resentment.

I miss Trent. I miss him every day.

A hand slips under my elbow and squeezes. It's Storm. She somehow senses the turmoil inside me. She understands.

"To the toughest nut I've ever had the pleasure of cracking," Dr. Stayner announces, and we all clink glasses and sip.

"So, am I cured, Doc?" I ask, savoring the sweet fizzy liquid in my mouth. It reminds me of Trent's mouth, of the last time that he kissed me.

He winks. "I'll never use the word 'cured,' Kacey. 'Healed' is a better word. There's one last epic step in your recovery before I'd say you're on your way to healing properly, though."

My brow quirks. "Oh yeah? And what's that?"

"I can't tell you. You'll know when you know. Trust me."

"Trust a quack?"

"A very expensive quack," he adds with a wink.

Speaking of which . . . "So who is this friend of a friend of a friend of Dan's who got me in to see you? I should probably thank them," I ask innocently.

Dr. Stayner's eyes flash to Storm and then quickly avert to the bar. "Oh, look! Caviar!" He slips away to investigate a platter, which no doubt does *not* have caviar. That pretty much confirms it for me, but I play along anyway. "Livie?"

She looks like the proverbial cat who swallowed the canary. "Don't get mad?"

I wait, smoothing my expression.

"Trent's dad paid for it all."

I mock gasp and level her with my best glare.

Livie rushes to explain, all flustered and red-faced. "You needed help, Kacey, and it's really expensive help. I didn't want to put you in some government-paid shitty program because they didn't help you last time, and the wait lists were too long, and—" Tears well up. "Carter had you listed as Dr. Stayner's patient in under an hour. Dr. Stayner is a friend of theirs and he's really good, and—" The tears are streaming now. "Please don't regress. You're doing so well. Please don't."

"Livie!" I grab hold of her shoulders and shake her. "It's okay. I figured it out already. And you did the right thing."

She swallows. "I did?" There's a pause and then she punches my arm, her face twisting in a scowl. "You knew and you let me freak out?"

I laugh and pull her to me in a tight hug. "Yes, Livie. You always do the right thing. You know, I always think I need to take care of you, but in truth you're the one who takes care of me. You always have."

She laughs softly as she rubs tears away with the back of her hand.

I pause, not sure if I should ask, but I do anyway. "Have you talked to Carter about Trent?"

Livie nods and offers me a gentle smile. I told her about Trent's goodbye. I'm pretty sure I heard her crying through the phone. Even she can't hate Trent. "Carter calls me every few weeks to check in. Trent's doing well, Kacey. Really well," she whispers.

"Good," I nod, smiling. I don't ask any more. It's best that we stay apart; I know that. But it still hurts inside. God, it still hurts. But feeling is okay, I tell myself. I won't hurt forever.

"So, girls, I have to tell you something," Storm interrupts us and looks up at Dan. With a nod from him, she announces, "I'm leaving Penny's. I'm going to open up an acrobatics school!"

Livie and I must be mirror images, both of our jaws are hanging open.

"But that's not all. Dan just bought a house on the beach, and he's asked Mia and me to move in with him and I said yes. Well," —she rolls her eyes—"Mia said yes, and what she says goes."

There's a moment of silence before Livie throws her arms around Storm. "That's great, Storm!" She begins to cry again. "Oh, these are happy tears, really. But I'm going to miss you so much."

Bittersweet delight washes over me as Storm and I exchange a glance over Livie's shoulder. I'm going to miss living next to her. Everything's changing. Everyone's moving on.

"I was counting on that, because"—Storm pushes Livie back for a moment and takes a deep breath, suddenly nervous—"the house is big. I mean, huge. Dan inherited money from his grandma. We have five bedrooms there. And . . . well . . . you two have become such an important part of our lives and I want it to stay that way. So we were thinking you guys could move in with us."

I look from Livie to Storm to Dan. "Are you sure *you* don't need therapy, Dan?" I ask with all seriousness. He only chuckles, pulling Storm close to him.

Storm plows on. "Livie, you can concentrate on getting into Princeton. Kacey"—she fixes me with a stern look, taking hold of my hands in hers—"figure out what you want in life and go after it. I'm here for you every step of the way. I'm not going anywhere."

I nod, biting my lip to stop myself from crying. It doesn't work. Soon, I can't see her through my tears.

My happy tears.

• • •

"Sure is going to be quiet without you ladies around here," Tanner says, scratching his head as he sits down beside me on the park bench in the commons. It's nine at night and dark. The movers are coming in the morning for our things.

"Like what you've done with the place, Tanner," I say as I take in the tiny white Christmas lights strung through freshly pruned bushes. The gardens are weeded and cut back, and there are a few tiny purple flowers blooming. A new barbecue sits next to a picnic table and, judging by the lingering scent of grilled meat in the air, I'd say the commons is finally getting some use.

"That's all your sister's doing," Tanner mumbles. "Kept herself busy while you were away." He leans back and settles crossed arms on his protruding belly. "So now I've got three apartments to fill. Yours, Storm's, and 1D."

Without meaning to, I peer over my shoulder at the dark window and feel sadness. "You haven't rented it yet? Trent's been gone for months." Saying his name makes my mouth dry up and a hollowness blossoms inside me.

"Yeah, I know. But he paid for six months. Plus I was hopin' he might show up again." He picks at his fingernails in silence for a moment. "I heard the whole story. Livie told me. Tough thing for both of you."

I nod slowly.

Tanner stretches his legs out. "Did I ever tell you about my brother?"

"Uh . . . no . . . ?"

"Name was Bob. He went out one night with his girlfriend.

Had one beer too many. Thought he was fine to drive. Hey, it happens. No excuse, but it happens. Wrapped his car around a tree. Killed his girlfriend." I wait quietly for Tanner to continue, watching his hands fumble and his leg jitter. "He was never the same after that. I found him hanging in Dad's barn six months later."

"I . . ." I swallow as I reach forward tentatively and pat Tanner on the shoulder. "I'm so sorry, Tanner." That's all I can manage to say.

He nods, accepting my condolences. "It's a terrible accident on all fronts. The wrongdoer. The victims. They all suffer somethin' fierce, don't you think?"

"Yes, you're right," I answer hoarsely, concentrating on the tiny Christmas lights, wondering if Tanner needed two months of intense therapy to come to that realization.

"Well, anyway." Tanner stands up. "I hope Bob's at peace now. I like to think he met up with Kimmy in heaven. Maybe she forgave him for what he did to her." Tanner walks away with his hands in his pockets, leaving me to stare at the dark window in 1D.

And suddenly I know what I need to do.

I can barely dial Dr. Stayner's number, my hands are trembling so badly. He gave it to me in case of emergencies. This is an emergency.

"Hello?" the smooth voice answers, and I picture him sitting in a wing chair by a fire with his glasses sitting on his nose, reading a *Shrinks Today* magazine.

"Dr. Stayner?"

"Yes, Kacey? Are you all right?"

"Yes, I am. Dr. Stayner, I have a favor to ask of you. I know it's probably an abuse of our relationship and confidentiality, but—"

"What is it, Kacey?" I can hear the patient smile in his voice.

"Tell him that I forgive him. For everything." There's a long pause. "Dr. Stayner? Can you do that? Please?"

"I certainly can, Kacey."

stage nine

■ ■ ■

FORGIVENESS

TWENTY-TWO

Waves lap at my feet as I walk along the shoreline toward home, watching the sun sink below the horizon. When Storm said "the beach," I didn't know she meant a property that backs right onto Miami Beach. And when she said "a big house," I didn't know she meant a sprawling three-story mansion with wraparound balconies and a separate wing for Livie and me. Apparently, Grandma Ryder had her wrinkly fingers in the oil fields and her only grandchild, Officer Dan, made out like a fox in a henhouse.

We've been here almost five months and I still haven't quite settled. I don't know if it's because it's too beautiful to be real or if it's missing something.

Or someone.

Every night I walk along the beach, listening to the calm waves lap up onto the shore, appreciating the fact that I can walk, and run, and breathe. And love. And I wonder where Trent is. And how he's doing. If he's found a good coping mechanism to help him heal. Dr. Stayner never updated me after that phone call. I trust that he passed on the message; I have no doubt about that. I can only hope that it has brought Trent some level of peace.

But I haven't pushed further. I have no right. I've asked Livie a few times if she's heard about Trent from Carter. Carter makes a point of calling her every other Sunday to check in on us and ask her how school is going. I think Livie really likes that. It's as though she has a father figure in her life to help fill the vast hole left after the accident. Maybe, in time, I'll be able to talk to him, too. I don't know . . .

Every time I ask about Trent, though, she all but pleads with me not to hurt him or myself by reopening those wounds. Of course Livie's right. Livie always knows what's best.

I try not to think about Trent moving on with his life, even though he probably has. Thinking of him with his arms around anyone else only feeds the deep ache in my chest. I need more time before I can face that reality. And my love for him—well, I don't know that it will ever fade. I'll just move on with my life, a part of me always wishing he were in it. Moving on . . . something I haven't done since my parents died.

My feet slow as I gaze out at the sun dropping below the horizon, its last light dancing over thousands of ripples, and I thank God for giving me a second chance.

"I think I like this meeting place better than the laundry room."

The sound of that deep voice stops my heart dead. I gasp and spin around to find blue eyes and a mess of golden-brown hair.

Trent is standing in front of me with his hands in his pockets. Here, in person.

I struggle to kick-start my breathing as my heart starts up again. A jumble of emotions slam into me and I stand frozen, trying to separate and understand each one so I can deal with them. Not suppress them. No more bottling.

I feel happiness. Happiness that Trent is here.

Longing. Longing to feel him against my skin again, his arms protecting me, his mouth on mine.

Love. Whatever happened between us, it was real. I know it was real. And I love him for letting me experience that.

Hope. Hope that something beautiful may come from this tragic story.

Fear. Fear that it won't.

Forgiveness . . . forgiveness.

"Why are you here?" I blurt out without thinking, my body trembling.

"Livie asked me to come."

Livie! Always the surprise. Trent's voice is so low and smooth. I could close my eyes and listen to it vibrate in my eardrums all night long, but I don't because I'm terrified he'll disappear. So I stare at him, at his parted lips, at his blue-on-blue irises as they roam over my face.

"I guess she's convinced you don't stuff kittens into ATMs anymore," I finally manage to say.

He chuckles, his eyes twinkling. "No, I suppose that's one less worry for her."

He's a mere five feet away, three steps from my arms, and I can't close the distance. I want to, so badly. But it's not my right. That lean, strong body, that face, that smile, that heart—none of it belongs to me anymore, outside of my dreams. Someone else will enjoy that blessing. Maybe someone already does. "Does Dr. Stayner know you're here?"

I watch Trent's chest rise and fall with a deep breath. "Yeah, I told him. I don't hide anything from him anymore."

"Oh." I hug myself tightly. "So how are you doing?"

He gazes at me for a long moment before he smiles. "I'm good, Kacey." There's a pause. "But not great."

"Why? What's wrong? Is therapy not working?"

"What's wrong?" Trent's brow arches as he takes two steps

forward, closing the distance between us, his hands firmly gripping the sides of my waist. I gasp, his proximity to my body both alarming and intoxicating. "What's wrong is that every morning and every night, I lie in bed wondering why you're not beside me."

My legs start to wobble. "You know why," I answer in a low, defeated voice. Inside I'm screaming, cursing reality.

"No, I knew why before. But you set me free, Kacey, remember?"

I forgive you. I nod and swallow. His hand lifts to stroke my cheek.

"And there's nowhere I'd rather be than with you." His thumb grazes my bottom lip.

I can't seem to catch a breath. My hand shakes as I push a lock of hair back behind my ear. "What does Dr. Stayner say about this? Isn't this wrong?"

"Oh, Kace." Trent's lips curve and he flashes me the deepest set of dimples I've ever seen, buckling my knees. "Nothing's ever been more right."

That's all I need to hear. I barrel into his arms, my mouth connecting with his.

Seizing him. Feeling him. Loving him.

EPILOGUE

A light breeze ruffles the folds of Storm's dress as she and Dan stand for pictures with the ocean and a fall sunset behind them. She's the most beautiful bride I've ever seen, all the more so with her swollen belly. The baby is due in just three months, and Mia has taken to referring to it as "Alien Baby X." I don't know where she comes up with this stuff. Dan, probably. The baby is another girl. Dan jokes that he's doomed, but secretly, I think he misses all the female companionship. The beach house is a little less estrogen-laden these days with Livie in New Jersey and me dividing my time between there, school, and Trent's condo five minutes away.

"Who knew there'd be so many hot women at a wedding?" Trent sidles up behind me, hanging his arm around my shoulders. My stomach does a nervous somersault flutter. It always does that when Trent touches me. Even after three years, he can do things to me with a look that I thought impossible. I hope that never fades.

"By so many, you mean one, right?" I murmur as I tip my head back and nuzzle my nose against his jawline.

He groans. "You trying to give me an erection in front of my parents?"

I laugh and gaze over to see Carter and Bonnie watching us from a distance, and they're beaming. During therapy, I realized that me barring them from my and Livie's life after the accident didn't allow them the chance to heal as a family. After Trent and I reconnected, I made a point of writing a heartfelt note to them, welcoming them into our lives. First Bonnie appeared at my door in tears, then Carter. One thing led to another and here they are, hand in hand, a family again.

The wind carries Livie's soft giggle to us. She's with Mia, who's busy showing her all her new grown-up teeth. Livie was accepted into Princeton like we all expected, so we don't see her much anymore. I'm so proud of her. I know Dad would be, too.

But I miss her like crazy.

And I think she's dating someone, though I'm not sure. She's remaining vague about whatever's going on, which is usually a sign that a man is involved. I hope she is. Livie deserves that and so much more.

I look out over the crowd of friendly faces. They're all there. Cain and Nate—as dashing in suits as any two men can be. Tanner, with a lady friend whom he met online. Even Ben, arm in arm with a blond-bombshell lawyer from the firm he just joined. He catches me watching him and he winks. I can't help but chuckle. *Oh, Ben.*

"You want to go to Vegas next week?" Trent whispers, biting my ear playfully.

I giggle. "I've got midterms, remember?" I just finished my first year of psychology at college. I plan on specializing in post-traumatic stress disorder therapy and I already have a killer reference from the renowned and unorthodox Dr. Stayner.

"Just a quick trip. To the chapel and back."

"Yeah?" I lean back and look into his eyes to see if he's joking but I see nothing but love.

His fingers graze my cheek lovingly. "Oh yeah."

Trent has kept his promise. He makes me smile every day.

ACKNOWLEDGMENTS

Writing this book has been a whirlwind of excitement and fear. I've gone beyond my comfort zone, stretched into a genre I have never written before, and pulled forward some of my deepest fears to write a story that I adore. I couldn't do all of that without the help of some truly amazing people.

To my beta readers, Heather Self and Kathryn Spell Grimes. You two gave me courage. All that talk of nipples had my stomach in knots and my confidence wavering. You, with your loud screams of encouragement, made me believe that I could do this exciting New Adult genre justice. Thank you.

To my amazing fellow authors, especially Tiffany King, Amy Jones, Nancy Straight, Sarah Ross, C. A. Kunz, Ella James, and Adriane Boyd, who jumped at the chance to read *TTB* before it came out. It is hard to make time for all of the fantastic books releasing and I appreciate that you made the time for this one. Thank you.

To all of the amazing bloggers and readers out there who have supported me. I seriously can't name every single one of you here because I'd forget someone and then I'd want to crawl into a hole and die (true story . . . takes me back to my wedding day when I forgot to thank my photographer). You know who you are and I can't say enough about you all. You are AMAZING people and I appreciate having each of you by my (cyber) side through this journey. Thank you.

To my agent, Stacey Donaghy, for your unwavering dedication, your absurd work hours, your words of encouragement, and for believing in me from day one. And for living close enough to me that we can drink Starbucks and take random pictures together whenever we feel like it. Thank you.

To Kelly Simmon of Inkslinger PR, thank you for reading my manuscript—uglies and all—and seeing the potential hidden beneath. Thank you, friend.

To my editor, Amy Tannenbaum, for believing in *TTB* and in me as a writer. And for just being awesome to work with. To Judith Curr for taking a chance on this Canadian. To the team at Atria Books: Ben Lee, Valerie Vennix, Kimberly Goldstein, and Alysha Bullock, for working their magic and making this book shine. Thank you.

To my friends and family who support me in my writing career and deal with my reclusive behavior. Thank you.

To my husband, for stealing my only proof copy and taking it with him to Dallas to read. It speaks volumes. Thank you.

The topic of drunk driving and the aftermath is one that has always scared me to death. Now that I have children, I can't describe my level of fear. Lives are lost, futures destroyed, and hearts broken every single day by judgment calls when people aren't capable of making sound judgment calls. If this book stops even one person from getting behind the wheel of a car after a few drinks, then it will have accomplished something monumental.

ABOUT THE AUTHOR

Born in small-town Ontario, Canada, K.A. Tucker published her first book at the age of six with the help of her elementary school librarian and a box of crayons. She is a voracious reader and the farthest thing from a genre snob, loving everything from high fantasy to chick lit. She currently resides in a quaint small town outside of Toronto with her husband, two beautiful girls, and an exhausting brood of four-legged creatures.

For more information on K.A. Tucker, visit her at:

Author website
www.katuckerbooks.com

Facebook
www.facebook.com/K.A.Tucker.Author

Twitter
@kathleenatucker

Goodreads
http://www.goodreads.com/author/show/4866520.K_A_Tucker

Atria Books/Simon & Schuster Author Page
http://authors.simonandschuster.com/K-A-Tucker/412040858